The Royles Saga Book Four:

HEIR TO A THRONE

The Royles Saga Book Four:

HEIR TO A THRONE

Virginia Coffman

This first world edition published in Great Britain 1995 by
SEVERN HOUSE PUBLISHERS LTD of
9–15 High Street, Sutton, Surrey SM1 1DF.
First published in the USA 1995 by
SEVERN HOUSE PUBLISHERS INC of
595 Madison Avenue, New York, NY 10022.

British Library Cataloguing in Publication Data

Coffman, Virginia
  Heir to a Throne
  I. Title
  813.54 [F]

  ISBN 0-7278-4825-9

Typeset by Palimpsest Book Production Limited,
Polmont, Stirlingshire.
Printed and bound in Great Britain by
Hartnolls Ltd, Bodmin, Cornwall.

PART ONE

Miravel, England

CHAPTER ONE

Her daughter dug her fingernails into the upholstery and cried, "Watch it! Someone is walking in the road."

Garnett ignored this filial lack of confidence in her driving. She swung her new 1955 red roadster around the curve onto the Miravel Estate Road and started down the steep incline. The car passed the young pedestrian ahead of them with at least a yard to spare and Garnett leaned on the horn, complaining, "What the devil is a child like that doing on the Estate Road? Looks like a gamin."

Alexia looked back. "Make that *gamine*. And she's not a child."

"I don't care if she's young Queen Elizabeth. She's not Nick's type at all, whatever that is. And what is this one doing on my Estate Road?"

"Undoubtedly hoping Nick will sponsor some new charity." Alexia did not add that after his long stewardship of Miravel Estate most of the shire considered it Nick Chance's Estate Road.

"Dear old Nick. Using my profits on his trip to sainthood," Garnett grumbled. "Good God! Could she be a girlfriend, at her age? Nick is over fifty."

Alexia smiled. There was cynicism in her amusement. Everyone in her mother's world except Garnett herself had learned the low value of manners and morality since the war. As for Nick Chance, known to the gossips of Miravel Village as Garnett's bastard brother, he was appointed Estate Manager at Miravel before Alexia herself was born, and during the ten years since the end of the Second World War he had produced even fewer profits for Garnett, the Estate's legal owner. Nick collected rentals over what seemed like half the beautiful Shropshire fields, plus some of the canal traffic and the excellent quality wool. He sold the vegetables, herbs, spices and the occasional bits and pieces of Miravel Estate to Londoners looking for fresh vegetables, a weekend retreat, or to be put up in a badly cared for cottage beyond the canal.

But whenever Garnett complained about Nick's lack of any accounts, not to mention profits, he became the local saint. The Miravel Home for Elderly Females, the Orphanage, a nursing home, and a school for children of London's Blitz casualties, were all sponsored by noble Nick Chance, at Garnett's expense. Whenever Garnett questioned some of the charities by asking for correct accountings, it was the Vicar of Miravel himself who led the gentle protests, reminding Garnett, and sometimes her daughter Alexia, that the Kingdom of Heaven was not entirely populated by accountants.

In the last three years the money from Miravel had been more important than ever before, to the Estate's owner, Princess Garnett. At this very minute the political future of her invalid husband, Prince Maximilian, was being discussed in tiny, Middle-European Lichtenbourg.

The Communist governments of Hungary, Czechoslovakia, and neutral Austria were crowding Lichtenbourg on all sides. She hardly considered it lucky that her son-in-law, Prince Stefan, the vice-chancellor, was being touted by the Western Powers as Maximilian's successor. As Garnett had pointed out repeatedly to her daughter, Alexia, "everyone knew" that Prince Stefan had only married Alexia in order to get his hands on the threadbare Lichtenbourg throne some day.

Alexia did not need her mother's constant reminders of Stefan's "treachery". She had been cut to the quick by what was very likely the truth. Stefan actually had married her with just this contingency in mind. She couldn't understand why that wise patriarch of the family, her great-grandfather, "Tiger" Royle, hadn't agreed with her. For some strange reason he actually thought Stefan would be the strong man Lichtenbourg needed and that her own father must step down, in spite of his illness and his gentle but sincere efforts to get along with his Communist neighbours.

Alexia hadn't broken with Stefan yet. She prayed that something would happen, some kindness to her father, that would make it unnecessary to break with the man she loved. She still hoped that he would remain in his present status as a kind of "assistant" to Prince Maximilian. Surely, that would make everyone happy, even the USSR which preferred to deal with a sick man. Life without Stefan would be a hard price to pay for Alexia's own loyalty to her feckless parents. The sound of Stefan's voice, the sight of him, still made her think of their bed and what she had believed was his genuine warmth and passion for her.

But there was her father, perhaps dying, and her mother, Garnett, to keep Stefan's treachery alive in their daughter's conscience. All the same, Alexia found Garnett Miravel Kuragin a poor substitute for Stefan's company. Garnett's own mind, as usual, was still on her woes, mostly financial. In England, at Miravel where she had been born, Garnett's bastard brother was cheating her out of their mutual profits.

"Nick knows perfectly well that he owes me over a year's profits, probably more. It's even more important, now that your wretched husband has failed to defend Max. Imagine, Lichtenbourg actually in the process of voting Max out of his own principality!"

"Never mind that, Mother. Just concentrate on getting your fifty per cent profit here at Miravel. Maybe you could use Nick's payments to bribe that nasty little People's Democratic Labour Party into voting our way."

Her mother was shocked. "But it is only a pittance we are talking about, actually. Not enough for bribes, at all. And I must remember how important it will be for me to look my very best when we fight off that disgusting plebiscite, or whatever they call their stupid vote."

Alexia gave up, but Princess Garnett was far from through. "I wonder why Nick really is so careful to avoid paying his debt to me? He doesn't have the Red Armies breathing down his neck as Max does. Come to think of it, I may have to put Grandfather Tige onto him. That should settle things. Nick's terrified of displeasing Tige."

Alexia suspected that her great-grandfather, "Tiger" Royle, was far too busy halfway across the world after the Korean "Police Action", to worry about Nick's peccadilloes but she said nothing, stopped by her mother's next remark which was spoken almost to herself.

"He can't possibly have a scheme for cheating me . . . Can he? I mean Nick."

"His charities on the Estate and in Miravel Village?" Alexia suggested dubiously. But that excuse was pretty well worn. Glancing at her mother, she was surprised to see the beginnings of a frown on that celebrated and still unmarked brow. Alexia was aware of a prickling suspicion. She herself wasn't sure what she suspected but with Princess Garnett anything was possible.

"Mother, tell me the truth. Does Nick have any hold over you?"

Garnett almost stalled the motor.

"What on earth do you mean? How could he possibly blackmail me? That is what you are hinting at, isn't it? But what can he know that would harm me?"

What indeed? The notion was unpleasant, even sinister. Nevertheless, it had been planted and it seemed to Alexia that something about her mother's behaviour only fed her suspicion. What could Garnett have done that Nick Chance, with his lifetime grudge against his legitimate sister, might – and undoubtedly would – use against her?

Alexia looked back. She saw the honey-haired girl, agile and thin as a rail, waving her arms and hurrying to catch the red sports car.

"Please wait. Oh, Miss . . . Madam, the vicar sent me to see Mr Chance, and maybe help the cook."

She was certainly an original. At a time when most women had barely begun spraying "Italian" haircuts and wearing ponytails, this pert creature's soft, fine hair was worn in an even closer crop that was almost boyish, but it did reveal a shapely skull which might have been a sculptured "gamine".

At Alexia's nudge Garnett pulled up with a melodramatic sigh. Alexia reached out to the girl. "Squeeze yourself in."

Most people were surprised by Alexia's Yankee accent acquired during her California schooling under the aegis of her famed great-grandfather, "Tiger" Royle. But the gamine didn't seem surprised. She was obviously too interested in Miravel Hall which loomed up ahead of her.

"Warmish pink bricks. I like your house. The Pater always said he wished our old broken-down castle was a bit less forbidding."

"The Pater?" Alexia echoed but showing no amusement. At the same time her mother gave Alexia a sideways glance, repeating, "Castle?" Clearly, she didn't believe a word of it.

The gamine shrugged. "Well, that was before the war."

She ignored Alexia's hand and flipped her thin legs over the door and into the car. She took up surprisingly little space as she wriggled in beside Alexia on the seat. She almost sounded pleased. At close range she was older than she looked, at least twenty, maybe more, but still saw herself as a heroine.

"May I proceed now?" Garnett asked with heavy sarcasm.

Before Alexia could open her mouth the girl treated the question with Garnett's own authority.

"Yes. Yes. Of course. The vicar said I must be there before sunset. Mrs Skinner is very particular."

Alexia laughed as Garnett started up the car with a roar, demanding of no one in particular, "Do you mean to tell me you are Skinner's kitchen help?"

The girl shrugged. "Why not? Someone has to be, and a job is a job. If Mr Chance agrees, of course."

Alexia nodded. "Very sensible. I only wish I had a job at this minute. What is your name?"

The girl was busy studying the beauty of the three-storey Miravel Hall, its mellow symmetry at its most impressive as it caught the late afternoon sun on its southwest front.

"Your name, dear?" Garnett asked, reverting to the light, warm tone so familiar in her years as a reigning princess in Lichtenbourg. Alexia suspected her mother wanted the gracious "Princess Garnett" reputation to be spread once more on her native Miravel Estate.

The girl said, "Oh, sorry. Actually, it's just Julie. Like Garbo."

That even startled Alexia. "Like Garbo?" She caught herself and added quickly, "Glad to know you, Miss Garbo."

Julie did not correct her. Garnett didn't see the humour in what she thought was the girl's impertinence. After another look at Alexia who pretended not to notice, Garnett drove onto the gravel road around the house, passed the building's main entrance facing the southwest, and headed the little car to the garage on the east side. It had formerly been the stables and was still a haphazard collection of stalls which served their newer purpose except when a Miravel Ball was in progress.

Miravel balls occurred on only two occasions nowadays, the first when Garnett graciously welcomed all those good citizens of the Miravel Estate who remembered that Her Highness expected a curtsy, and second, when the Vicar and Mrs Tenby wanted to promote a charity, assisted by their generous patron, Nick Chance.

Before Garnett was out of the car two servants from the Hall, the stableboy and the chauffeur, hurried across the gravel to offer her their assistance. As always, Garnett was at her best in such situations and greeted them with her warm laughter and two beautifully gloved hands.

"Well, Durkin, I'm home again. Would you be a dear

and lend me your boy? The new kitchen girl is expected and you know how difficult that dear old Skinner can be if these girls are late."

The stableboy, looking pleased, rubbed his freckled pug nose and then wiped the palms of his hands on his overalls. Having bowed to Garnett and Alexia, he was about to bow in Julie's direction but Garnett waved him away. "Skinner is in a rush. Do run along."

The boy and Julie, who didn't seem to be offended, started off to the right. Feeling something else was called for, Alexia wished Julie, "Good luck. Give Mrs Skinner my best. Tell her I'll be in to see her."

Julie nodded without looking back. She kept up with the stableboy quite well.

Garnett stared after the girl a few seconds, then muttered to Alexia, "Who the devil is that girl, really? Did you ever hear such impertinence? Garbo, indeed!"

Alexia grinned. "She didn't say she was Garbo. Merely Julie. You said once that Grandpapa David had to get drunk to sire Nick Chance. Maybe Julie has similar ancestral problems. It certainly isn't her fault."

Garnett was not amused. She glanced at the old chauffeur's face but he had not been in the Miravel household over thirty years without learning discretion. He was gazing innocently at the long windows of the small salon, the heart of the family's private quarters, and looking deaf, if not dumb.

The old chauffeur held the side door into the entrance hall open for the two women. Distantly, Nick Chance could be seen on the great staircase which descended to the entrance hall, effectively cutting the east half from the west half of the four-hundred year old building.

Alexia wondered if he deliberately chose to stand

there above them until the women paid the tribute of looking up at him from the foot of the staircase. Garnett certainly had done so during her reign as Princess Royal of Lichtenbourg.

A graceful, greying man of only middle height, Nick Chance looked taller than he was. He had always been attractive in his subtly amused way. He seemed to find the whole world an ironic mess. As both Garnett and Nick aged, they looked less and less alike but in some ways, resembled each other more. Alexia often wondered if they would end by accepting the true bond between them. Not on Nick's part, she assumed, until the Royle and Miravel families acknowledged his right to the Miravel name.

Garnett reached the foot of the staircase, looked up casually, and remarked, "What? We've caught the squire at home in his snug little cottage? I expected to find you out doing good works. Are there no dear old ladies waiting to do you honour for the mutton, or was it fish, you sent over for their dinner?"

Nick came down toward them. Alexia offered her hand but Nick was too busy bowing elaborately to his half-sister.

"Dear Highness, you are looking shamefully – one might even say – vulgarly beautiful for this shabby little village. But you never minded that, I know. And Alexia, welcome." He took her offered hand, adding after looking her over, "I see your mother's unerring good taste has not washed off upon you, fortunately."

Alexia expected her mother to be offended, but Garnett merely laughed. "Don't be coarse, dear fellow. And mind your manners. We are here on business."

Watching him, Alexia thought, *so that's what they*

mean when they say "his brows knit". He was aware of trouble ahead.

"Delightful of you to warn me. But where the devil is Horwich? Drunk, I suppose, though how an old wretch his age can manage it without losing his liver, I don't know."

Horwich, the butler, had been at Miravel since before Garnett's birth, and when he appeared silently behind the two women he carried his stout self with the poise he had used when Alexia, and even Garnett, had been children.

He cleared his throat. "Sir, Your Highness," and to Alexia, "Your Highness," not missing anyone, in spite of Nick's accusations, "A person is in the kitchen asking to see Mrs Skinner. May I ask what is to be done with the young . . . person?"

Since Garnett did not care in the least, Alexia reminded her, "It's the young woman we met on the road. Julie Something."

Nick said, "Don't tell me. Another relative of the late Lord Miravel? Still waters do run deep. May I ask why she is deposited in the kitchen?"

Garnett was amused. "I'm sure it's all some sort of trick to make herself mysterious. The vicar sent her. Obviously, she is a charity case. To help Mrs Skinner."

"Very likely, Your Highness," Horwich put in, then cleared his throat discreetly. "I'll have a word with her and remove the young person from the Estate if she has lied about her background."

Nick waved away the problem. "No. My mistake, Horwich. I have some business with the young person, after she has been dismissed by Skinner." Alexia noticed the look he gave to Garnett and felt a renewal of her first uneasiness. No doubt about it, he had some matter

12

to attend to. Knowing him, it was bound to be secret, unpleasant, and directed against his legitimate sister, Princess Garnett.

Alexia shivered. Nick Chance had this effect upon her.

CHAPTER TWO

Left alone in the spacious kitchen Julie went around examining the open hearth, no longer used, the big pre-war stove, a new refrigerator, much used, and outside the kitchen door a flourishing herb garden. The cutting table in the centre of the room showed the scars of age but made her think of the good food that must have been prepared here. It was like the glorious period cinema that was so much a part of her life. One of the good things about being an orphan, Julie found, was that she could go to see the movies when she had a couple of shillings, and become whatever she fancied on the screen. It was all hers, theoretically.

She couldn't remember all the households to which she had been sent as help, first by the Hospice for Blitz Children, then, during the years since VE Day, she had been sent to an assortment of "temporaries", all of which gave her fuel for quite a different series of cinematic dreams. But this one, so closely connected with Miravel Village, was currently her favourite. The Reverend Tenby of Miravel had "rescued" her from the pub in London and promised she would find Miravel Hall as glamorous as any of her favorite cinemas.

In fact, the vicar saw himself as a saviour of souls, removing her from "sin". No need to tell him then that the pub owner's wife kept one sharp eye on Julie's morals and the other on the meagre tips she made. How could the old harpy know that Julie wasn't about to sacrifice her virtue for anything but the highest price? Julie hadn't decided what that would be. A little dreaming was profitable, but at around twenty (she wasn't sure how far around twenty) with her dreams of success, she had already found temptation easily resisted, except in her dreams.

She looked out the window above the old-fashioned sink, seeing the conglomeration of wooden barns that had once been stables and now were "the garages".

Rich people. What odd ways they found to save money. This method looked shabby. It didn't suit a wonderful old house like Miravel.

Julie sighed and hearing a telephone somewhere, wandered over to the door through which the two ever-so-elegant ladies had disappeared into a dark hall. She opened the door, remembering almost too late to assume the respectful manner she had been laboriously taught, consisting of a lowered glance, her lashes fluttering just a trifle.

She did not feel humble. She knew nothing would ever make her genuinely humble. Underneath the modest demeanour, she was anything she wanted to be, and right now she was "Julie" (antecedents unknown) child of war and aristocratic parents – why not dream of the best? – and down on her luck, but quite the equal of any Miravel.

As a child she had been haunted by strange snatches of memory, horrors of music and sadness and the stench of death all mixed up, These were brought on, she knew, by the tales of other girls who obviously made up stories as they went along. But time and the wonderful make-believe life of the cinema had gradually blotted out the horrors, leaving her what she considered perfectly self-reliant.

The telephone receiver was lying on the stand in the hall beside an impressive central staircase. Whoever answered it must have gone to find the recipient of the call. But surely, these fancy Miravels had more than one extension to their telephone system!

Julie looked around, much impressed by the Regency reception hall that ran from the southwest entrance to the staircase. She had never seen anything she coveted more, the minute she saw the Hepplewhite furnishings, with the crystal lustres of the chandelier high above the staircase, giving off a rainbow of light from the setting sun.

When I'm rich, she thought, *I'm going to have my house furnished just like this.*

Meanwhile, behind her, the telephone was making odd, squawking noises. She glanced around, saw that she was still alone in this lovely house, and decided someone had to answer that caller. It was only common courtesy.

She took up the receiver and listened for a few seconds. The elderly male voice on the other end of the call was not only angry, he was pompous and insulted as well.

"Do you hear me? Is anyone there? This is a trunk call from London, the Lichtenbourg Consulate. His Serene Highness, Prince Stefan von Elsbach, the Vice-Chancellor of Lichtenbourg is calling."

A live prince whose secretary – or whoever – used the telephone and spoke English. Who would believe it? And talking, well, almost, talking to Julie herself.

Except for brief views now and then of the late king and his lovely queen, and once a sight of Princess Elizabeth and the Princess Margaret Rose, Julie had always regarded royalty as beyond the pale, hardly

16

human. She knew that the two women she had met on the Miravel Estate Road were royalty on a small scale, but that wasn't the same thing at all, and she couldn't let this chance slip by. After clearing her throat and counting mentally to three, she spoke into the telephone.

"Yes, sir. Would you put His Highness on?"

She reminded herself that she hadn't really lied, just let the royal secretary in the London consulate assume she had some official standing.

There was a scramble of some sort at the other end of the line and a deep, exciting voice thrilled her.

"Stefan Elsbach here. I take it that my wife is occupied."

"Well, sir, I'm afraid so." How could anyone desert a man, a prince, with a voice like that?

"I understand. Don't concern yourself, Miss . . ."

"Julie."

"Julie?" He was waiting for the rest of it.

"Just Julie." She hadn't meant to blurt that out. She heard his questioning "Oh?" and hurried on. "The vicar says it makes one special."

"I understand." He sounded kind, as if he really did understand. "I wonder if you would tell my wife to expect me soon, possibly in the morning. I am wrapping up my business here in London at the consulate."

"I'll be happy to tell Her Highness, sir."

"Thank you. You might tell her I wish to see her about a legal matter, in the event she – " He hesitated, then added, "Thank you again, Miss – Just Julie."

She heard his warm laugh and wished him "a safe trip, sir," but wasn't sure whether he heard her or not as the connection between them was broken. She hated to lose

17

contact but maybe things would improve when Prince Stefan arrived tomorrow at Miravel.

It did not occur to her until she saw the pompous face and stout body of the butler, Horwich, as he descended the staircase above her that she was by no means sure of her own presence here tomorrow. Clearly, she had committed a serious error in answering the telephone, or at least, in cutting off the connection, but she allowed herself the excuse that Prince Stefan had cut the connection first. She flashed a nervous on-and-off smile, "He rang off, sir, I'm afraid."

Horwich's eyebrows raised. "Before I could bring Her Highness to the extension, I take it?"

"I'm afraid so."

But he was not fooled by her apologetic manner. "Young woman, I think we had better have a talk with Mrs Skinner."

She followed him back into the passage that joined the kitchen with the various household offices, the house-keeper's private parlour being the first. They found the pleasantly plump cook-housekeeper coming up the cellar steps into the back passage, armed with jars of preserves, jellies, a wrapped package of meat, and what appeared to be a shrouded leg of lamb.

Horwich began solemnly, "With Their Highnesses arriving you asked for someone to assist you. This young person is here for that purpose. Later, Mr Chance wishes to speak with her. Meanwhile, she has been very busy answering calls from people who ring down expecting to hear from Their Highnesses."

Mrs Skinner did not reply until she set everything down on the kitchen table. She scarcely glanced at Julie but busied herself sorting out all these cellar treasures.

18

"Well, Mr Horwich, I am glad there was someone who knew her duty and answered the telephone. Will you be so good as to set the meat in the bottom of the ice chest? It won't be needed until tomorrow."

Horwich was deeply offended but managed to say with dignity, "I am happy to assist you, Mrs Skinner. I believe you said 'the bottom of the refrigerator'."

"Quite so. In the ice chest."

This time Mrs Skinner glanced at Julie and to the latter's surprise, gave her a knowing little smile.

Horwich dropped the meat in as instructed, slammed the refrigerator shut, and stalked out of the kitchen. Watching him, Julie began to giggle but was wise enough to stifle her amusement. It was very well for a woman in Mrs Skinner's position to have a little fun with the arrogant butler, but most unwise for a new kitchen-girl to do the same.

"Now, my girl," the cook said when he had gone, "Wash your hands at the sink and then fetch out the dough I was working. Go to the end of the table, while I get the pork pies ready for the oven."

As Julie obeyed her, the cook looked around the kitchen. "You'll not be telling me you came without luggage."

This sounded promising. Julie liked the motherly Mrs Skinner already. "Mrs Tenby thought I best make myself useful this evening and then return to the village tonight. In case I'm temporary."

Mrs Skinner got her an all-covering pinafore, then began to rattle beautiful Waterford Crystal dessert dishes around, filling them and slipping them into the refrigerator. She stopped momentarily to watch Julie return from the sink and start to work on the slab of half-worked dough. The woman said, as if to herself, "Still, I don't favour the notion of a wee chit walking the village road after dark. Things have changed since the war, what with those young troublemakers from London and the rest."

Julie's heart beat faster. A head taller than Mrs Skinner, she was not by any manner of means "a wee chit", but she let the good lady think what she liked.

Mrs Skinner said no more on the subject and Julie could only hope. But her busy imagination began to picture herself living in this glorious house, a house soon to be inhabited by a real prince with a wonderfully deep, sexy voice.

And he had seemed to like her a little.

Julie had learned early in life that the more tasks she learned, and the better she learned them, the more likely she was to advance beyond her fellow orphans. Many of the latter came from loving parents lost during the Blitz or the Buzz Bombs, in battle or in hospitals.

These were losses that only involved Julie in a peripheral way. She had never known her parents, being abandoned in her infancy, and having been blessed with the ability to look ahead in the last few years. Along with this more recent optimism, so unlike the haunting fears of her childhood, went ambition and a certain degree of shrewdness picked up from a street urchin whose reputation was enhanced by hints of a gangster father in Chicago. Eventually, he was whisked away to the States by the missing father who turned out to be a reasonably innocent merchant marine. But the lesson of the boy's lies was not lost on Julie.

Imagination had helped to clothe her dreams so that she told herself she could be anything, rise to any heights, since her roots were anywhere she chose to plant them.

Right now her object was to please Mrs Skinner who would be her most important superior for the time being. Horwich, the butler, was a bag of wind, and the two princesses weren't likely to involve themselves with her at the moment, or vice versa. But things were definitely looking up.

"Would you happen to know anything about serving?" Mrs Skinner asked just when Julie had the dough kneaded to the nth degree. "Not that I approve of females in the dining room, but the war left us not quite so choosy."

"Ay, Mum. I mean, yes, Ma'am." She almost burst into a brogue she had picked up at her last post. That had been one of her rare mistakes. Mrs O'Halloran had thought she was being mimicked. But Mrs Skinner only pursed her wrinkled lips as if hiding a smile.

Royalty ate very well at Miravel. Julie loved the many odours of roasted meats, the fresh, local fish, the herbs and vegetables home grown, all quite superior to the food she was familiar with in London. Although the war had been over for ten years, London, one of the standard bearers in that victory, had reaped few profits and could only hope that at least the food would improve sometime in the future.

Mrs Skinner hesitated about permitting Julie to lay the table in the formal dining room, and Julie was amused to see that the boy in training who called himself a footman, stumbled through his task, dropping several heavy pieces of silver on the worn Axminister carpet and was caught wiping the knives on his livery.

Julie was wise enough not to let Mrs Skinner see her grin, however, and went about her work, washing the dishes as the courses were finished. It had always shocked her to see how much food was wasted by the *noveau riche* since the war, but these old-time aristocrats were different. She developed a surprised respect for them, although the older beauty whom they called Princess Garnett was a little more wasteful, and had probably never seen the inside of a kitchen, Julie thought.

She was putting the carefully dried dishes in their neat cloth pockets when a big, noisy sedan pulled up outside the makeshift garages. Mrs Skinner stood on tiptoe, looked over Julie's dark head and stiffened with excitement.

"It can't be. But bless me! – It's "The Tiger" himself. And me with not a warm bite for him to eat." She began to bustle around. "A great man, that Tige Royle. Let's see. Yesterday's beef, and the creamed turnips. He's partial to my turnips. My dear, he's the glue that holds the Miravels and the Kuragins and even the Elsbachs together."

Julie's eyes widened. Her interest grew. Mrs Skinner fussed on. "His daughter married the last of the male Miravels. That was back in 1900."

Julie looked back toward the dining room. "I thought Mr Nick was. Something the vicar said."

"Sh!" Mrs Skinner put a finger over her lips. "It's not talked about by the staff. Mr Nick was not born in the marriage-bed, so to speak." She sighed again. "Well, we must do our best for Mr Tige. He's a Yankee who's used to the finer things in life."

This was all too complicated for Julie. Besides, she had never thought very highly of Yankees. Except for her Chicago friend, Yankees they were too impudent by half. She turned from the window and finished putting away the freshly dried china.

Instead of coming in by the entrance hall and heading for the formal dining room which the family were about to

22

vacate, clearly, Tige Royle knew his way around the great house and the habits of its denizens, he first threw open the kitchen door beside the herb garden. Further surprising Julie, he held out his arms and enfolded Mrs Skinner who blushed and looked enormously thrilled. Tige Royle was a powerful man with hard, weathered flesh, eyes that looked boyish with enthusiasm, and movements that belied his great age and full brush of white hair. He must be past seventy, even eighty.

But much as Mrs Skinner liked him, she broke away from his embrace to remind him. "Ye're wasting time on an old female, sir. Miss Garnett and Miss Alexia are in the dining room serving coffee to Mr Nick."

"The Sainted Master, you mean?" Tige corrected her with a holy look that made Mrs Skinner laugh, though she punched him lightly on the upper arm.

"Don't let His Holiness hear you, sir. He's dead-earnest."

"Likely." The big man did not treat this news with suitable gravity. "Never you mind. It's Lexy I came to see. My great-granddaughter needs cheering up. She's worried about her dad's illness."

He broke from the cook and swung around thoughtlessly, almost bumping into Julie. His grin was infectious.

"Sorry. Didn't mean to upset you, young lady. Don't you let this dragon overwork you."

Julie was pleased to hear herself called a young lady, but even more surprised at Mrs Skinner's giggle over her own nickname.

"No, sir. She's been most kind."

"That's our Dear Dragon." He pinched Mrs Skinner's wrinkled cheek and started toward the imposing dining room opening off the entrance hall.

The cook began getting pots and pans ready to heat a late supper for the patriarch. Clearly, he was the acknowledged king of this domain.

Julie's lively eyes crinkled with amusement at the cook-housekeeper's excitement. "He likes you, Ma'am."

Mrs Skinner was not displeased. "I don't know what Miravel would have done if Miss Garnett's dear mother hadn't married Lord David Miravel. That's long gone by now, of course, but the money still flows in when needed. Here, my girl. You slice and heat up the beef. I'll get the vegetables. Tige Royle has a man's appetite. He got his start in the silver mines in the States. A real man is the Tiger."

There was a new electricity in the air. By the time Tige Royle's supper had been served and the others were finishing their coffee, Julie found herself surprisingly tired. Like Mrs Skinner, she had worked faster and harder since the famous old patriarch had entered Miravel.

She finished her work and jumped lightly down from the stool. "What's next, Ma'am?"

The cook looked around the big kitchen. "I expect that will be all for this night. Since Mr Royle's come so unexpected-like, Mr Nick probably won't have time to interview you tonight. But you come back tomorrow. And you'll be needed to help in here if you've a mind to."

"Yes, Mrs Skinner. Of course."

The cook-housekeeper looked around, fussed by her new problems with the arrival of Tige Royle. "The question is, how are we to go about getting you home to the village? That's a problem. Annoying business. If only the village was nearer."

Julie was aware of a sinking feeling. This was what came of too much optimism. When the problem was not immediate, before dinner, it was swept aside. Julie was sure she had done everything to make herself useful. Evidently not. Now, she was a liability. The woman might resent calling on her in future. Julie couldn't have that.

She cut in brightly, "But Ma'am, I've often walked a deal further. Just a matter of putting one foot before the other, so to speak. The vicar's lady lent me a room in the vicarage. All private. I don't share it. Just me. It has a real casement window, like the olden days. An attic room, in fact."

Obviously, Mrs Skinner had never slept in a dormitory with a half-dozen other girls, some of whom had adenoids.

"But like I said, it's mine, while I'm with the Tenbys. I don't share it. When I had the pneumonia back in the summer, Mrs Tenby herself brought me rice broth and real fruit juice and mutton stew. Got me right on my feet, so she did."

The cook was still troubled, but she certainly had been relieved when Julie tried to make things easier for her.

"A good heart, has Mrs Tenby. I'd never say no to that." Mrs Skinner sighed. "Well, if you believe it's not an imposition, I'll thank you, child. I do need the stable boy tonight, and the new footman and the two maids, though heaven knows they've never been trained to serve royalty. Thanks to Mr Nick's nursing of every shilling."

Half an hour later Julie shrugged into her coat, pulling the collar up around her youthful, pointed chin, reflecting that if she ran some distance she would reach the village considerably before midnight.

In the doorway to the herb garden she heard a woman's voice call, "Julie? That is your name?"

Julie stopped. "Yes, Ma'am?"

Alexia crossed the kitchen to her. "My mother tells me, somewhat belatedly, that Prince Stefan left a telephone message for me."

Julie realized that between the butler, Horwich, and Princess Garnett, they intended to blame her for the failed message. She recovered quickly.

"Ay, Ma'am . . . Your Highness. The telephone was untended for quite a spell. I thought it was forgotten."

"Quite true, Ma'am," Mrs Skinner put in generously. "Horwich left it untended."

Julie hurried on. "Then Mr Horwich ordered me off to the kitchen. Didn't he deliver His Highness's message?"

"Apparently, he delivered it to my mother." Princess Alexia frowned, but her anger seemed to be reserved for her mother and the butler. Why on earth would Princess Alexia's own mother keep the message from her?

With an innocent eagerness Julie said quickly, "He asked that Mr Horwich tell you he was arriving tomorrow." She rattled on by rote before she realized the princess did not want to hear the crucial addition. "He said to tell Your Highness it was a business matter."

Alexia's beautiful features lost their brightness and Julie bit her tongue. It was never wise to emphasize what her employers did not wish to hear.

Nick Chance's voice, light and easy, with an edge of sarcasm, interrupted this painful moment. "What, Little Princess? Secrets in the kitchen with the servants?"

The three women turned, each of them startled, but Alexia seemed the most angry. She snapped to Julie, "Thank you. That will be all." She turned and left the kitchen, passing Nick Chance as if he were invisible.

He seemed amused by her attitude, looked after her, smiling faintly, then said to Julie, "I want to talk to

26

you. Come along, please." Puzzled, Julie glanced at Mrs Skinner who shrugged and nodded. Julie went after the Estate Manager, into the entrance hall and on to a dusty little library, obviously unused, but with windows looking out on a view of the Estate Road, already dotted with the first rain drops of the evening.

This interview with Mr Chance was strange. She had begun to think the cook-housekeeper decided such matters. And she had forgotten to bob a little curtsy to him. It was old-fashioned, but Mr Chance might expect it. People in his dubious position, not owners, not quite employees, were sticklers for the formalities.

There was a long, heavy walnut desk in the middle of the room. The legs had lots of curlicues and must be devilish to dust. Nick Chance threw one leg nonchalantly over a corner of the desk and in that position, half-standing, half-sitting, he studied Julie. His shrewd eyes missed nothing from her pert crop of fine, dusty-gold hair down over her leggy torso to her narrow feet in their walking shoes.

What on earth did he think he was employing, a chorus girl? Surely, not one of those females the GI's picked up in Piccadilly. It was almost insulting to admit, but men seldom pursued her for "that sort of thing". She cleared her throat but stubbornly refused to speak first or to act as if she were uncomfortable.

He spoke suddenly. "I'm told you don't know your full name."

"No, sir. But Old Mrs – the lady at one of the places I was sent to when I was four – during the Blitz – said it didn't matter. Sometimes I was called Jones. Julie Jones. I hated it."

His eyebrows went up. "Why? It's perfectly respectable. Quite as good as Chance. My mother's husband obliged me with his noble name."

"Oh, but I like that. It's so exciting. Chance. Better than Jones. Nothing ever happens to a Jones."

Evidently, her genuine enthusiasm didn't suit him. He waved aside her words.

"Don't trouble to please me, Jones. This is not an employment interview. I leave those matters to Skinner."

She was relieved but puzzled too. What was he getting at? She looked around the dusty, book-lined old room as a hint that she must have been summoned here for some reason. He was still studying her in that odd way, tilting his head to get a better view of her profile.

She wondered if he had dismissed her without saying so, but that wouldn't match his curious remark that this wasn't an interview; so it had to be something else. She backed away two steps before he got to the point and said, "I haven't dismissed you, Jones." She opened her mouth to reply but he asked, "What does Merribelle mean to you?"

An easy enough question. Obviously, he had mistaken her for someone else.

"I never heard of it, sir. What is it?"

He considered her face carefully, frowning. "It's a woman's name, we think. You were very young. Do you remember anything about your infancy?"

She wondered if he could be drunk, or just making some silly joke. But he seemed sober. She shrugged.

"No, sir. Just being with children who talked – you know, funny. Foreign." She closed her eyes, seeing snatches of faces and most of all, hearing voices. They kept changing. People adopted or maybe claimed them.

28

Children brought over from the Continent between the time of the Spanish Civil War and the London Blitz. Long ago, when she was very young, she had heard stories about Spain and the suffering in the war. For some years the bloody stories remained with her, accompanied by a dread of Spanish music.

"The woman died recently," Chance explained. "Our Vicar Tenby had met her at some charity hospital in London. She mentioned either Miravel or Merribelle."

Excitement gripped her along with a prick of dread. Maybe . . . Maybe, it was someone who had known Julie's parents. But she didn't want to know. Would the truth end all the dreams she had created in every local movie house? Besides, if it was Merribelle, it certainly wasn't Julie. The idea was like a double-edged knife. Maybe the very odd Mr Chance recognized her doubt.

"Aren't you a trifle curious, Jones?"

Since he seemed anxious for her to say something, she obliged him. "Yes, sir. Very much. But I never knew a lady named – what you said. And I've been staying with the Tenbys. They never mentioned it to me."

He made a little gesture as if dismissing the Tenbys and their incompetence.

"Well, no matter. We know very few of the details at present. Don't raise your hopes. Run along. Did Skinner tell you she will need you tomorrow? As you see, we are entertaining royalty, such as it is."

Confused and anxious, Julie backed out nervously. "Thank you, sir. I'll be pleased to do anything I can for Mrs Skinner."

"Naturally." He didn't sound too impressed. As she was leaving the stuffy little room he called out suddenly, "Our conversation about your past remains between us.

Such rumours may bring unwanted attention to the Hall, especially while our royal guests are here. If that happens, I am afraid we must dispense with your services. You understand?"

Baffled by his mention of unknown events in her infancy, Julie hurried through the elegant reception hall to the front doors of Miravel and started up the Estate Road. She was not at all sure why Mr Chance's prying questions had troubled her so much. Perhaps because she had spent most of her life trying to blot out those early memories of her babyhood, memories that were, in all likelihood, just nightmares based on stupid stories by fellow orphans.

As for people who had known her in those times full of nightmares, she knew she had grown self-sufficient and shaken them off. She didn't want to find herself suddenly in the emotional power of strangers about whom she knew nothing but who knew everything about her. They might try to take her back to the nightmares of her childhood.

CHAPTER THREE

Julie bundled herself up against the cool night with her fingers stuck into the sleeves of her coat. The wind had risen, bringing with it the smell of wet leaves from the mist and the water gardens around her.

Normally, none of this would matter. In fact, she enjoyed it, except for the all-important question that nagged at her. Would all that silly business about an orphan at Miravel or whatever, prevent her job at Miravel? And almost as important, would they prevent her from getting a sight of her new hero, the warm and friendly Prince Stefan? Also, from a purely business standpoint, such an acquaintance wouldn't hurt either.

She started up the Estate Road, hardly frightened, but well aware of the heavy darkness within the woods where a carpet of bluebells always spread out earlier in the season. Telling herself she wanted to get "home" to the vicarage before the rain, she hurried her steps.

She was a fast walker and was soon out of the Estate Road which was something of a relief. After a few minutes on the road west from the railway station and about to take the village road which clung to the side of a grassy, treeless hill, she made out a peculiar sight. It was what appeared to be a giant lump – perhaps a lorry or some kind of vehicle – and from between the wheels something protruded, very like the legs of a man. At least, they were long enough and wore slacks. Obviously, an accident. She took a few steps in the easterly direction, toward the station and the silent vehicle.

Nothing moved, even the legs.

The night was so dark she couldn't make out the silhouette distinctly, but it had to be unnatural, probably an accident which had thrown the driver out of his vehicle, or lorry. She hesitated, reflecting that no other cars, and certainly no pedestrians were around, but something had to be done. Common sense dictated that the wounded man required aid. He might even reward her in some small way. It did not occur to her that she might not have the strength to help him. She seldom failed at anything she tackled.

She approached the shadowy vehicle in a gingerly way. It was always possible some Teddy Boy from London would leap out at her. Sure enough, the car was continental, probably German and there were definitely legs sticking out from beneath the underbelly of the car.

She knelt, noticing that the man's boots looked quite expensive in the shroud of misty light, She called suddenly, "Are you hurt?"

There was a dull thud underneath the machine, followed by a deep voice growling something in a foreign language, possibly German. The legs slithered out on the road with the aid of two lean, sinewy hands holding onto the underpinnings of the car. Eventually, the upper torso and head appeared, hawk-faced, with a prominent, straight nose and black eyes frowning at her. Then the man grinned.

"I beg your pardon. You startled me. Like an idiot, I raised up and hit my head."

Before he finished speaking she knew that voice and was thrilled by her own terrific luck. As if she didn't recognize him, he held out one hand to her, explaining, "Elsbach. Stefan."

Delighted, she took his mud-stained hand, uttering the hated name, "Jones. Julie."

"What luck! We know each other. You *are* 'Just Julie', aren't you?" he teased.

She studied his broad forehead. "I think you'll have a bruise there, below your hairline. I'm so sorry. Can I help?"

"It was hardly your fault that I was clumsy. In any case, this machine is a mystery to me. I never was mechanical."

He got to his feet, ignoring the hand she held out again to help him. After brushing off the dust of the road which was just beginning to dapple with rain drops, he shrugged at his car. "I've no notion what is wrong with it except that I haven't run out of petrol. Even I know that." He scowled into the sky and laughed when he had to blink away drops of rain. He asked himself, "Shall I take the road to the village or to Miravel Hall? I've never considered which is shorter."

She reminded him, "There is a garage on the Square. It faces the old Tudor Inn. Timothy is very good with cars. Foreign ones, too." She added as he looked both ways, "I'm on my way to the vicarage where I'm staying, for now. I could show you the garage."

He smacked his dusty hands against his thighs. "Excellent. I shall have company. You must tell me all about 'Just Julie'."

He would hardly be interested in the many names she had chosen in her childhood, just before the war.

Princes were not interested in people with her dismal past. Just before the war, she called herself Julie Garland. Then, when she sighed and dreamed over Errol Flynn after being taken to a movie house in Leicester Square by a very charitable lady who belonged to the Royal Family, she had sighed and dreamed over Errol Flynn and decided she would be Julie de Havilland after Errol's lovely leading lady. Unfortunately, she couldn't carry it off. It was the "de". Nobody ever believed that. People laughed. Her Chicago friend, who was nothing if not frank, told her she was just like a terribly low-class character in a Fredric March film called *Les Misèrables*. The character was a street girl and she died in a gory mess at the end of the film. For a few days Julie had been depressed, catching glimpses of this "gamine" in shop windows and mirrors, but finally, she made the best of it. If she was a gamine type she would concentrate on being the best. No second-billing for Julie!

Seeing that his remark had upset his young guide, Prince Stefan asked, offering his arm gallantly, "Shall we try to beat the storm to the village?"

Feeling very like a real princess, Julie took his arm and they strode along the village road which was somewhat sheltered from the windy shower by the hillside.

"You are one of the Reverend Tenby's protégées?" the prince asked, obviously trying to make conversation, although his mind was on an other subject entirely. Of course, it was always possible that he was really curious about her background. An encouraging thought.

Two pre-war sedans passed them but though Julie called to the drivers, no one stopped. One of the drivers, who frequented the Tudor Inn and was somewhat the worse for his pint of ale, raced by them so recklessly Julie cursed him and waved her fist. She was embarrassed to be caught in such unladylike conduct. It certainly wouldn't be the behaviour of her companion's elegant wife, but the prince laughed.

"You took the words out of my mouth, Just Julie. But we are nearly there. I can see the village across the bridge."

Anxious to keep his mind off her conduct, she pointed out the church below them, beyond the fairly dry riverbed where Miravel Village rambled over the ground to the west.

"There is where I go. You see the square tower of the church? The top is all crenellated. That's what they call it."

"I haven't been here since a visit in 1941," the prince went on. "I thought the war activity would enlarge the place but I am happy to see it has shrunk back to its neat little size. Lovely spot." He added something she would rather not have heard. "I fell in love with my wife here. She was coming to the deathbed of her grandfather, the last Lord Miravel." He looked down at her, smiling at the picture she must make, all speckled with rain drops and blown by the wind. "I hope you are warm enough."

"Oh, yes." The mere thought of her proximity to her companion made her warm.

"You gave my message to my wife, the Princess Alexia?"

She tried not to let him think she had failed him, which she had, in a way. "I'm afraid Mr Horwich took the message first. He went upstairs to put Her Highness on an extension, and there must have been some mix-up. The other lady heard about the call instead."

"Her mother." His mouth looked hard, angry.

Obviously, he and Princess Garnett had little love for each other. She hoped he would be pleased by her efficiency when she said eagerly, "But later, in the kitchen, the Princess Alexia came to see Mrs Skinner, so I told her what you said about it being a matter of business."

He didn't look pleased. Seeing this, she apologized. "I'm sorry. I thought . . ." Her voice drifted off as his fingers squeezed hers in a reassuring way.

"It isn't your fault. I only added that excuse because I was afraid she wouldn't see me when I came."

"Wouldn't see you?" she repeated, outraged. "But that's dreadful."

He laughed at her indignation. "How good to have a kind little friend in my corner! Ah, here we are at the church. I remember the vicarage. Good. The lights are still on."

She wished they hadn't been. It would be heavenly if this wonderful man felt responsible for her tonight. But they had barely reached the gravel path to the vicarage when the ever-trusty Mrs Tenby, a tall, kindly woman who managed her husband without seeming to, opened the door. She was concerned and hurried Julie into the vestibule, paying no attention to the prince.

"My dear child, we've been ever so worried. Mrs Skinner called. She blames herself entirely for sending you off alone. She tells me that between the Lichtenbourg ladies and Mr Horwich she was all of a heap. It seems they must prepare now for Miss Alexia's husband, as if two royalties weren't . . . Good heavens! I do beg your pardon, sir."

She had just seen the rain-soaked prince who was shaking himself like a half-drowned wolfhound. He

36

waved away Mrs Tenby's curtsy. Julie was delighted that a prince could be so gracious.

"My fault entirely, Madam. I saw the chance to spend a few hours at Miravel, my business at the Consulate being concluded until we discover how the voting comes out. Our friends, the Commies, are pretty active." He offered one damp hand which the vicar's wife took after rubbing her own palm on her sleeve.

"I'm sure we are all sorry, sir," Mrs Tenby said. "I mean, about those dreadful Commies trying to throw your family out."

Less interested in politics, Julie cut in, "His car stopped. It was out on the station road. He hit his head."

"Good heavens, Your Highness!" Mrs Tenby's kind heart was all a flutter. "We must get some gauze and a plaster."

"Please don't trouble yourself. I'll leave Miss – er – Julie – in your good hands and see if anyone is stirring at the garage."

Mrs Tenby was aghast. "But that can be attended to later, sir. My husband has driven out to find Julie. When he returns he will be happy to drive you to the Hall . . . Julie, my dear, it is past bedtime. Have you eaten dinner? Do go and see the cook. She has a pan of chops and vegetables heating for you."

It now occurred to Julie that she was hungry. She had been so excited by her companion that she hadn't once thought of dinner. She glanced at Prince Stefan who took both her cold hands in his, shook them and thanked her for coming to his aid tonight.

"My young rescuer, in a manner of speaking."

She was embarrassed but excited by the effect his kindness, his voice and his dark eyes had on her. She had never been embarrassed in quite this way before. Few people ever put her at a disadvantage, no matter what their intentions might be.

"Yes, sir. Thank you, sir." *Good Lord*! she thought. *I sound like a Victorian waif.*

She slipped her fingers out of his clasp and hurried off through the warm, homely parlour to the rear quarters of the house. She wondered if he was watching her. When she looked back, he wasn't.

Mrs Tenby thought she understood Julie's excitement. "I suppose Mr Chance discussed my husband's secret with you."

Julie wanted to think about her romantic encounter with His Highness and shook her head.

Good-natured Mrs Tenby was disappointed. "I can't seem to find out what it is all about. Are you sure it doesn't involve you? Maybe you've inherited some money?"

"Not likely, Ma'am. I'm going to make my own way."

Mrs Tenby sighed. "I'm sure I hope you will."

Or marry a prince, Julie thought, aware that her heart was beating faster. After all, anything was possible. Look at this morning, she had never dreamed she would meet a prince before the day was out. Much less a romantic one.

CHAPTER FOUR

Alexia was always surprised by the persisting friendship, or plain generosity that existed between her great-
grandfather Tige Royle, and most of the far-flung Miravel
Family, with all its global ramifications. He never let
Alexia's trouble with Prince Stefan, or Nick Chance's
undoubted bastardy interfere with his friendship or his
business connections. He didn't trust Nick, who had
once made life miserable for Tige's nephew, Christopher
Royle, but he remained his friend, wary, yet generous. He
seemed to feel that the family owed it to Nick.

Although Tige arrived when the family had finished
dinner and were in the process of leaving the dining room,
Garnett insisted that everyone sit down again, as she put
it, "to give our poor Tige some company."

Alexia was more than willing. She adored her great-
grandfather, known to all the financial and political world,
and to his family, simply as "Tige".

In the late 1930s Tige Royle had suggested that his
great-granddaughter, Alexia, take her four college years
at Berkeley, California, commuting across the Bay from
Tige's luxurious apartment building in San Francisco.

"It'll teach you how the other half live," Tige had
claimed. "Cosmopolitan, that's our Alexia."

Since Alexia's parents, the Prince and Princess Royal

of Lichtenbourg, were far too close to the Third Reich for comfort, Alexia's years in California had been satisfactory all around. The Second World War and Alexia's romantic marriage to Prince Stefan von Elsbach, a rival claimant to the Lichtenbourg throne, had brought her home again.

But the one stable influence in the family remained Tige Royle. Alexia hugged her great-grandfather now when he came around the dining table with arms outstretched.

"Here, what's this?" he demanded, holding her off from him and making fun of her tears. "That's no way to greet Old Tige."

With her famous flashing smile Princess Garnett came between them, holding her arms out to her grandfather. On her beautifully shaped third finger was a cluster of diamonds surrounding an impressive and heavily insured emerald. The ring was the gift of her husband, Prince Maximilian, who adored her. If he should have his little country taken from him by the cold-blooded ambition of his son-in-law, at least Garnett could have her revenge by breaking up her daughter's marriage to Stefan von Elsbach.

Garnett cried, "Dear Grand– Sorry, Tige, how good to see you!"

Tige left Alexia long enough to kiss his granddaughter Garnett's still flawless forehead.

"I was in Seoul about this Panumjom Armistice in Korea which threatens to break off any minute, and I decided to pop over to England to see you. I have some business with Stefan and we thought it better to talk in private. Lichtenbourg is too full of Russky spies."

"Prince Stefan! Over my husband's dead body!" Garnett cried indignantly.

Alexia winced. "Mother! For heaven's sake! Father

40

is still very much alive and the plebiscite has barely begun."

Tige avoided this unpleasant subject of the bitterness within his family. "Anyway, it seemed a nice idea for me to come and see you. And my girl Lexy here. And Nick, of course."

"Very good of you, sir," Nick put in meekly.

Garnett gave Nick Chance a quick look before explaining to Tige, "You're psychic. You knew we needed you, dear. What with the business we must settle at Miravel."

Alexia saw Nick's sardonic gaze shift from Garnett to Alexia and felt uncomfortable. It was absurd that he should make her feel guilty. She was wondering if the dynastic quarrel in Lichtenbourg would make her leave Stefan. On the other hand, Nick would always have a home at Miravel, according to Lord David Miravel's will, providing he paid his legitimate sister, Garnett, half of the profits from the Estate.

Alexia's own life had been topsy-turvy since the Royal Council in Lichtenbourg decided her father was too weak, physically and mentally, to hold the country against the Soviet influence which threatened to suffocate Lichtenbourg. She had suspected her husband, Stefan, of his ambition to rule Lichtenbourg long ago when they first met on the train to Miravel. Then had come the courtship, played through all the hectic days of late 1941, the marriage heartily endorsed by the neighbouring Führer himself, who believed so strongly in the Elsbach loyalty in Lichtenbourg that wedding gifts and presents of various sorts were sent by him. The fact that Hitler was badly mistaken in that friendship had saved the country during the post-war upheaval in pro-Nazi countries. But where the Swastika had been torn down, there were the Reds to worry about now.

What was Stefan doing tonight in London? Planning the takeover of the principality from Prince Maximilian? He had almost completely fooled Alexia into thinking he loved her during the years he may well have been betraying her poor father. Whatever he did in London, the "business" he wished to discuss with Alexia was undoubtedly in order to install himself as reigning prince. The pain ached like an old, deep wound.

Mrs Skinner, who must have been hovering outside the hall doors, knocked with some difficulty and shuffled in balancing a tray of leftovers made appetizing by her efforts.

Alexia could see that Nick was very much onstage, playing a role with Tige Royle that he had played before, smooth, acquiescent, looking to the Great Tige for advice and knowledge. He would end by doing things his own way. He had an intelligent but devious will. Princess Garnett began on her problems almost at once. "How good it is to see you, Tige! It's almost like the old days at Miravel. With, of course, the one dreadful exception of my poor Max's illness. He was in that Viennese Hospital two weeks ago. People sent him tons of flowers and every loving gift you could imagine. They wanted the world to know how much they care for him."

"The loss of Prince Maximilian would be tragic," Nick murmured.

Tige, who was busy rearranging his silverware, looked over at Nick. He too could be sardonic, Alexia thought. His look made Nick Chance flush a little as he added, "That is to say, His Serene Highness is certainly superior to – " He was in hot water again. "I suppose if Miss Alexia's

42

husband takes over, the State funds and crown jewels et cetera will be at Prince Stefan's disposal."

Tige's knife came down hard on the china as he cut his meat. "Are you referring to Max's property, by any chance? Let me tell you, his investments since VE Day have not been wise. I'm afraid he never would listen to the rest of us. It's Stefan I'm concerned about. If he wins the election he will have to repair the damage. I did my part to get the Western Allies to step in with a few diplomatic and financial squeezes against the Russkies. But it was like talking to a stone wall. And there was this Korea thing that took precedence."

Alexia glanced at her mother and suddenly realized Garnett knew all the time that Stefan was treating her and Max, not to mention Alexia herself, most generously. She hated the thought; humiliating, degrading. She and her family could hardly say their souls were their own because they had all been bought.

Garnett shook her head. "My darling Max. He never did understand money. But so generous. When Stefan has tried to usurp the throne these past months, it was nothing more than a stab in the back."

"Mother—" Alexia began, but broke off. She wanted to say, *Why did you take and take from Stefan, only to put yourselves under obligation to him?* But Garnett wouldn't know what she was talking about.

Tige interrupted her. "No stabs in the back about it. Max has been hopeless. Old Stefan has been an excellent vice-chancellor. Now, let's say no more about this until we all get a night's sleep."

Garnett hesitated. Maximilian had always been her cavalier, slave, companion and lover from the time her first memories began. Poems and columns in almost

43

every European language had paid tribute to her beauty, but in spite of what Alexia knew were her mother's occasional interests elsewhere, only Max had been her devoted slave.

Garnett smiled finally. "My dears, I do feel just a bit tired. Must be my age. How dreadful to be getting old!" She wrinkled her perfectly sculptured nose, waiting, as her audience knew, for the gallant denial.

"Rubbish, Your Highness," Nick put in with his slightly edged gallantry. "Tige and I may look old, but not you. Not ever."

She studied her fingers, her lips parting with pleasure. She was happy again.

Nick remained in the dining room doorway watching the two women, escorted by Tige. Alexia wondered if Nick would manage to get in the first word to Tige about the long overdue profits from Miravel which, by the last will of Lord Miravel, would go equally to his daughter, Garnett, and to his illegitimate son and Estate Manager, Nick Chance.

Tige manoeuvered Princess Garnett around the Gallery Landing, past the four-hundred-year-old stiff and arrogant Miravel family portraits. "Here you are, honey. I suppose you have the bridal suite. But how you can put up with all those old Miravels staring at you from the gallery, I can't imagine."

Garnett smiled and patted her grandfather's hand as he opened the door. "You forget. I was a Miravel. A Royle-Miravel."

She went inside where one of the Miravel maids waited with bored attention, to run her bath.

Tige turned to Alexia. "Now for you, Lexy. Your usual suite? The one where you dreamed of marrying Stefan?"

"No. Not that one." Everything in the bedroom and dressing room made her think of those few nights in 1941 when she was hoping Stefan would love her. Of course, he wanted to marry her. He was next in line for the Lichtenbourg throne. He needed only one additional argument on his side, a marriage to Alexia Kuragin, the only other claimant to the throne. But he had been kind, strong and understanding, a partner whose sexual prowess, she knew now, had blunted her suspicions. What a fool she was, how easily won!

She saw Tige watching her, curious over her hesitation. She tried to play it lightly. "So I'll pick another room. She walked on to another door. I think I'd enjoy sleeping here."

"Well, that's better." he pushed open the door, and looked over her shoulder at the room with its pleasant pink glow from a lamp beside the bed. It was a virginal room, with a long window giving a misty view of the Azalea Path leading to the fountain pool where, in 1900, Tige's beloved daughter had been married to Lord David Miravel, a ceremony witnessed by, amongst others, the jovial Prince of Wales who became King Edward VII.

The sight of that spot made Tige blink. A large part of his personal life had gone out of him long ago at his daughter's death. This must be why he enjoyed meddling kindly in other people's lives, Alexia thought. He turned and left her. His memories occupied him.

Alexia went into the dressing room, removed her make-up at the mirrored sink across the narrow room, and ran her own bath in the next room. Her mother had never been without servants but Alexia's years in the States, especially California, had given her an independence that made personal maids and bodyguards a nuisance to her.

It was past eleven before she got to bed. She was deep in her first sleep when a car descended the Estate Road and stopped before the southwest entrance, the headlights dimmed so they wouldn't flash across the elegant fanlight over the door. After a brief stop the car swung around and headed up the road again.

About five minutes later Alexia was shocked out of a sound sleep by the door opening and the ceiling cluster of lights snapped on. She sat straight up in bed, frowning. For a moment she was too startled and confused to recognize the tall man with the dark complexion and the strange, piercing eyes she could never forget.

Prince Stefan, her husband, had arrived and was standing there looking almost as surprised as she was, but at least he was able to speak: "Good God! Is it you?"

Not a very romantic greeting, but understandable, in the circumstances.

CHAPTER FIVE

Alexia avoided going into the reasons, if any, that she had for the change of rooms. He undoubtedly guessed, and if any of his old affection for her remained, assuming it hadn't all been phoney, it would hurt him now to realize she didn't want to be reminded of those years unless he surrendered his claim to the Lichtenbourg throne.

"I thought you were getting in tomorrow." She tried not to sound critical or snappish but in his usual, whimsical way, he reminded her.

"This is tomorrow. It's after midnight. I finished my London work early. Diplomacy of sorts. Got this far afterwards."

Probably he was building up his image against her father's illness or weakness, she thought, but he went on without any further reference to politics. "Well, in any case, I started for Miravel but my car broke down just this side of that little railway station. Had to walk to the village for help. And the garage was closed, naturally."

Concerned, she sat up, not aware for a moment that the layers of flesh-coloured chiffon in her nightgown were nearly transparent. He was startled momentarily at the sight of her neat, pale, well-rounded breasts, almost bare, and she remembered the touch of his always exciting mouth on her flesh.

Though he moved across the bedroom without hurry, he was much closer now, looking her over in a way that aroused her body in spite of herself. Since he had joined the Royal Council in "suggesting" Prince Maximilian's retirement, she had worked hard to forget his physical effect on her. There were other males, even in her somewhat constricted world, whose physical attractions equalled or surpassed those of this tall, lean, hardy man with his rather frightening strength of mind and body.

When he reached her bed and leaned over her body to kiss her she found herself unable to avoid his touch. She could only pretend indifference. Her body betrayed her.

"Hello, darling," he murmured in his deep, well-remembered voice, and when she opened her mouth to return his greeting casually, he covered her lips with his own. She felt as if she were being drawn into his body as he had so often been drawn into hers in their unforgettable moments of sexual contact.

Breathless and ashamed of her weakness, a betrayal of her dying father, she finally broke from him. She was deeply aware that only his strong, voluptuous mouth and the old, remembered passion had held her to him. She tried to make a joke of the feelings he aroused in her. "I suppose it's too late to say 'hello'."

He laughed. "Not at all. It is never too late to show my feelings for my wife. Have you forgiven me yet for my tactless way of telling you the truth about Max?"

Getting a tight grip on her angry emotions, she asked finally, "How did you get here if your car broke down? You should have called. We would have sent a car."

He explained matter-of-factly, "The worthy Reverend Tenby brought me. He was expecting to pick up a young lady who had been left to her own devices after working here at the Hall tonight."

She felt the guilt of that. "Good heavens! And it's been raining, too. I'm sorry. I guess everyone thought someone else had attended to the matter."

His inconvenience did not seem to matter to him. Her great-grandfather, Tige, had once said Stefan was a rare "princeling". Whatever that meant.

"The young lady and I had a delightful walk to the village."

She stiffened. She looked tousled after sleep but the ghostly light from the window cut across the light of the little crystal lustres and touched her figure with silver. He seemed to be enjoying this while she said, "I'm sorry, but Mother doesn't seem to approve of her."

"That, of course, should weigh heavily with all of us."

That brought a smile. As Tige Royle had once observed, "Stefan has Garnett's number. He sees through her a hell of a lot better than poor old Max does."

But though his comment brought out her smile, she found it sad that Garnett's conduct was so obvious her own grandfather had made such a remark.

Stefan leaned over her, his eyes glowing with that old desire she found hard to resist. He reached for her. "That's my lovely, smiling girl. There's an old song somewhere. 'Moonlight Becomes You'."

She wanted to resist but was glad his strength overcame all her doubts at this moment. He lifted her to him, pulling her hard, almost painfully, against his breast. Under the impetus of his muscular strength, she yielded to her own hunger for him. He sensed her growing excitement and ordered in that deep, husky voice

49

she loved, "Like the old days, sweetheart. I've waited so long."

His command brought back all the erotic memories. She freed her hands which had been crushed tight against his groin and began to remove first his coat and then the belt around his slacks. She felt the growing hardness of him against her own flanks that were barely covered by the wisp of a silken nightgown.

She loved this proof that she could arouse him. In spite of elections and the knowledge that he could destroy her dying father, he must feel a genuine sexual desire for her.

He was ready yet he held himself until he pushed her gown above her tightening breasts and then entered her. The heat of his swollen flesh seemed to pierce her body and she closed her legs upon him, a captive to her long hunger. She heard herself uttering whispers of lust that matched his, and wondered how she could have lived for weeks without this wild, hot sensation.

Even when they rolled over on her tumbled silk sheets they remained locked together until breath was burned out of them and they broke apart breathing heavily. In this moment, while he changed his position and closed his lips on one of her breasts, she whispered, "Can't we go back to those days? Forget politics and elections? Let my father die proudly, without being disgraced by the deposition?"

His body moved slowly away from hers. He sat up, and began to dress. It was like a glass of cold water thrown in her face. His voice too was cold, authoritative, and worst of all, sarcastic. "I hadn't realized before. You really are your mother's daughter."

While she watched him, speechless, he got up and

strode across the room toward the door. She tried once to amend her bad timing. "Where are you going?"

Over his shoulder he dismissed her. "May I take it that there is an unoccupied bedroom somewhere? Some little corner that Horwich is better informed about?"

She recovered with an effort. "Yes. Of course. Just beyond Mother's suite. I'm sure Horwich put Tige in his own room."

He stopped. "Oh? So Tige is here. Good. I want to thank him for his efforts with the Western Powers on Lichtenbourg's behalf."

Stefan went his way, closing the door behind him. How easily he recovered from several minutes of a supreme passion!

Alexia crawled back under her silk sheets, a Christmas present from her father before his latest heart attack. He had reminded her then, "All princesses, especially ours, should have silk sheets." Poor Father. He meant so well.

When Alexia was a girl she had resented Prince Maximilian, the reigning prince of little Lichtenbourg, because he lacked the courage to punish his heroic father's assassins. He knew if he did so he would arouse the deadly wrath of Adolf Hitler, who was responsible for those killers.

Years of living with only the Austrian border between the Third Reich and her father's principality had shown her that it took shrewd, clever and exceedingly brave men to fight an underground war against Hitler. Her father was none of these things.

Now, he might die and would never know that his daughter understood.

Her family's rivals, the Elsbachs, had been different.

She found their bravery, like that of her great-grandfather, Tige Royle, once more of a kind that her father would never have been able to match. She was sure that today Stefan cared only about outwitting the USSR who had taken over from the Nazis their push-and-shove tactics, along with their unpleasant and often unsolved murders.

And what the devil was Stefan doing, walking along dark county roads in the rain with a girl almost young enough to be his daughter? A conniving little liar, Garnett had guessed. She called them as she saw them, and she could be surprisingly right on occasions.

Eventually, and not very happily, Alexia went to sleep.

Mrs Tenby handed up the breakfast plates to Julie on her kitchen chair and remarked with her warm smile, "You're looking very dreamy this morning, Julie. No nightmares for you, I take it."

Giving herself a minute to make up something, Julie stacked the plates on the wall-of-dishes as she had been taught by a Scottish employer.

"It was an awfully nice dream, Ma'am, a lovely dinner at Buckingham Palace, with young Queen Elizabeth and her husband. So handsome!" She sighed and reached down for the breakfast tray service.

Mrs Tenby teased, "I do hope there was room at the dinner for the Reverend Tenby and me. I've always wanted to dine with royalty."

"Oh, indeed, Ma'am. It was you that got me in."

Mrs Tenby laughed. "I doubt that, Julie. If your charm couldn't do it, I'm quite sure my husband and I would be found at the nearest Lyons' eating a salad."

That made Julie laugh too, but she was trying to hold

the fragment of her dream: Prince Stefan riding a black stallion with Julie perched up in front of him, held in place by his strong arms.

It seemed like the answer to her dream when the Reverend Tenby came in from his study with one finger marking his place in the Bible for his next sermon. He told Julie, "You are quite the most popular young lady in Miravel; did you know that? A gentleman is asking for you. A very special gentleman. He won't even wait inside. Says the village fascinates him."

"Aha!" Mrs Tenby put in. "I told you to be kind to that nice boy in the tobacconist's shop. You see? You've captured his heart."

But Julie's thoughts and hopes were far from the lanky snaggle-toothed boy in Mr Miller's combined postal service and tobacco shop. She almost dropped Mrs Tenby's favourite souvenir teapot. "Oh, yes, please. May I go and see him?"

Mrs Tenby gave her a playful little push. "Certainly, dear. In the village we consider him very special indeed."

It seemed just like Prince Stefan to admire this funny little village. Julie hurried off, trailing her dust cloth which she had to run back and pick up and hand to the Reverend Tenby with breathless apologies. He chuckled at her panic, remarking to his wife, "Puts me in mind of those days when I used to call on you at your father's house. What a panic I was in!"

Hearing this as she ran, Julie had a sudden twinge of depression. It seemed strange to think people as old as the kind Tenbys had ever been eager and young. And sensual? The sadness was partly selfish. Would she ever be so old and still think herself romantic? She had enough

53

trouble thinking she was romantically attractive at twenty or whatever she was. What would she be like at forty?

As she reached the spacious double parlour used for Christmas and midsummer celebrations, she slowed to a sedate walk. Suppose the person waiting for her really was the toothy boy from the tobacconist's shop? What a disappointment!

The deaf old lady from Elder Home, who had been knitting a wool vest for Mrs Tenby to wear over her dresses this winter, looked up to see Julie flying by. She shook her head at this exuberant behaviour. Clearly, in her day, hired girls Julie's age didn't go running about in the vicar's parlour. Julie gave her a fleeting smile, not caring what the old lady thought but aware that if she wasn't careful the rumour would get around that the hired girl at the vicarage was fast in more ways than one.

Suddenly nervous as she reached the partly open door at the end of the little passage, Julie smoothed her honey-coloured, sleek hair, took a deep breath and opened the door wider.

A stranger stood there with one arm propped negligently against the brick wall. Not quite a stranger, she realized. She had seen him before when he came like a whirlwind into the Miravel kitchen from the garage. He was Tige Royle, the Yankee everyone practically worshipped. Must be his money. What was he doing here?

For an old man he was surprisingly virile and attractive, with hard, tight flesh, and not an ounce of excess weight. Having heard something of his background, Julie suspected he might not always be as jovial as he looked. Still, like most people, she was disarmed by his friendly air.

"So you're the famous Just Julie. Get your duds on.

54

You're needed at the Hall. His Reverence said you liked working there."

That made her a little nervous. Prince Stefan should not call attention to his joke about her name. She pretended to take his remark in a light spirit. "Somebody once thought it would be nice to call me Julie Jones. That was awful." She gave him her innocent, faintly wistful smile. "You see, they don't know what my birth name was. It might be anything. Even Windsor. Nobody can say for sure it isn't."

She was relieved by his chuckle. "Your logic is almost flawless."

"Almost?" she repeated, rather daringly.

"Well, nobody is perfect. Even me."

That made her laugh. "I'm sure people think you are."

"I doubt it. Now, run along and get ready. I've delegated myself to drive you to the Hall. Your friend, the prince, wanted to, but he had business with my great-granddaughter, so I made it my pleasure."

The prince had wanted to come and get her. Prince Stefan did remember her. She hurriedly untied Mrs Tenby's old apron and went running into Mrs Tenby's dining room.

That dear lady and the vicar were thrilled at Julie's popularity. Mrs Tenby said, "Mrs Skinner is most particular. My dear, it does you credit that she wants you back. Of course, you may go."

The vicar added mildly, "It was careless of them not to get you home to the village last night. I didn't mind, for myself, but it worried my wife, I know."

"Rubbish, dear. You were just as worried as I was." Mrs Tenby then gave Julie the glad assurance, "And

Mr Tenby was quite taken with His Highness, the prince. So democratic, didn't you say, dear, when you drove him over to Miravel."

Julie's heart beat faster. "I thought so too." It had been too much to hope that Prince Stefan might have mentioned a kitchen-girl who led him to a useless garage, but the vicar – bless him! – said, "By the way, His Highness thought you were a remarkably self-possessed young lady, Julie. His very words. Run and get your coat."

"And your knitted cap. You don't want to catch a chill," Mrs Tenby added as Julie flew out of the dining room toward her steep attic stairs.

Julie wrinkled her nose at the notion of wearing a cap that made her look like a leprechaun, but she didn't want to disobey Mrs Tenby who had been a good friend.

When she returned, having dabbed on a little lipstick and powdered her nose, she found the vicar talking about the village with Tige Royle, who was still propped in the open doorway of the reception hall.

Julie had started down the attic stairs at a run but it occurred to her that the famous Tige Royle must be used to everyone running to oblige him, so she tried to relax. She crossed the big room with as much dignity as she could muster in her aged, all-weather coat that was much too young for her, but the high collar was handy and besides, she tried to wear the coat with a certain style. The fashion magazines at Mr Miller's shop were wonderfully helpful, when she wasn't caught studying them.

The Reverend Tenby turned around with his usual pleasant greeting, presenting Julie to Mr Royle.

"One of our favourite little – pupils, I think would be the word. Very obliging and quite the most intelligent young person my wife and I have encountered in some time. She's from London, you know. Originally, from the Hospice for Blitz Orphans, those who were unknown."

"That's good enough for me." Tige reached for her hand which she hadn't yet gotten out of her warm sleeve. She pulled it out fast and her fingers were swallowed up in his. Surprised that a man who was old enough to be a great-grandfather should be so strong, she winced. Not that it mattered.

What must it be like to know that the blood of strong "doers" in the world ran in your veins? Those princesses at Miravel Hall were doubly lucky. At least, Princess Alexia was. To have an ancestor strong and powerful as Tige Royle, and a thrilling and sexy husband like Prince Stefan was almost more than one woman deserved.

Long ago Julie used to tell herself that life wasn't fair. Other children found their parents, or were found, or they were wanted. It was only a few years ago that she got away from that and began to plan her own life which she could choose for herself and be whatever she wanted to be.

Somehow, meeting people like the prince and the famous man they called "Tiger" Royle, with the Tenbys to bring them together, Julie was sure all the cards were right. She once had a fascinating friend at the pub who read the Tarot Cards. She was a gypsy and didn't work long at one job. Julie never had seen her again, but the fortune she predicted for Julie was almost, if not quite, perfect: "Julie would get what she wanted out of life, providing, of course, she made up her mind precisely what that was". Right now, her head was full of mixed-up dreams. She had to straighten that out first.

The vicar watched Julie and Tige Royle go down the path to the street. He smiled at Julie's attempts to keep up with the big man's stride. Julie's thin, leggy figure kept up with most people. Tige looked down at her and grinned.

"You'll do, little one. You put me in mind of someone who was rather like you at your age. Nothing would stop him. He is still in there pitching, as we say."

"Really, sir? Was he one of us or a Yankee?"

"Oh, very much one of you. His mother was from this village. Girl named – what the devil was it? Chance was her husband's name, actually."

Nick Chance? She became alert. Nick Chance seemed to know secrets about her. Everyone called him the most generous man in Miravel. But she didn't like him. She was sure the two princesses didn't like him either. And old Mrs Tether, who had been the former vicar's housekeeper, hadn't any use for him at all. But Mrs Tether lived at Elder Home and was even older than Tige Royle. Her memory probably wasn't as good as it might be. Still, Nick Chance sounded like a man who had succeeded in life. He lived at Miravel Hall and even the two princesses treated him like an equal.

Julie admitted, "I don't think I could be as generous and good as Mr Chance."

Tige laughed. "Rubbish. He's no angel. Not that I don't admire the fellow. He was quick to learn. I like that. And he made himself in spite of his mother. Bit of a rip, that female. Died years ago in 1918, during the Great War."

"How awful! Poor Mr Chance."

He looked down at her. "He didn't let that stop him. Don't you let anything stop you, Missy."

"No, sir. I don't." As a matter of fact, it was the most solemn of all her secret vows.

He helped her into the front seat of his big car, making her feel like a princess herself. Nobody else except the vicar ever did that. Her luck was changing already.

Funny thing about Mr Chance. In spite of his reputation, he didn't look like a very nice person, certainly not likable, and a fancied similarity between his character and Julie's seemed to be an 'open sesame' to the interest of the great Tige Royle. He must enjoy manoeuvering lives around. She didn't mind, as long as it was to her advantage.

They drove through the main square of the village, past the public garage, open for a change, and across the bridge onto the road that hugged the side of the green hills. Julie was sure that several villagers saw her seated elegantly beside Tige Royle but made no attempt to wave or call anyone's attention to her. She knew enough about human nature to assume that if she acted as though she was used to this elegance, others might assume it as well.

Tige said after a few minutes of silence, "My great-granddaughter's husband was impressed by you, Julie."

She gave him a side-glance out of her tawny eyes with their oblique and mischievous slant. "Was he, really? He was awfully kind."

"Yes. A fine fellow. And an excellent ruler, I wish I could persuade Alexia of his good points; he loves her very much."

He looked at her and she wondered if his comment was based on something in Prince Stefan's attitude when he spoke of Julie. A thrilling thought. And a warning? *Stay away from my great-granddaughter's husband?*

This could mean that she had to be particularly careful. Tige Royle looked like a man who might read her thoughts, and could crush her like a flea if he chose.

CHAPTER SIX

Driving along the east front of Miravel Hall as a guest of the celebrated Tige Royle struck Julie as quite a different thing from her unwanted presence in Princess Garnett's car yesterday. Nor was she despised by Mr Royle. He had already told her, "Call me Tige. Everyone does."

When they reached the big, ramshackle garage she tried to show him she knew her place. "I'd best go in through the kitchen door by the herb garden. Mrs Skinner will expect it. I know the two ladies – I mean the princesses – wouldn't like me bouncing in past the family rooms."

She was almost out of the car by the time Tige came around to her side and gave her a helping hand down from the front seat. He grinned at her quick movements. "Now, nobody's going to gobble you up. If you're setting out to be a lady, like you told me, you have to make the gents do a little work. That's what we're here for."

Unlike Prince Stefan he then let her make her way to the house without his hand under her elbow. He probably figured rightly that in spite of his words she didn't need any stranger's help.

As they crossed the pebbled ground she half-apologized. "Don't you worry, sir. I learn fast."

"I'll just bet you do. But never mind the kitchen for now. Garnett, my granddaughter, has just quarrelled with one of the Miravel maids and you might fit the bill. Have you ever played ladies' maid before?"

She hesitated. Who wanted to be a servant kicked about by that arrogant beauty? She was about to say "no" to his question when he added, "Stefan – Prince Stefan, that is – suggested you when he and Nick and I were having breakfast. That lad seems to think you can do almost anything."

This changed matters entirely. She gave him a wide-eyed, hopeful look. "Oh, yes. I only hope I can please him. I mean the lady. The princess."

"Well, we'll see. It's only temporary, but who knows? My granddaughter was spoiled from the word 'go'. I wish you were working for Alexia. She's a hell of a lot more like Garnett's mother used to be. My daughter was very special." He shrugged and threw off a painful memory. "However, that's neither here nor there."

Mrs Skinner had come to a window of the small salon which was the scene of most of the Miravel Family's activities. She crooked her finger, beckoning to Julie while she bowed her head in homage to Tige.

When they reached her on the kitchen stoop surrounded by the still-flourishing herb garden, she said, "Do hurry, Julie. Her Highness has been complaining about your tardiness this hour."

"Impossible," Tige cut in. Julie rushed past him, not not wanting to displease the imperious beauty on her first day's work.

Tige called after Julie, "Slow down. Tell her it's my jalopy. Good luck." He went on to the cook-housekeeper, "Well, Skinner, my girl, has my granddaughter been giving you a bad time? Garnett will have to get used to the idea that she's not the only pebble on the beach."

Julie hurried through the entrance hall to the great main staircase before she realized she didn't know where she was going. She found herself nervous and hoping for the best when Princess Alexia called to her from the elegant, Regency reception hall.

"Julie? You must be looking for my mother. I'll take you to her." She came up the stairs, joining Julie on the first landing. She looked tired, a little harried, but she was kind and quite lovely. Almost beautiful.

She must suspect that Julie was nervous, not sure what would be the best approach with a woman who hadn't liked Julie from the first minute she gave her a lift on the Miravel Estate Road.

"I hope I can please Her Highness," Julie remarked, voicing her thoughts.

"Do your best. That is all any of us can do."

No wonder Prince Stefan loved her, Julie thought enviously. But there was always hope. Princess Alexia was not living with her husband. He would be bound to get tired of hanging on to a woman who no longer wanted him.

Alexia went on calmly, "Flatter my mother, if you feel you can do it subtly."

"Thank you, Your Highness." Julie meant it. This young woman did not talk about her mother like others Julie had known. There were others who were most disrespectful to their mothers, but they did a good deal of pretending. In Alexia's case there seemed to be a definite coolness regarding her mother, but that was no problem to Julie. She wasn't enraptured by Princess Garnett either.

As they turned at the gallery floor Alexia corrected her. "At Miravel I am Miss Alexia. I prefer it."

"Yes, Ma'am . . ." First error. Julie made a mental

note. "Yes, Miss." But she thought it very odd. If Alexia von Elsbach really was a princess, why not call herself one? Unless of course, she was afraid of meeting the hideous fate of the Czar and his family after the First World War.

Alexia led the way on the gallery floor past the now divided staircases, coiling their way up to the next floor and the attic floor above that. Between the two staircases with their wrought iron railings, hung an impressive chandelier, its many prisms catching the daylight. The gold ropes of the chandelier were anchored to the high, domed glass ceiling. Julie was properly dazzled but as Alexia was already knocking on the panelled door of the centre suite, she hurried her own steps, trying to appear calm and efficient.

She found it less and less easy in such a setting. The job meant more to her than any she had ever applied for. Who knew what future splendours it would lead to?

The door was opened by Prince Stefan before Alexia could raise her hand a second time. Julie saw Prince Stefan's face and wondered how his estranged wife could remain indifferent to the tenderness in his dark eyes and the tentative smile that must tell her he still cared.

She must be made of stone, Julie thought, envying her as she had never envied any other female, even the bejewelled women who visited "The Blitz Hospice". Those women were dream figures, appearing and disappearing, sometimes taking the hand of a nervous child whom the Blitz Girls never saw again.

The Estate Manager, Nick Chance, was looking out of the long windows at the water gardens below. He turned when Alexia entered with Julie. He looked Julie up and down and then gave Princess Garnett a sardonic smile.

"You'll have trouble with that one. She's not the docile doormat you usually pick out."

The princess shrugged. She had been standing in her dressing room doorway. The silver back of a hair brush in her hand caught the light from the windows. "Probably not, my dear, but until I receive my share of the last four quarterly profits I shan't be able to afford anything better."

"Good God!" said Stefan disgustedly at the same time as Alexia objected. "Mother, for heaven's sake!", and followed this with a few angry words in German.

Julie didn't like her new employer's remark but was delighted by Prince Stefan's quick anger on her behalf. She was very much aware that the woman's arrogance and tactlessness only helped Julie's own case with Prince Stefan.

Nick Chance replied to Garnett's financial reminder by the promise, "Our good-hearted vicar will explain about Miravel's so-called profits. You must be patient, he had several appointments this morning. Doing his Christian duty."

"Christian duty!" Garnett mocked. "Very likely . . . You there, young woman, let's see if you can rearrange my hair. This bouffant style is absurd on me."

Julie hurriedly obeyed, trying to remember how the prettiest girl at the Miravel Midsummer Social had arranged her hair. While she worked, vaguely aware that Princess Garnett was watching her in the dressing table mirror, she tried to hear the conversation through the open doorway between Prince Stefan and Alexia.

It wasn't going well, and it didn't get better when Nick Chance put in his own advice, reminding Alexia that she and her mother need no longer concern themselves with how the well-groomed Royal Consort appeared to the world.

"When Prince Stefan takes over, you will be free as birds. Like us common folk. A pleasant chance, I should imagine."

Evidently aware of the man's maliciousness, Stefan told Nick Chance, "Stay out of this. Lichtenbourg's affairs are no concern of yours."

"By all means," the Estate Manager agreed amiably.

"At least," Garnett put in with a feline purr, "Stefan may soon be on the run if the Soviets have anything to say."

Julie had known other people, male and female, children and adults, like Nick Chance and Princess Garnett. She could believe the gossip between Mrs Tenby and the old ladies visiting from Elder Home, gossip which had told Julie, to her surprise, that Nick Chance really was, very likely, Princess Garnett's bastard brother. He must have built up his hatred against the legitimate side of the family for a long time.

In a way, Julie could understand the man's resentment and perhaps his revenge. Too bad he was not more likable. But he probably wouldn't appreciate or even want sympathy. Besides, she was fully aware that her concern in the present conversation was a selfish hope that Prince Stefan and his wife would remain alienated.

"Do attend to your work," Princess Garnett reminded her more languidly than sharply. "That mascara brush belongs on my lashes, not my cheek."

Julie recovered rapidly, furious at her own wandering thoughts. "Indeed, Your Highness. But you don't really need any of these silly paints. Everyone says Your

Highness is more beautiful than any of those Miravel portraits in the gallery."

Garnett laughed. "My dear, there were one or two real beauties among those gargoyles." She studied her reflection and adding a satisfied, "However . . ." which made Julie want to smile.

Besides, Julie told herself, it was almost true. In appearance the lady was just about flawless. The trouble was, she knew it.

Julie managed to please Garnett by the simple method of following the princess's fingers. Garnett tucked up and pulled out fine locks of hair here and there and since she looked her glamorous self as always, she smiled at Julie's reflection and congratulated her on an excellent job.

Julie caught snatches of Prince Stefan's deep voice and slipped a little nearer the open doorway of the white and gold dressing room. Surely, very soon, she would learn what Prince Stefan would do to become the ruler of Lichtenbourg.

"I was prepared for everything but the desecration of my mother's tomb in the Cathedral. Work of the Reds, of course."

Alexia admitted, "I know what Lichtenbourg owes your mother. No one owes more to her memory. But Lichtenbourg is trying to toss out my father, too, and he has certainly given a lifetime to his country."

Garnett got up and came to the doorway. "Ilsa von Elsbach, that dyed blonde! What did she ever do for her country?"

Prince Stefan and Alexia looked at each other. Evidently, they shared some knowledge unknown to Princess Garnett.

Alexia startled everyone by her outburst. "Who cares

if she dyed her hair in polka dots? Stefan's mother was a beautiful woman, by the way, but that's neither here nor there. She did more than anyone in Lichtenbourg against the Nazis, and none of us knew it until too late. Look at the people she saved, smuggled out of—"

Stefan cut in with a warning. "Alexia, the Soviets may feel that as she worked against the Nazis, others in her family may work against Communist influence."

Alexia broke off, glanced at Nick Chance, apparently to see if he had noticed, and said no more.

Stefan went on. "We needn't go into that now. It will be important to our country if things blow up next door in Budapest. As usual, Lichtenbourg will be in the middle."

Tige Royle nodded. "There is a good deal of uneasiness in Hungary. It may go up any day."

Julie was excited by all this intrigue and puzzled by the fact that the undercurrents obviously pleased Nick Chance. She shivered and wondered why she did so. She did not intend to cross him or make trouble for him. Even the details of her employment here seemed to have shifted to others, for which she was relieved.

Garnett dismissed Julie casually. "Dear, why don't you run down and see what you can do to help Mrs Skinner?"

Alexia was going out the door and Julie slipped out after her. Alexia's thoughts were on matters far from a local servant girl and she went off quietly to her own quarters while Julie hurried down the great staircase.

Just as she reached the lower floor and the entrance hall towards the kitchen quarters, she heard the voice that was already chilling to her. It was a stupid reaction. Nick Chance had merely hinted that someone she'd never heard of might be related to her. What was so bad about that? But at this age, beyond childood, even beyond girlhood, she was repulsed by the idea of "belonging" to some stranger, dead or alive. The dreams she had made up were far better than a drab or sordid truth, which might even put up a barrier to her fierce ambition.

She stopped but with one foot forward, as if ready to scurry off. "Yes, sir? Excuse me, sir, but Mrs Skinner will be wanting me.'

He reached for her wrist. His fingers were thin and surprisingly hard. She winced but looked up into his cold eyes with more boldness than she felt.

"Well, sir?"

"You haven't babbled to the vicarage about that dying old woman in London and her talk of Miravel? They did not wish it discussed."

He was still harping on about that business. "Why should I? I never heard of the woman who died."

"Good. I'll find out what I can for you, but I shouldn't count on much if I were you."

She didn't like to be manhandled, and she couldn't resist an angry, teasing little laugh. "But I'm not, sir. And I do have a good memory of my babyhood and childhood."

"Excellent. I'm sure you wouldn't care to be claimed by the connections of such a female. One of the dubious sort, I should think. No money there, if that is what you have in mind."

"No, sir."

"And then there was her curious ramblings as she lay in her delirium. Something in Spanish."

For one breathtaking instant Julie felt stiff with icy dread of an old childhood fear. She sometimes felt that way when she heard certain sounds, like the deep thrumming of a guitar. She had no head for music, one of the matrons had complained when she was about ten. Perhaps it was true.

"Well," she said lightly, "then it couldn't be me she was talking about. I certainly don't feel Spanish and positively loathe their music."

"What a naughty thing to say about some of the world's most beautiful sounds!"

It was Nick Chance who saw that they were not alone. She looked over her shoulder. Tige Royle's leonine presence had a startling effect on the Estate Manager. He then dismissed her, "That will be all, Jones," and became humbly obliging to the old patriarch. "Were you looking for me, sir?"

"Looking for you? Now, why should I be doing that?" Tige asked, his still plentiful white eyebrows rising with an amused scorn that the younger man read immediately.

"I only meant – " Nick had to take out his annoyance and humiliation on someone. "Jones, will you please go about your work? Skinner is – " He saw Tige's bright eyes on him and cleared his throat. "Mrs Skinner will be wondering what has happened to you." Then, ignoring her as she moved on, he explained gently to Tige, "They will insist on listening in upon the conversation of their betters whenever the opportunity arises."

To Julie's surprise and delight Tige looked after her, saying in his easy way, "I shouldn't think Miss Julie regards any of us as her betters."

Julie didn't look at Nick Chance, but went along towards the service area, not quickly enough, however,

69

to miss Tige's next question of the Estate Manager. "What is this about Spain then?"

"Spanish music, sir. The girl was singing on duty. She annoyed Princess Garnett. You know how Her Highness dislikes anything Spanish."

Liar! Julie stopped in the darkness near the service doors.

Tige then asked, "Oh? Is the girl Spanish?"

The idea made Julie tense.

"Certainly not, sir." What made Nick Chance so emphatic? "It was just something from an old Hollywood film, I believe."

Tige dismissed the matter for the moment. "Have Alexia and her husband made any progress toward a truce?" He started up the stairs with Nick following.

"I'm not sure, sir. I rather fancy they are still at odds."

"Too bad. I am sorry about the damage to Ilsa von Elsbach's tomb. She almost outwitted Hitler. Not that very many knew it," Tige replied.

"But you did, obviously."

Tige didn't like to be contradicted. True to Nick Chance's suspicions of her, Julie remained in her corner to hear the voices until they faded out as the men reached the gallery floor.

"Obviously," Tige echoed, but with a snap to the word. "I knew because I had some dealings with her that even her son, Stefan did not know. She ran a kind of Underground – or is it an Undersea Movement – that the Scandinavians were running across the Baltic Sea or the Kattegat to safety in Sweden. She was our linchpin in Nazi territory. Damned clever, Stefan's mother."

"Yes, sir, indeed!"

Julie went into the kitchen. All that talk about the unknown dying woman who mentioned Julie, and Spain, still troubled her.

It was such a cowardly, childish admission, that she had been frightened of the stories told by some mischievous older girl in the orphans' home. They were stories of suffering and horror in some war – obviously the Spanish Civil War – which the other girls accompanied with music on a cheap record player. Appropriately enough, the music had been the deep, plaintive, passionate music of a Spanish guitar.

And here she was, a score of years later, still haunted by the made-up stories of a mischievous girl who had undoubtedly never been to Spain, but she had obviously known a gullible child like Julie when she saw one.

CHAPTER SEVEN

The Reverend Tenby, flashing a nervous smile, arrived that afternoon between the Miravels' old-fashioned early dinner and teatime. He came through the little herb garden and the kitchen entrance, explaining to Mrs Skinner that as soon as he had a few words with Mr Chance and Julie Jones, he would take the girl back to the village and not interfere with the coming meal.

Mrs Skinner greeted him in her respectful but dignified way. "A very obliging help she is, Reverend. In some ways, the best you've sent us." Puzzled and curious, she added, "You did say you wished to speak with Nick Chance *and* Julie? Together?"

"If there is no objection, yes. Both are acquainted with the matter."

Mrs Skinner's jaw tightened. "Not to put too fine an edge on it, sir, but when Nick Chance is involved with a help it's usually a complaint, and I'll brook no complaints about that girl. She is sharp and willing."

It seemed to Julie, who heard this from the cold storage room, that Mrs Skinner had struck a nerve in the vicar. He straightened to his full, modest height. "I cannot allow aspersions upon our patron, Mrs Skinner. As for Julie, my good wife is perfectly aware of Julie's useful ways. This happens to be a personal matter concerning Julie's – ah – past."

"Her past! That child? Lord love us! What will Nick Chance think of next?" Mrs Skinner took a deep breath. "Well then, take her along. But mind no ill-natured remarks from that – Mr Chance."

The vicar assured her with dignity, "You must be aware, Madam, that I give deep consideration to the welfare of the young people placed in my care."

Mrs Skinner sniffed, obviously not convinced. "I devoutly hope so. Not – " she added, remembering she spoke to a man of the Cloth, "Not that you would do otherwise, Reverend, sir. It's just that it was Nick Chance I had reference to."

"A good Christian, Madam." Turning from her to graver matters, the Reverend Tenby held out his hand to Julie.

Julie, who had been the object of insults in the past, both earned and unearned, threw off her apron and went along with the vicar after a grateful smile at Mrs Skinner. She had a very strong feeling that someone was going to discuss the subject of the late Mrs What's-Her-Name who had obviously confused Julie with a long lost relative. *Why couldn't someone like Prince Stefan claim me for a relative?* she thought. Not that she wanted to be related to that prince by blood. It would ruin all her dreams.

Along the reception hall on their way to Nick Chance's small study they passed the billiard room. Both doors were open and Julie saw Prince Stefan facing her from the far side of the table. Tige Royle had his back to the doorway and was heavily engaged in making his shot. She felt that he was a man who always won whatever he played, games or business.

Julie was too much like that herself to feel any warmth for him, such as she felt for the prince, who raised one hand to her and gave her his delightful smile.

Seeing his gesture, Tige raised his head and looked over his shoulder. To Julie his frown was more thoughtful than disapproving, but she wondered what he was thinking and wished he would stop acting as if he expected her to steal the silver.

Nick Chance was waiting for the vicar in the tight, crowded little study that Julie thought could use a good dusting and some polish. The light filtering in between the portières at the windows only called attention to the dust motes in the air. It was clear that Mrs Skinner spent a good deal more time at her cook's post than as a housekeeper.

How strange that the two princesses had spent much of their lives in tiny, dangerous Middle-European Lichtenbourg when they might have lived here, at least half of each year. There was no accounting for tastes.

Nick Chance surprised and amused Julie by his careful posture behind the desk, in an old-fashioned, squeaky chair that leaned back dangerously now and then. She suspected he was imitating someone, perhaps his father, Lord David Miravel, who had never recognized his legitimacy and probably wasn't worth imitating anyway. People who didn't recognize their own children had long ago fallen beneath Julie's contempt.

She remained modestly attentive, trying not to speak until she was spoken to. Reverend Tenby seemed eager but a little nervous, too. "The woman's final words seemed promising; don't you agree, Mr Chance? It was not Christian of her to keep silent so long but she does give an explanation of sorts."

Nick Chance was holding a letter-opener between his two hands, moving his prominent thumbs over the blade to a steel rose on the haft which he referred to now.

"The white rose of the House of York. They made the fortunes of this family." He shrugged. "Then came the Tudors and the white rose was proscribed. We have been at outs with Royal Houses ever since. I don't suppose it matters to the Windsors. However – "

While Julie noted his inclusion of himself among the Miravels and thought of herself, with her own ambitious dream life, the vicar bit his lip but managed to contain his eagerness to get the subject back on track.

"To be sure. But I do remember hearing that the Miravels entertained King Edward VII."

"That would be due to Tige Royle, I imagine. No one seems to have refused his company . . . odd really. He began as a miner, you know, and no one has the slightest knowledge of his antecedents. Those were deep mines, mind you. Nevada silver. He took me there once. I shouldn't like to have found myself that far under the earth." He chuckled, inviting them to laugh with him, though his eyes remained hooded as always. "Not at least until I am in my coffin."

"Which we sincerely trust will not be for many a day," the vicar put in and corrected himself. "But what am I saying? Our benefactor deserves many a *year*. Such kindness to the Elder Home, and now the children! Which puts me in mind of our young miss here. You do agree that the woman's dying words deserve to be given investigation."

"My dear fellow," Nick Chance waved his letter-opener, with the glistening point toward the vicar. "A good deal of rubbish is spoken in one's final hours. I remember my own father's last words, in this very house. How tenderly he spoke to me; yet you processed the will. You, above all, should know how little credence we may place in Lord Miravel's last words."

Tenby murmured, "But sir, this matter has no similarity to anything that your – I mean Lord Miravel – may have said. Very likely, no money and no estate are involved. It is only Julie's name that we are trying to verify."

"Only her name," Nick repeated softly and dug the point of the opener into the ink-stained blotter. "She may find it easier to remain Julie Jones, or whatever she is called."

Julie surprised them both, hoping to end this business. Sooner or later someone was sure to bring up the haunting nightmares of her babyhood. "Yes, sir. When I was young I dreamed all sorts of things, being a princess, or a star in the cinema. But not any more. I want to be me, not some imaginary character."

Nick Chance regarded her with more interest. "Quite so. Very intelligent of you. So, my friend, I think we may dispense with any hopes that the young woman will turn out to be a great heiress, or possibly the Queen of Spain."

Julie shivered and then wondered why he had said that odd thing. It was not the title she found frightening. It was . . . but of course, it had always been that. Spain.

Both men sensed her reaction, each in his own way. Nick Chance studied her with his chilling curiosity. The vicar obviously was disappointed. "Now, Julie, you are being very childish. This is all for the best. Somewhere, someone loved you and lost you long ago. You must think of your loved ones who may still be alive, still searching."

Then Nick retorted, "I doubt that, sir, not after all these years. You said this old woman merely hinted that an orphan, either at Miravel or named Merribelle, was known to her long ago."

But the vicar was stubborn. "No, sir, I said the dying woman had reacted immediately to the name of my parish, or to this Estate. She said several words: 'orphan', and 'Miravel' or 'Merribelle'. One of the hospital's patrons, a gentleman named Athlone discussed the matter with the nursing sisters. He believed that the woman was a midwife known to his own dead wife long ago. His wife had employed the woman in Spain on some charity work in the early Thirties. Athlone thought his own son might be concerned. The boy was also adopted. But this sounds to me like wishful thinking, since it does not explain Miravel's part in it."

"But much more likely," Nick put in. Clearly, the notion of another person connected with his own special dream of Miravel was unwelcome to him. The unknown creature might even be a rival who could be entitled to a part of the Miravel Estate.

"I don't know any Athlone, and I was never in Spain," Julie protested, backing toward the door. She was relieved to hear the two billiard players talking in the hall. Surely, they would change the subject. She raised her voice. "Please, it had nothing to do with me."

Out of the corner of her eye she saw the two men stop in the hall. She had caught their attention. Prince Stefan came forward, moving to the doorway between Julie and her inquisitors. She thought of his gesture as protective and admired him more than ever. He nodded to the Reverend Tenby but addressed the Estate Manager.

"What is this all about, Nick? Can't you take her word

for it? Julie says this business has nothing to do with her. Leave it at that."

Julie was too nervous to utter a word.

Nick yawned, tapping the palm of his hand against his mouth. "Quite so. And may I point out, Your Highness, that I agree with you in every particular. The dying woman said nothing of this girl."

The vicar concentrated deeply. "I believe – that is, the nurses and I found the poor woman so near death she might have said anything. I did get the impression, however, that there was a Spanish connection. Also, the nurses seemed divided in their opinion of the woman's word 'Miravel' which they took as correct because the dying woman was jarred to some remembrance when she heard the name of my parish. Possibly those who believed she said 'Merribelle' were right, after all." He added modestly, "Our charities here include quarterly contributions to the nursing home and hospital in London, so they know me fairly well."

"And is there a connection with the village?" Tige asked, behind the prince.

The vicar shook his head in perplexity. "I cannot in all conscience, swear to anything about the matter, only what I assumed I heard, and that could be either word."

"It's all much too 'iffy'," the prince said, after a glance at Julie who was as uneasy as ever. "There seems to be an inquisition against Julie here. I imagine you were right in your surmise, Nick. This Athlone probably is closer to the matter than we are."

"Very likely, Your Highness," the vicar put in, still in what the rest thought was an annoying tone of doubt. "I'm afraid I jumped to conclusions. But my dear wife thought

78

it would be lovely if our Julie should find she was the daughter of – well, important parents."

Stefan and Tige looked at each other. The prince said quietly, "I think our young lady will remain 'Just Julie' and make her own way in the world. When we leave here she will have to find a new post, I imagine. I doubt that you will need her services, Nick."

"Not in the least," Nick assured him.

"If you like, Julie," the prince went on, "I'll speak to Princess Garnett once we reach Lichtenbourg. There should be something for a capable young lady like you."

Julie burst out eagerly, "If I can be of service to the ladies, sir . . ."

As Julie had suspected, very few things, even nuances, escaped Tige Royle. "Nick, what do you know yourself about this business in London? What is your interest?"

"Nothing whatever, beyond what the Reverend Tenby has told us as a pure conjecture."

He's lying, Julie thought. She had known many liars in her life. Sometimes, as in her own case, lies were for self-protection, but what did Nick Chance expect to get out of this affair which had nothing to do with him?

Tige stared at Nick in a way that would have made Julie exceedingly uncomfortable. Then he dismissed the matter. "Stefan, I want to talk to you about your plans. I need some exercise. Suppose you take a stroll with me out past the water gardens. If you should be voted in, and the People's Democratic gang come in second, Colonel Grigori Vukhasin will take your old job as Vice-Chancellor. That is in your constitution; isn't it?"

Prince Stefan grinned, playing it lightly. "Just what I need, Comrade Stalin breathing down my neck."

Everyone was surprised when Tige, who seemed to

be acquainted with half the world, said "That's to be seen. Vukhasin may be dangerous. In fact, I'd say he is, especially after he had the gall to manoeuvre his way into citizenship in your country. But he's one of those you can't seem to kill. Metaphorically speaking. I knew him years ago in Barcelona, about the time the Civil War started, with Hitler and Mussolini supporting Franco. Vukhasin was lending Stalin's light touch to the Loyalists in the fracas. Ugly bastard, Grigori, but we were buddies during the Hitler days. Who knows? Our 'old pal' routine may still be useful to you and your country."

Julie was afraid they would forget Prince Stefan's suggestion about her future and she put in, "I can type, sir. Mrs Tenby says I'm quite fair at it."

Tige ignored this impatiently. "We are getting away from matters at hand. Stefan, you're missing a bit, not looking into the NATO problem. It's one way to get the Western sympathies on your side."

"And the USSR on my back," he replied.

The vicar, like Julie, had other matters on his mind, more important than all this political wrangling. "My dear wife and I are very fond of Julie, but if she can better herself in Lichtenbourg, and if there is nothing that concerns her in London, we won't stand in her way. But I think we must clear up this London matter first, even though it is probably all a misunderstanding."

Julie groaned, but it was obvious that Prince Stefan and Tige considered international affairs took top priority.

"Good. I'm sure Mrs Tenby and you will handle matters for Julie's best interests. Now, Tige, let's get to the water gardens and that infernal NATO problem."

As the two men were leaving, Nick Chance put in, "So now, Your Highness, it would seem to me, the new

Lichtenbourg elections will make the world your oyster."
He glanced at Julie, adding, "In every way."

Whatever he implied by his reference to Julie, Stefan ignored it. Tige didn't like it but had the last word, as he often did. "It would seem to me my dear fellow, that even if that were the case, you would have nothing to say about it."

CHAPTER EIGHT

At a late supper on their last night at Miravel, Garnett was celebrating her "triumph" over Nick Chance's book-keeping. Nick looked modest, even innocent, a feat which Alexia found both amusing and suspicious. Who had given Nick the wherewithal to pay Garnett a year's profits after the careful shearing off of his own?

Alexia saw Stefan's side-glance at Tige and decided to ask Tige if he was the 'Good Samaritan'. She felt that his constant bailing out of Nick Chance would certainly put her mother in Nick's class as far as Tige was concerned. It was one of the many reasons she was glad when Tige defended Stefan for his behaviour about the Lichtenbourg elections. It gave her the excuse she wanted in order to return home with Stefan and to hope that the elections would make him come to his senses, perhaps even insist, with his new power, that Prince Maximilian be kept on as a figurehead. That might save her father's life. Partly for Garnett's sake, Max cared so very much about retaining the social eminence he had held since he was a youth.

Meanwhile, once again, the Miravels were in debt to Tige who must have paid Nick Chance to clear his debt with Garnett.

But Tige enjoyed it, and not, Alexia thought, out of the generous streak which Tige certainly possessed. He probably felt that no one else was going to repay Nick for a lifetime of illegitimacy and the injustices of his father, Lord David Miravel.

Two hours later Alexia was on her way to her bedchamber when she passed her mother's suite. Garnett was nowhere in sight but the elegant, panelled door was wide open and to her surprise, Julie, was jumping up and down on one of Princess Garnett's packed Vuitton steamer trunks.

Although this conduct was not guaranteed to give the case a long life Alexia could not help laughing. She called from the open doorway, "Julie, that used to be my job. But I seem to have been replaced in my old age."

Julie jumped down in a fluster.

"I'm sorry, Miss Alexia. But His Highness said it was the only way to get it shut and locked."

Alexia stepped into the room with its green and gold fittings so perfectly suited to Princess Garnett's colouring. The first thing Alexia saw was her husband, Stefan, trying to bring the two sides of a big wardrobe trunk together so the hasp would work. He had one knee pressed against the trunk and was pulling with both arms. At sight of her he gave one more pull, fastened the trunk, laughed and wiped his face. "Not easy, I can tell you. But I've been assured that everything in here is an absolute and incontrovertible necessity."

"That's mother, all right." Alexia saw the other trunk gaping open and ordered Julie to help her.

Julie looked anxiously from Alexia to Stefan who nodded as if Alexia couldn't give an order without his OK. Julie joined her and then gasped in horror as the princess pushed the unfastened trunk wide open and began to take out a wooden hanger with an exquisite Dior gown which required a corset to get into it.

"That goes out. And this black and white Chanel. She always says she looks terrible in black . . . And Stefan, how did she persuade you to let her take the red Dotted Swiss? It's more suited to a teenager. Like Julie here."

Stefan turned to the wide-eyed, hopeful Julie. "You see? My wife is not only the most beautiful woman in the world, but she can manage that Gorgon mother of hers."

Julie looked around hastily but Garnett was still missing. Alexia threw the Dotted Swiss to her. It fell at Julie's feet. Obviously, the girl couldn't believe this was happening to her.

"Here," Alexia said. "Wear it in good health. But for heaven's sake, not before my mother."

Julie swallowed and hesitated but anybody could see she loved the summery dress. Stefan picked it up, made an elaborate bow and handed it to Julie with the excellent advice, "Her Serene Highness won't miss it after she makes her usual purchases as we pass through Paris on our way home."

"Then I do thank you, sir, and Your Highness, with all my heart. It's terribly kind of you," Julie gushed.

"Say rather, it's terribly kind of Princess Garnett," Stefan remarked, obviously enjoying himself.

How delightful he could be when in the right mood, Alexia thought and then, feeling that she read too much into that teasing manner, she returned to business, removing a couple of lengthy Oriental scarves from one of the trunk's several drawers. The scarves must weigh a pound apiece. The designs were heavily encrusted with real silver bits. The trunk drawer could close easier now, especially after she removed a pair of pumps from the bottom drawer which had been stuck against the drawer above.

She followed this with other depredations. "And this jacket." She reached for the hangers again and shook out the sable in its wrappings.

Stefan was a bit rueful. "I'm afraid your mother alone is responsible for the depletion of wildlife." He handed the jacket to Julie who hung it temporarily in the closet before leaving. Stefan remarked, "No wonder she came storming over to Miravel for her share of the profits."

Alexia smiled but shook her head. "I'm afraid she charged all this to you, darling." That endearment slipped out. She pretended she hadn't noticed it. She couldn't tell whether he had made anything of it. Probably not. She did have to admit that Garnett was a bit hard to take, in spite of her celebrated charm and beauty. Tige once said Garnett had the misfortune to take after Lady Phoebe Miravel, the mother of Garnett's late father, Lord David Miravel. Alexia doubted very much if it had been meant as a compliment, or even a joke.

She and Stefan shared a knowing look of exasperation over the current Princess Royal of Lichtenbourg. He dismissed Julie with thanks and his warm smile which obviously pleased the young woman. To Alexia she still looked like a leggy, stringy girl, an ageless gamine.

The girl hesitated, glanced back in time to see Stefan draw Alexia to him. Then she left the suite.

Alexia warmed to him and to his hard arm that enclosed her. She longed to believe he was, and had always been, sincere in his devotion.

When he lowered his head over hers she raised her face, anticipating his heavy, passionate lips that looked hard, sometimes ruthless, but had always absorbed her doubts and fears with his own passion, as he did now.

A minute later, still with her body close, one of his long legs pinning her to him, he asked her in his low-pitched voice, "Am I forgiven, Liebchen?"

"Don't joke." She was annoyed that he should take this minute to say such an absurd thing, as if it had been some domestic spat over a trivial household matter. "Nothing can be settled until the elections are over."

Her reminder had reacted upon him. She felt that he was drawing away from her emotionally, if not physically. "Then, hadn't we better settle it now, so we can get on with our lives?"

She took a long breath. "Stefan, back in 1941, when we met on the train to Miravel, you planned to meet me, didn't you? You followed me out of the air raid shelter after the All Clear and deliberately found a seat in my railway carriage."

"Your memory is faultless. Congratulations."

She hesitated, then blurted out, "You said you were Count Andross."

"That was and is one of my names. My father's, as it happened. My mother was married twice. Not entirely unknown."

She had always been afraid to charge him with the fears which had never completely left her. What if he admitted the true reason he had lied to her when they met? When she had found out that he belonged to a rival family with a claim on Lichtenbourg's Royal House, she was already in love with him. Her own parents, needing his political power and that of his mother, had urged the marriage.

It had been easy to bury her first suspicions when she learned his real identity. Everyone, including Stefan, joined in assuring her his love for her came first and he had no desire to supersede her father. But in the end her father might be deposed, and die in defeat, if not in disgrace, while Stefan's original ambition was fulfilled.

He let her go, his arms slipping away from her. His voice even and too calm. "Would there be any use in assuring you that I loved you then and I love you now?"

"You arranged to meet me then for political reasons."

"I never denied it. If you are talking about those first days," he replied.

Something inside her wanted to cry out, *Deny it! I don't want the truth.* But she laughed abruptly to hide her feelings. "Thanks for being so patient with Mother tonight."

He locked one of Princess Garnett's cases with a loud, crisp snap, dismissing Alexia without looking at her. "I certainly deserve your thanks for that, at least."

The next morning Alexia was ironically amused, as always, to note the instructions on her mother's two Vuitton trunks and her eleven Vuitton cases of assorted sizes. Engraved instructions on gold name plates read:

FOR HER SERENE HIGHNESS, PRINCESS GARNETT PHOEBE MIRAVEL KURAGIN, THE NEW PALACE, LICHTENBOURG CITY, LICHTENBOURG, CARE OF THE ROYAL HOUSEHOLD STAFF, DIPLOMATIC AND CUSTOMS INSPECTION TO BE WAIVED.

Garnett had always been a traveller in the grand style, and Alexia wondered how much good all these grandiose flourishes would do. She doubted if any stray Commissar around the Hungarian border would pay any attention to her imperious order. If the plane carrying them made a stop in Budapest, where the underground revolt was seething against Communist rule, Garnett might wind up minus a wardrobe at the very least.

However, election or no election in Lichtenbourg, someone would reimburse Garnett for a wardrobe. Someone always took care of the 'Garnetts' of the world.

Looking at all the well-travelled luggage with its obvious purpose of reminding the world of her mother's regal identity, Alexia wondered, not for the first time, if her mother had been faithful to Maximilian. She certainly enjoyed her travels and her high expenses, and she could hardly live without an entourage of handsome young men around her. Probably the same admirers were a part of her expected decor. But it was within the realm of possibility that there may have been more to Garnett's past than her daughter had guessed. She hoped her father would never find out, if such a thing had happened in Garnett's life. It would certainly kill Maximilian.

While stout, hard-breathing Horwich and the old chauffeur, Durkin, made Garnett and Alexia comfortable in the back of the limousine, Tige leaned in at the back window facing Alexia who probably looked as she felt, worried over the future with a man who had virtually overthrown her father.

Meanwhile, assuming her grandfather's interest was directed at her, Garnett extended an exquisitely gloved hand. "Tige, dear, do give me one more peck on the cheek and show me you wish us well in those horrid elections."

Tige brushed her cheek and then touched Alexia's hand. "Honey, if you need me for anything, just contact my San Francisco number. You know the one. They'll get me, any place in the world."

After a handshake with Tige, Stefan started the car with a deep roar of the powerful engine.

The limousine rolled around the front of the Hall toward the slope of the Estate Road. Nick Chance came out the southwest doors of the Hall with the Reverend Tenby and Julie Jones beside him. All three waved to the limousine. Looking back, it seemed to Alexia that, as usual, Nick's gesture was flippant, like a child whose mother waves his reluctant hand.

Stefan shared her curiosity about the two men. Or one of them in particular. "Clever fellow, that Nick," he said, more or less to himself. "Maybe too clever for his own good."

"Good heavens, why?" Garnett asked. "Nick is out for one person. Himself. Simple."

Alexia thought, *like brother, like sister*, but she asked instead, "What particularly clever thing has he done now?"

Stefan glanced back at Alexia. "Just that business about young Julie. He seems to know something and he certainly doesn't want us to know whatever it is. I mentioned it to Tige but sometimes he plays his cards too close to his chest. I can't tell whether Tige is interested or not."

Alexia was surprised at his interest in Julie Jones. But it was Garnett who gave the remark the indifference it probably deserved.

"Oh well, it can hardly be our concern."

PART TWO

Lichtenbourg

CHAPTER NINE

Julie suspected that all the other passengers in the badly worn, post-war train compartments were staring, enraptured, out the windows at the passing Austrian scene. The country might be green with promise, having traded away its useless belligerent rights for freedom from the four Allied Powers, but it held less interest for Julie than her very own passport and two precious letters, one warm and full of good wishes from Mrs Tenby, and the other, a formal page, typed, and headed by the impressive eagle of Lichtenbourg's reigning family, the Kuragins:

His Highness Prince Stefan Andross von Elsbach wishes me to inform you that your stenographic services will be accepted in the Foreign Department following upon conclusion of the elections proclaimed by His Serene Highness, Prince Maximilian Kuragin.

Enclosed are your First Class tickets for the Paris–Wien–Lichtenbourg City portion of the Express on the date indicated. Your train will follow the route of what was formerly known as the Arlburg Orient Express.

Also enclosed is a voucher for your personal needs. The staff of the Lichtenbourg Consulate in Paris will assist you in obtaining the requisite funds in French Francs, Austrian and Lichtenbourg Schillings.

For His Highness Prince Stefan,
(signed)
Count Sigismund Thallin von und Zu
Helgemain

It was all even better than she had dreamed of. Certainly, the money was phenomenal to her. In Paris, with only hours to spare, she had shopped in several small but delightful places off the fantastic Champs Elysées and one on the Left Bank. The styles, being for middle-class customers, were still very much in the romantic and flattering Christian Dior style which she was thin enough to wear even without a new corset, though she bought one anyway. Nothing like impressing the Lichtenbourgers! Not to mention her generous dream lover, Prince Stefan.

The trip itself was nerve-racking in some ways, especially when she was interrogated by customs officers and border police. It was really an anxious time when the train was stopped at the Rhine border between France and the Federal Republic of West Germany, but the customs men weren't at all like Nazis in the movies. She managed a big, wavering smile and was delighted when the customs officer with two front teeth missing gave her a friendly grin.

There were a few formalities at the border between the Federal Republic and something called "Ostereich" which proved to be Austria. Some passengers got on at Salzburg and the train rushed on to Wien, which turned out to be Vienna. She was now within an hour of Lichtenbourg.

As she peered out the window, admiring the beauty of

green fields and gentle hills, a train attendant knocked on the door of her compartment. The attendant opened the door and stuck his head in. He seemed to have trouble explaining some problem. He was French and his English was not clear to her. Nervously, she tried to make things easier for him. After all, whatever the trouble was, his language problems weren't any worse than hers. What little French she knew had come from her days as the handy-girl at a Belgian refugee's beauty shop in London.

While she and the frustrated little attendant were trying to put together what he wanted to explain, a young man with unruly hair and an air of cool indifference shifted the attendant aside and slid an expensive overnight bag along the carpet.

Without giving Julie much attention he explained in a businesslike way, "Second Class compartments are shared, Miss. However, we needn't put up with each other for long." Then he looked over at her, giving her a moment of discomfort since she couldn't see his eyes. He didn't smile and she doubted if his interest was flattering. Was he memorizing her face? Why?

"I didn't know it was Second Class," she excused herself, trying to remain haughtily unaware of having deliberately chosen a Second Class compartment rather than the First Class one Prince Stefan had paid for. She knew perfectly well that she had changed the tickets so she could have a little more money for her small but carefully chosen wardrobe.

The attendant gave up, shrugged and closed the door, leaving them alone. The young man kicked his suitcase aside to make room for his crossed legs as he sat down on the edge of the bed. Having nudged the case against

95

her own suitcase which was packed and ready for her departure, he surprised her again by glancing over to read her neat gold tab:

J JONES
NEW PALACE
LICHTENBOURG CITY
LICHTENBOURG

Julie had considered that what was good enough for Princess Garnett was good enough for her, but now she found herself slightly embarrassed again, as if she travelled under false pretenses.

Her new companion looked up from her suitcases and studied her face. Then he said, "Pardon me. Are you, by chance, one of the Royal Family?"

She was not going to let him reduce her to her true status. She had lived for the last few days in the pleasant aura of an unspoken identification with the "Royals".

"Certainly not. It is my destination address."

He glanced at her make-up case with its two tags. "Then you come from . . . Miravel. In England?"

"In Shropshire, yes." She wanted to ask his own identity but decided to play the cool uninterested aristocrat instead. Aristocratic heroines in films didn't usually blab out their life stories on first acquaintance with rude men.

She wished he would stop staring – no – studying her. It made her wonder if something was wrong. Her make-up on crooked? Her pillbox hat too far back? But she didn't dare to rectify these possible faults. They could at once call attention to her insecurity.

She meant to show him that she was not anyone you could stare at, but eventually, tired of this game and uneasy over its purpose, she turned her head, and looked out the window, pretending to be enthralled by the view of a distant chalet nestled in a grove of trees on the hillside.

Barriers loomed up, cutting across the fields and ruining whatever had been planted there, since deep trenches had been dug on both sides of the wire barriers. They must be approaching tiny Lichtenbourg, which, in spite of its size, still assumed the same border rights as its more powerful neighbours, Austria, Hungary and beyond the Danube, another Communist-dominated country, Czechoslovakia.

She started to smooth on her carefully unsoiled white kid gloves which she had heard that Grace Kelly wore off the screen, when her unwanted companion surprised her by remarking. "Well now, it seems we share the same destination."

He must know that. He had read her baggage tag. But she shrugged in her most sophisticated way. "Of course," and then added, because she was genuinely curious, "have you business in Lichtenbourg City?"

He seemed almost civil. "In a sense. I am visiting the British Consul, General Sir George Athlone." Then he surprised her again by asking, "Do you know the name?"

"I've never heard of it. Should I?"

He smiled with his eyes still fixed on her. "Shouldn't you? I wonder if you know a nursing home in London, some little distance from Victoria Station. Off the beaten path, I would say. A hospital built over the ruins of some mews that were bombed in the Blitz."

She stiffened. She had the absurd thought that he might be a friend of Mr Chance, quizzing her about that old lady who mentioned Miravel and then died.

"I've no idea what you are talking about. I've never been to a charity nursing home in that area."

"Of course not. I beg your pardon." He gently moved her suitcase with the toe of his shoe. "But then, how did you know the place was a charity nursing home?"

What difference did it make? And especially, what difference did it make to him? She snapped out haughtily, "They usually are; aren't they?"

"Of course. Invariably."

She knew that was sarcasm but pretended to take his words at face value and gave him one of her aloof, movie star shrugs.

He surrendered his quiz, to her intense relief, and got up to take down her sleek French coat with its reserved but elegant Chanel cut. "Yours, I believe, Miss – "

She didn't answer but got into her coat before he could help her.

He seemed to find her oddly interesting, or was it only amusing? Not that it mattered. They were pulling into a city with Germanic architecture right out of a Grimm's fairy tale, ancient houses leaning over narrow streets, two and three storey houses with roofs like peaked gables.

She forgot her pique at the young man who shared her compartment and raised her voice in her excitement. "It looks like it wasn't bombed here. And so weird, like a wicked witch with a pointed hat would come out any minute to sweep those funny cobbled alleys."

"It is an ancient city," he replied. "Early Middle Ages. Thank God it wasn't bombed during the war, except down by the railway yards. You've never seen it before?"

"No. Never. It's wonderful. Just like a fairy tale. A little scarey though." Then the train moved on, slowly now, and the scene changed. She strained against the window, looking out at what appeared to be the heart of the city. This was a long, wide boulevard, heading down from the station which loomed ahead of the train. The boulevard moved down to a busy circle outlined by a Gothic cathedral on one side and numerous public buildings on the other. At the far end of the boulevard, on a slight rise, was a long stone building protected by a barrier of wrought iron fence and impressive gates.

Julie opened her eyes wide. "Is that a jail? I mean, like old Newgate and Wormwood Scrubs?"

Her companion looked at her. He seemed amused but then he explained in a friendly way. "Not quite. That's your destination – the New Palace."

"That ancient wreck? I thought it would be – " She bit her lip. "Well, they ought to at least clean it once a century."

"I certainly agree to that. However, some of the public rooms are quite nice. I can't speak for the private ones."

The train slowed to a gentle stop, followed by a great deal of activity on and off the train. A stocky little man in a tight uniform made his way through the crowd. With a rapidly beating heart Julie wondered if it was even vaguely possible that the uniformed man, holding his cap respectfully in the hollow under one arm, was sent by Prince Stefan to receive her.

The attendant knocked and opened the compartment door. "The luggage, Mademoiselle?"

Her companion had already picked up his case and waved her ahead of him. She went past him with her best smile, thinking how surprised he would be if the uniformed man had come to meet and escort her to the palace.

She went down the steps as gracefully as possible, not with her usual pell-mell descent. She didn't want to fall on her face in front of everyone. When she reached the platform of the big, glass-roofed station the train attendant set her two bags down beside her, waiting a fraction of a minute until she remembered her duty and took out a French Franc note with staggering figures. There had been talk about "New Francs" coming but the bank in Paris had given her these. They looked like the entire war debt.

The little uniformed man was striding her way, and her nervousness eased. Her recent companion was just behind her, so he was bound to see her reception. As the uniformed man reached her she smiled appreciatively, only to have him look past her to that very curious young man. She couldn't miss the exchange of greetings, though she pretended to be deaf to the whole incident.

The little man had signs of a brogue, probably Irish. "Well, sir, good to be seeing you again. And did the old lady oblige you now?"

"Not quite, Lukey. Matter of fact, she was on her deathbed. Died while I was there. A form of pneumonia, they said. Poor devil. A good amount of coughing . . . How is my father?"

The two passed Julie. She was surprised to see that the young man carried his own bag. The chauffeur put on his cap as they went across the platform to the waiting room doors. One thing she could say for the inquisitive fellow, he was very democratic.

Meanwhile, no one came for her. It was Miravel – and several other assignments in her life – all over again. *Get there the best way you can. You're not one of us.*

She lifted her two bags and walked out after the rest of the crowd. Behind her the Express gave a long mournful whistle and started off toward the brewing political troubles of Budapest.

But they were not Julie's concern. Right now she had one problem, to find a bus (they were cheaper than taxis). It was not a good sign that no one had come to collect her.

Maybe it would be better to walk down that boulevard decorated with all the political banners and signs pertaining to an election. If she got tired before she started up from the big circle with its church and all, to the long stone "New" Palace, she could find a pavement café like those in Paris, and have what the Parisians called "a Sanzano" though it was spelled Cinzano. That would make her feel more like her aggressive self.

Julie pushed one of the doors open with her knee and went through a little hall to the outside doors. A number of cars of all makes had been parked facing the station with a funereal black limousine having pride of place. It must belong to the British Consul, General What's-His-Name, because the little uniformed chauffeur and Julie's recent train companion were headed toward it.

Talk about uniforms!

A large, solid-looking man of middle years got out of the limousine. The chest of a British military uniform, heavy with braid, ribbons and medals, told Julie that he must be the British Consul himself. He looked jovial and jowly. The young man from the train came to him and they exchanged embraces with resounding slaps on the back. The chauffeur held the door open for them but the young man said something to the general who looked over at Julie. He seemed surprised for a moment, then nodded and to Julie's astonishment, waved her over to the limousine.

Well, this was something else! What on earth had induced her recent companion to mention her to the general? He couldn't be attracted to her. He hadn't shown the slightest sign of that. Quite the contrary. She had felt wavelengths of dislike between them. Maybe he was sorry for having behaved so oddly. But even so, what did he say that made the general (if this was the general) summon her to that glamorous car? Well, why not find out?

It was possible her train companion really did believe she was someone important at the palace. That struck her as a good joke. She swung her cases around, tried to behave with the friendly, yet regal elegance of Prince Stefan's wife, and walked towards them, careful not to appear too eager.

The general's face was flushed. Maybe, Julie thought, he drank. He didn't look at all like the young man who must be his son, judging by their slaps on the back and their clear affection for each other. But the general seemed as easy and friendly towards a stranger like Julie as if they had been warm acquaintances for years. She was careful not to go overboard by trying to bow or show too much respect. He wasn't a prince, after all.

When she reached the general, he looked at the young man who said, "My father, General Athlone, suggests that since your palace escorts are delayed, we might stop by the palace with you, if you like, Miss Miravel."

"Jones," she corrected him, sure he had read the name on her baggage tags and remembered it.

"Of course. Careless of me."

Before he could make amends for his "mistake" his father extended a beefy hand and squeezed her fingers painfully. "Do join us, my dear. We'll get you there safe and sound. You won't have time to share a spot of tea at the consulate, I daresay. Or is it sherry with young people now?"

"Father," his son cut in.

"No. Sorry," the general went on in excellent spirits. "Before the war – considerably before – 'Gin and It' was the thing. But I'm rambling on. Brett never ceases to remind me. You are all back to whisky now."

"Father, the young lady is waiting."

"To be sure. Do join me, Miss Miravel. We'll let my boy sit opposite us to eavesdrop."

She smiled sweetly at Brett Athlone. "I'm sure he does that supremely well."

The general took this as a droll bit of humour but the younger man turned to stare at her. She refused to be cowed but at the same time was surprised to discover that the dark-haired young man had blue eyes. Deeply blue. They did not soften his expression as he stared at her.

What have I done to this ridiculous fellow, she wondered and decided to simply ignore him.

As they arranged themselves, thanks to the general's helping hand, Brett Athlone got in opposite Julie. His eyes remained fixed on her in a most uncomfortable way.

"So you are from Shropshire, young lady," the general said, obviously trying to start a jovial conversation.

"No, sir." She decided to confound Brett Athlone, since this false impression had clearly come from him. "I've lived most of my life in London, except during that horrid bombing. They moved us out then and we lived around the countryside where it was usually safer."

"We?" the general's son asked.

"The children orphaned by the war."

"Sad business. Sad, indeed," murmured the general. "Personally, I shouldn't like to repeat my own experiences. We were pitted against a fairly skillful Jerry. Name of Rommel. But you are an orphan, then?"

Brett raised his head, looked at his father and appeared extraordinarily cynical to Julie. For no reason at all that Julie could see, he said three words: "There. You see?"

"Rubbish, my boy. You leap ahead too fast." He turned to Julie, seated beside him in luxurious splendour. "My boy Brett was an orphan long ago, of course. In the mid-thirties. My dear wife took him under her wing. I was off in some hellish place Kipling used to write about. Matter of fact, we were somewhere between Rangoon and Mandelay. Didn't feel like singing about it, though. Didn't like this possible adoption back home, either. A boy near on four years old? But Brett was a clever little monkey. Said he'd not have me for a father. Imagine that."

Julie could imagine it. She smiled, a smile that didn't escape the younger Athlone. "So you adopted him in spite of his dislike? That was goodhearted of you." But remembering her own fears, she added, "I wouldn't like it myself. But being Irish and all, he had something in common with you."

Brett Athlone raised his glasses. She was keenly aware of that piercing gaze.

"Not at all. The name they gave me in the Home was Conrad. I was born in Spain, just before the Civil War." She stiffened and was aware that the general, close beside her, had noticed her reaction and was puzzled. To her annoyance, nothing escaped his son.

"You don't like Spain, Miss Jones?" he asked her.

"How'd I know? I've never seen the place," she blurted out and added, as they moved up the rise in the boulevard, "we're fairly near the New Palace now. Maybe you'd best let me out here." Abandoning all pretence, she explained, "I think I'm to enter in the employees' gate. I'm in the Foreign Department."

The general was surprisingly pleased. "Excellent. Excellent. Then we shall be doing business with you. What with all the congratulations and what-not about the election. They must have the results at the Chancellery any time now."

Just as she might have expected, Brett Athlone tapped on the partition and then leaned over, and opened the door for her. He must be frightfully eager to be rid of her. She got up. He swung out with ease and held a hand to her as the chauffeur set her bags beside her.

To her astonishment the younger Athlone smiled at her. On the whole it was a pleasant smile, but there was also something teasing about it. "Goodbye for now, Miss Jones. We must get together soon and have a little chat about Spain. Maybe I can convert you to the fair country where I was born."

A tiny British MG tooted behind the limousine. Julie ignored the MG and was so puzzled over the last few minutes, she forgot to take the hand Brett offered. The limousine hurried away a second after he leaped back into the car. She saw the general at the window, waving enthusiastically.

She was still trying to figure out the Athlone twosome when the little MG drove up beside her and Her Highness, Princess Alexia, called out, "Thought you'd been kidnapped. Hop in. I'll show you around to the staff entrance. The garages are in the back, just this side of the gardens. Practically like Miravel."

Julie did not bob a curtsy but she bowed her head, just

before hopping in beside the princess. She hoped the bow would take care of protocol. She appreciated the offer of the princess. It was very democratic. But it wasn't part of her dream, that Prince Stefan would come zooming up to the railway station, rush in breathlessly to meet her, and say something like: "It seems ages since I saw you. I've so much to say. Did you miss me?"

Princess Alexia tooted the car's little horn and some gates opened down Palace Boulevard from the great, gilded main gates. The princess drove in through the staff gates, meanwhile assuring Julie, "We're delighted at your arrival, Julie. Things are such a mess right now and we need girls who know English, what with the final results of the elections and my father's illness. You will have your work cut out for you, answering all the election congratulations from foreign dignitaries. I hope your shorthand is good. Father isn't up to doing any of it himself."

Julie sighed. So much for her stupid bragging at Miravel. This was not exactly what she had in mind when she received the formal letter of employment in Prince Stefan's name. But she said, "I'll do my best, Ma'am."

How she would manage that, she hadn't the faintest idea.

CHAPTER TEN

Alexia drove to the back of the palace into the area in front of the garages. Here a young attendant in the red-piped blue uniform of the Kuragin Royal Family hurried forward, reaching in to unlock the little open car and stand aside in stiff salute.

"Yes, yes, Raul. You may relax," Alexia told the young chauffeur.

Too much formality made Alexia impatient. She had spent many of her formative years in the United States, under the watchful eye of her great-grandfather, Tige Royle, and had never been quite able to fit into the careful protocol and formality of a royal residence. Besides, she was well aware that democratic Tige could buy and sell her parents' tiny country; so the elaborate royal life of Lichtenbourg had seemed quietly amusing.

Not that she ever mentioned this treasonable opinion to the Prince Royal, Maximilian, or even more importantly, to her mother, Garnett, the Princess Royal.

Motioning Julie to crawl out first, Alexia climbed out after her and instructed the young chauffeur, "Have it handy. I may need it to check the voting tallies again later. My father will be so anxious."

"Yes, indeed, Your Highness. So are we all. Not that Prince Stefan isn't doing an excellent job, but Prince

Maximilian has been in power so long. Ever since his father, of sacred memory . . . ”

Alexia surprised Julie by her sudden change of mood: she frowned and looked off over the gardens which extended from the hedges behind the garages well up the gentle slope towards a series of mountains which were surprisingly close. “Franz Kuragin. The greatest ruler Lichtenbourg ever had,” she explained. “I absolutely adored him when I was five . . . He was assassinated shortly after my birthday. Everyone blames the Reds but it was two of Hitler’s men.”

She glanced at Julie who didn’t seem sure what she was talking about. “And now the West German Republic is our friend and the Communists are the enemy, in a way. Life is strange.”

“Yes, Your Highness,” the young chauffeur said, but Alexia had a notion he didn’t understand her any more than Julie Jones did.

She dismissed him with a gesture and a smile, then ushered Julie up a flight of steps into the ground floor of the palace. She spoke as they went on up the next flight: “These are offices at this end of the palace. The important public rooms are open to the public on Wednesday, on this and the floor above. The private apartments are on this end of the two floors above us.”

“Excuse me,” Julie cleared her throat. She seemed to be consumed with curiosity. “If your father doesn’t win the election, won’t Prince Stefan win? Everybody says the Communists will come in a bad third. But I thought Prince Stefan was an excellent prince, I mean administrator.”

“So he is. But my father hasn’t long to live, and the least Stefan could have done was forbid the elections until Father was gone.”

No use in wasting her breath, Alexia thought. The girl wouldn't understand. In fact, no one would. In her childhood Alexia had been unfair to her father, blaming him because Franz Kuragin's assassins were not punished. Also, Alexia was more and more certain that her mother had been unfair to Max. In the pre-war years when he needed her support most, with Hitler breathing down his neck, and no help from the Western Powers, Garnett had been gallivanting around Europe, enjoying herself, and doubtlessly enjoying the attentions of her many admirers in France and Italy.

It was in order to repay her father for these early injustices by herself and others, that Alexia bitterly resented Stefan's rush to take over in his place.

There was another reason which shamed her and in many ways ruined her married life: she asked herself every day, and certainly, every night was it for this supreme position in Lichtenbourg that Stefan had married her fifteen years ago? The suspicion had troubled her before her marriage, and after lying quiescent for some years, had haunted her ever since Stefan's decision to let himself be run as a candidate against her father.

There was no answer to that question, especially if he should win the election. Her visit to the Chancellery today, before offering to pick Julie up at the station, had found the results dependent on the vote of the citizens outside the actual confines of Lichtenbourg City. Many of these citizens were shepherds, farmers and the owners of the Lichtenbourg Vineyards who were often what might be called "absentee voters".

She went on up the curving staircase with Julie, describing the various features of the offices concerned with royal business, but she was fairly sure the girl had something else on her mind. It was odd because Mrs Skinner at Miravel and the vicar's wife were both excellent judges of character, and they had assured Stefan, who assured Alexia, that Julie Jones could be counted upon. She might be an extraordinarily useful girl. True. This was not a kitchen job, but according to Mrs Tenby, Julie was able to take down any letters dictated, which would be important both to Alexia's father and here at the palace. Maybe the girl was just worried about her position here in the palace.

Alexia tried to relieve her on that score. "I'm sure you will suit us very well. Old Count Thallin's secretaries dictate a great deal in English, whether they work here for my husband or for my father, and they oversee most of the communication problems for us. You won't have to learn too much protocol all at once. Days may go by without your having to face all that bowing and scraping with my mother and Stefan. On the other hand, my father is different. A gentle person. Very democratic. He won't frighten you."

"Oh, no, Madam. His Highness, I mean Prince Stefan doesn't frighten me," Julie cried, loudly enough to attract the looks of two young footmen hurrying down the steps. They caught Alexia's glance, inclined their carefully coiffed heads in respect and hurried on.

Alexia wondered if there would be difficulties between Julie and the male staff, but the girl seemed unaware of them. She went on eagerly to Alexia, "Really, Madam, I can handle – I mean – I learn fast."

"I understand. But we'll proceed slowly. No rushing ahead. We all feel overawed at first when we have to bow and scrape. It happened to me when I came back from the States. I think we have just the place that will give you a chance to work your way slowly through this morass of titles. My father is badly in need of a secretary. People write and ask favours, or discuss his illness, or will – God forbid – pity him, if the voting has gone wrong."

Reaching the next floor whose high ceiling and rafters never looked free of dust or cobwebs, Alexia motioned to the right. "Until you are located, you might use a room on the west side. That means you overlook the Boulevard Kuragin. Not as pretty as the rooms on this side of the corridor. They face the gardens, which are also open to the public on Sundays. But you will like all the views at the Royal Chalet where my father is recuperating."

Watching her without appearing to do so, Alexia found Julie Jones suddenly subdued. Maybe she was oppressed by all this regal splendour. She would do much better when she started to work in Prince Max's service, across the city. He would be gently understanding as he had always been with Alexia, unless he was feeling particularly bad. Then he might be querulous, but he never forgot his good manners. By working for him Julie would also learn the protocol expected of her. He would enjoy doing it; keeping his mind off his illness and the political problems he faced. It was so much simpler for her to start in at the Royal Chalet. Alexia didn't like to think how close her father had come to death during his latest angina attack.

Alexia counted the tall, panelled and age-warped doors, found the one she was looking for and laughed as a chambermaid opened it almost in their faces. "Good heavens!" she exclaimed. "It's my old room. A suite, they used to call it."

The stout young chambermaid curtsied, looking flustered and pink-cheeked. "Highness, the suite should have been ready sooner, but there is such excitement with the voting and all. And of course, with the Fräulein occupying it for such a short time."

The maid's last words seemed to have surprised Julie Jones. Poor thing. Maybe she was hoping for more splendour, not less. "I understand," Alexia replied and went into the parlour with its heavy nineteenth century German furniture and shook her head. "Hasn't changed a bit."

But Julie gave her a weak smile. "I love it, Ma'am. It's so – royal."

As the maid took Julie's coat and little hat, Alexia asked, "Did you like the British Consul and his son? They are very social. Appearing at all the palace gatherings."

Julie did not seem to hear her. She was still looking around the parlour and getting a glimpse of the bedroom beyond.

Curious at her indifference, Alexia went on, "The son is quite good-looking, isn't he?"

Julie apologized. "To tell the truth, it's hard to say. I'm afraid I didn't notice."

Since Julie herself was noticeably attractive, Alexia suspected that Brett Athlone had been attentive and the girl resented it.

Julie had already begun to discuss with the chambermaid the factor that her possessions must wait here for further disposal when Alexia left the room, wishing Julie well. The girl's curtsies were cut off by the sound of running footsteps in the corridor. A young footman rushed up to Alexia as the chambermaid closed the door behind her.

Before the sweating footman could open his mouth, Alexia saw her husband striding along the corridor toward her. All this excitement was a bad sign. She girded herself for the worst.

Stefan waved away the footman who retreated towards the broad, regal steps at the far end of the corridor, but kept looking back.

Seeing the concern that relieved the normal harshness of his features, Alexia beat him to the announcement. "Is it to be Your *Serene* Highness now? Have they made it formal?"

"I'm afraid so. I want very much for you to understand, darling." He tried to take her hands but she drew them back.

She heard his deep voice that could be so tender, so passionate, and she determined not to be moved by it when he gave her his usual excuse, "You know as well as I do that in this Cold War climate the country has got to be in strong hands."

"Yours?" she asked in a sardonic voice.

He took a deep breath. "Who else is there?"

They had wrangled over this a hundred times. At least, she had wrangled, even humbled herself by pleading, without any discernible change in his expression, except that he had the grace to remain troubled, or was it pitying? God forbid! But answering his question she said sharply, "You haven't sent any formal deputation to my father yet, have you?"

"Certainly not! What do you take me for?" He seemed angry to think she had such an opinion of him. He added on a lighter note, "Of course, Her Serene Highness, Princess Garnett, knows. She was practically glued to the front gates."

Alexia groaned. "Poor Mother. What was her reaction?"

This time he smiled. "She told me she must consider her options."

"What!"

"Her options."

Alexia burst into laughter. How typical of Garnett! She would end by deciding her best option was to stand, loyal and faithful, beside the son-in-law she despised.

While her laughter hadn't swayed her feelings on the matter, it certainly didn't make her sick father's situation more bearable. She knew she would have to attend to him first. "Well, I must get to Father as soon as possible."

"Yes, of course," he agreed. "I'll be over to see him very shortly. There is a certain amount of red tape first, I'm afraid."

She started away, then remembered what she had been doing here. "By the way, the girl recommended by Mrs Tenby and Mrs Skinner has arrived. I left her in her rooms."

"What? 'Just Julie'?" He glanced down the corridor and back to her. "Good. That child ought to liven up this old heap of traditions."

She tried to move on but he had reached out to her once more, his fingers pressing into her shoulders, hard and firm. "Darling, are we still at odds?"

His dark eyes looked tired. She wasn't blind to their poignant plea. She gave him credit for still caring. But he must know what had finally happened in the voting was merely the culmination of their wedding vows. It had all been done with this end in mind.

"Go and show 'Just Julie' the ropes," she told him, using one of Tige Royle's favourite expressions.

When she had reached the wide steps leading down to the Great Hall of Receptions, she looked back as the footman had done. Her husband had taken her at her word and knocked on Julie's door. The poor girl would probably be discomfited at the sight of the country's new ruler. If young Athlone had been too much for her, Alexia wondered how she would behave to Stefan, His Serene Highness of Lichtenbourg.

CHAPTER ELEVEN

The suite of a real, live princess. Only temporary. But real.

Julie tried not to show how impressed she was before Wilhelmina, the young chambermaid, but she had never felt so near her dreams of a splendid future. If only she could be working for Prince Stefan!

This was true elegance, better than the great public rooms of a palace because it was more personal. Maybe she could come back to it when she finished working each day. It would give her a feeling that she lived like a true princess. Hadn't Her Serene Highness, Princess Alexia herself, lived here once? And look how high Alexia Kuragin had risen, married now to the real ruler of Lichtenbourg, in name as well as in fact.

Wilhelmina's heavily accented voice, interrupted her dreams. "I will go now, Fräulein Jones. I have three others I must do in this wing, before they come from the celebrations." She rustled by Julie, her big hips pumping as they piloted the girl across the worn carpet. She did not curtsy. After all, Julie was only a servant like herself and with no seniority. Julie knew she couldn't expect miracles, not this early in her campaign.

The girl went out, leaving Julie to explore the wonders of her very own rooms. Make that "suite", she amended in her thoughts. Julie Jones in a suite. It was the first time in her life that she had ever had a real room all to herself. Not to mention a suite.

"Until you need them, Fräulein, I will leave them here." Wilhelmina then hung up her carefully chosen Paris clothes. Not many. The money hadn't gone that far. But cleverly chosen, if she did say so. Thank heaven, dear Mrs Tenby had given her the name of a lady on the Left Bank, near the Odeon Metro stop. Julie had been just a tad afraid she might get lost in the huge complex of the Paris Underground. After all, she remembered the movie *Les Misérables* and knew the sewers of Paris were down there somewhere, but it had been wonderfully easy, yet exciting. When she walked out of the Metro and into the noisy Place de l'Odeon she felt that she had made her first foreign conquest.

The shop carried the very slender outfits worn by models during the fashion shows and a few of them were not too dusty and worn out. They had mostly been carefully cleaned. She didn't recognize some of the names, but who cared? The gold, raw-silk suit would be useful and stylish for several occasions, day and night. It brought out the highlights in her light, boyish hair style.

Optimist that she was, Julie had bought one black, clinging evening gown cut on the bias. It looked wonderfully like something Carole Lombard might have worn in the Thirties. And it was cheap. Luckily, the saleswoman said, no one could get into it but Julie, whose breasts were not large enough to cause trouble in the fitting department.

Then there was a three-piece day dress that could be worn as a suit and didn't look too out of style, though it had come to her in the charity bag at the vicarage, like her jeans and the only other outfit, the green skirt and sweater she wore now.

Seeing every item, even her faded jeans, hanging up in the dressing room beyond her bedroom, she felt a childish urge to clap her hands at her own luck. It needed only an added touch. At least one sight of her hero, Prince Stefan.

The knock on the corridor door came so opportunely, she rushed across the living room, desperately hoping it was him. She was just opening the heavy oaken door when she heard the prince's voice, speaking to someone else. "Good afternoon, haven't seen you in some time. The consul told us you were in London. Great city. I was there recently."

For Julie, there was a moment's pause. The other man was a few yards away and inaudible to Julie who had stopped with her hand on the door latch.

Then Prince Stefan said, "Yes. I wish the accursed thing had never been necessary. But it's over now. It was unfortunate that the Soviets made such a showing . . ."

Damn! The man would get the prince's attention and they would go off to talk politics. Taking a breath, she opened the door wide and looked out.

There he was, turned away from her door talking with, of all people, General Athlone's son. What was he doing here in the private sector of the palace? Just like him to ruin her chances for a perfectly harmless few minutes with Prince Stefan. She knew it couldn't be more than a few minutes, just long enough for him to greet her and wish her well. But it would mean so much.

Both men looked at her. At first the prince appeared careworn, older than she remembered him, but she would never forget his smile, and his genuine pleasure at her arrival. "Well, well, so our wandering young lady crossed

118

half of Europe to reach here and help us out. It is good to see you, Julie. Did you have any trouble on the way?"

She was too busy curtsying deeply to reply at first. But upon rising, flushed with pleasure, she caught Brett Athlone's interested gaze and stiffened with anger. How dare he come here into the private quarters of the palace with his nasty spying!

She addressed herself solely to the prince. "I'm deeply grateful, Your Highness. I hope I may be of help. Mrs Tenby said I served her very well, taking letters and all."

"I'm sure you will be a welcome sight to my father-in-law." He made a gesture of introducing her to his companion. "This sprite saved my life one dark and rainy night when my car broke down. She led me to Miravel Village and even persuaded the local vicar to drive me to Miravel Hall. Miss Julie Jones. But I shall always think of her by the name she insisted on that night. 'Just Julie'."

"Interesting." Keeping his deeply penetrating blue eyes on her, Athlone bowed. "I never would have guessed at her unearthly qualities. But you are fortunate. The young lady looks quite able to function at earthbound tasks." He ignored the prince's puzzled and not too pleased expression. "I encountered Her Serene Highness a minute ago in the Gold Room. She told me the young lady would be offering assistance to His Highness, Prince Maximilian. I might drive her there, after I return the earring she left in my father's car."

He held up a stunning bit of sapphire set in diamonds. "Yours, I believe, Miss – ah – Jones."

What was his game? Julie thought suspiciously. "I'm afraid you've made your trip for nothing, sir. I never wear diamonds."

119

Still puzzled, Stefan looked from one to the other of them. There was a peculiar tension here. He then said to Julie, "Would you rather wait until someone from the palace is free? But I do believe I can vouch for Mr Athlone." He forced a smile. "The Athlones have always been good friends of the throne."

"Then I'd be delighted, Your Highness, if the gentleman will wait for me to get my coat," she answered, wanting to please the prince at all costs.

"Good. Now then, Athlone, you will have to look elsewhere for the owner of that little bauble. Much too expensive for such casual treatment."

As Julie went for her coat, she wondered if the prince suspected the valuable earring had been a mere ploy for Brett Athlone to pursue this strange acquaintance. He certainly had no use for her. What else could be his motive? Had he really thought she would take advantage of his mistake (if mistake it was) to take a jewel that didn't belong to her?

When she came back the prince was gone and Athlone was leaning casually against the wall, watching her every movement. She felt distinctly uncomfortable. She said abruptly, "Shall we go? I hope you know the way."

He took her arm, saying airily, "Oh, yes. This won't be my first visit to the Chalet. Her Serene Highness, or I should say, the *late* Serene Highness, Princess Garnett, used to throw some choice parties there. My father was particularly attached to the place. He enjoys a little entertainment, like the rest of us."

Was he saying something about Princess Garnett, or wasn't he? It was perfectly possible, Julie felt, but not as likely to be true of the more reserved new Serene Highness, Princess Alexia.

The Athlone limousine had been impressive but Brett Athlone's white Porsche was an exciting substitute. He helped her into the car, though she suspected it was an afterthought. Probably he was acquiring the American habit. Her young Chicago friend, years ago, had boasted that nobody who was anybody had to help girls into a car. They climbed in quicker without help. In any case, these good manners made her feel more like a lady.

The car started off with a roar, heading north towards a hilly street whose narrow buildings leaned perilously forward, and were like pictures she had seen of Eastern Europe before the war. It was all very thrilling and new. She was so excited she forgot her companion's hostility and exclaimed in wonder, "It's like a wonderful movie."

Athlone looked at her oddly. She could sense his surprise and added in embarrassment, "I mean, just when I used to get settled I had to go to a different place, so I kept tight to my dreams and my movies. I knew it would happen some day, and it did."

"Just how many different places have there been?"

She wondered if she was imagining it, but his voice sounded slightly different. Not quite so flippant and sarcastic. Maybe he had never before met a person on her own and proud of it. She had better straighten him out or he would be pitying her next. A revolting thought.

She then said brightly, "It was fun, in a way. Not needing anyone, I mean. Except for having to deal with stupid employers. Even that was great training. I learned how to get on, no matter what. You never know in this world, when you might need it."

"Yes. I suppose that's true." He was looking ahead at the street which had turned into a country road and wound its way up one of the tiny country's many hills. "Then, if you found yourself suddenly with a great deal of money, or an important position in life, you'd do anything to get it because you've earned it."

"Why not? If it was mine, fair and square."

"And if it wasn't fair and square?"

She looked at him, wondering what all this fantasy talk was leading to. "But it would be. I don't dream like that. I knew a lady once who said: 'Don't be negative'. So I'm not."

He laughed shortly. "An excellent motto for forging ahead. I must remember that."

They were approaching a long, two and a half storey building, whose walls were relieved from austerity by large blue painted designs, some of which seemed to be the fierce Lichtenbourg Crest.

"You haven't seen the Chalet before?" Brett asked, noting her wide-eyed interest.

"That's a chalet? I thought a chalet was a little house in the mountains surrounded by snow."

He grinned. "And skaters headed for the lake with red tassels bouncing on their caps. Well, that goes on here too, in the heart of winter."

"I think it's darling." She let her enthusiasm get the better of her, though she knew he would sneer at her sentimentality. But who cared what he thought? Prince Stefan didn't mind it. He had acted as if he liked her chatter that rainy night on the road to Miravel Village.

He seemed amused but he didn't say anything nasty about her enthusiasm. "Do you skate?"

"I did once. I had to hold on to the wooden rail. Even then, I fell flat on my bottom."

He laughed. "Not much padding there, either. Were you born in snow country?"

Before she could resent his personal remark she felt the prickle of chills along her spine and shifted uncomfortably. "I was in the North to help clean up a children's hospital that was hit by a buzz bomb."

"Do you remember anything about your infancy? A flash or two of babyhood memories?"

She gave him an impudent grimace. "How could I? I was hatched."

He laughed again. Not an unpleasant sound. More of a chuckle, as they headed towards the chalet with the royal blue and red colours of Lichtenbourg flapping over the rooftop. He looked up at the flag. "They are going to have to change the Kuragin crest to the Elsbach. I imagine that ends the Kuragin Dynasty. Maybe the Elsbach too. Stefan Elsbach has no son and Princess Alexia doesn't seem receptive to him these days."

Maybe it's her fault, Julie thought, but for once was wise enough not to say so.

"Have you any idea what they want with you here?" he asked as he made the turn into the drive. He brought the car to a stop beside the steps where he was challenged by the sentry's rifle. The rifle bore had a hideous fascination for Julie. She clutched Brett Athlone's arm. He gave her icy hand a reassuring squeeze before he showed his passport to the sentry and then a little, nervous man hurried down the steps to greet him and Julie like old friends.

"Prince Max's valet," Brett told Julie as the man, breathing fast, rushed to Brett.

"Please accept my thanks, sir. I am Biddicombe, Prince Maximilian's valet, but you may have forgotten."

"Not at all. Delighted to see you again," Brett told the little man, to the valet's pleasure.

"So glad to see you. You are too gracious. His Serene

Highness – or do I mean, his Royal Highness now that he is no longer – but I must not skate too close to that. His Highness is not used to coping with the election result."

Brett Athlone nodded. "It will take time."

"But sir, he doesn't have time."

"You know I can't interfere, Biddicombe."

The little valet shrugged hopelessly. "No one has been to see him today, since the election finals. He is, if you will pardon the expression, 'a loser'. Just treating him with the respect he demanded might lift his spirits."

The sentry had lowered his rifle and approached as a deferential reminder. "Sir, His Highness has asked us to pass you in to his presence."

Brett took Julie's arm. "Yes. We are coming."

Julie was relieved that they would soon be out of sight of that long rifle.

The valet murmured, "He doesn't wish to see me as he's in one of his moods. I'll go to my quarters, sir."

But Brett was more interested in his companion's obvious fear of the rifle. As the doors at the top of the steps opened on a signal from the sentry, Brett asked, "Have you had any personal experience with guns?"

She shook her head. "Reminds me of things when I was a child. War and noise and all."

"I certainly hope they moved you out of London during the Blitz."

"Oh, yes. It brought back the nightmares, mostly. I'm over them now."

"I'm glad." But he looked doubtful and incredibly enough, seemed sorry for her. What pride she had carried with her on this ride was gone now and she could even accept his pity. Anything to free her mind of all those old horrors that had once haunted her dreams.

Her companion saw her looking around the spacious reception hall that ran the length of the building, with numerous panelled doors and staircases at either end. Hardly the little "love nest" chalet she had sighed over in the films.

Brett gave her a slight nudge. Startled, she looked up, saw the frail but impressively handsome man at the landing on the north staircase. The stairs were carpeted in royal blue designs that almost matched the uniform of the gentleman also waiting to greet them.

At the foot of the stairs, a uniformed usher cleared his throat and announced, "His Serene Highness, Prince Maximilian, Hereditary Prince Royal of Lichtenbourg."

With legs shaking Julie went down in a deep curtsy. It was embarrassing when Athlone, having bowed, had to give her a hand up, but the prince, while awesome, looked gentle and actually smiled at her near-miss.

He held out one thin hand to the British Consul's son. "My dear fellow, it is good to find at least the British Lion still recognizes me."

"Your Highness." Athlone left Julie for a moment to move up the stairs where he put the back of his hand under the prince's and bowed again. "Sir George asked me to present my profound regrets over the voting and to assure you he will pay his respects very soon. He also asked me to felicitate you on your recovery from your recent illness."

"Thank you. I am glad the Consul does not take the word of my physicians, especially the fellow my son-in-law insists is the best in the field. One cannot always take Stefan's word. Ambitious is the word for that one. You have only to see the results of the election he manoeuvered."

Brett Athlone said politely, "I am sure you are the best judge of your feelings, sir."

"Quite true. I sent this specialist – this Chalgrin – off to his precious charity ward at the hospital in Vienna today. I don't want him here when my wife visits me. His pessimism is depressing to a woman of her sensitivity."

Julie saw that Prince Maximilian looked more ill than she had imagined. One of the ladies Mrs Tenby had sent her to help at Elder Home suffered spells of great pain from a heart ailment. It seemed obvious that Prince Max was far from recovered. But how well he wore his uniform! He must be one of those royal figures born to play a "stage" prince.

The prince looked at Julie now and she coloured a little, hoping he could not read her thoughts.

Then he turned to Athlone. "My daughter Alexia told me to expect this young lady. I understand she is a secretary of no mean talents."

Brett Athlone took her arm, led her up to the landing, and presented her. "Miss Julie Jones, sir."

"I only hope I will not be too slow for Miss Jones," the prince apologized. "I must speed up for such an accomplished young lady."

Julie rushed to relieve him of this problem. "No, sir. Be as slow as you like. I won't mind."

Athlone laughed but the prince nodded gravely. "Thank you. That will be most satisfactory. And now, Athlone, you must join me for tea – or whisky, if you prefer. I keep Scotch on hand for my wife and Count Thallin, the head of my – " He hesitated, then corrected himself, "the head of the Foreign Secretariat of Lichtenbourg."

"Tea will be fine for me." Athlone glanced at Julie, obviously unsure if the invitation included her.

"And our Miss Jones, of course, while we get to know each other," the prince agreed, nodding to her in a flattering way.

It wasn't every day that a girl like Julie got to take tea with a real, live, reigning prince. Well, make that formerly reigning. Nervous but happy, she smiled her thanks and slowed her steps to accommodate the usher while the prince began discussing the faults of Lichtenbourg's election with Athlone.

The floor above the stately reception hall was light and cheerful, with exquisite silken wall coverings and faintly tinkling crystal lustres on the chandeliers. At the end of the hall the ceiling was decorated with painted figures which, all appeared to be staring down at them. Julie found the painted figures uncomfortable. They seemed to be having fun at her expense. Clearly, they asked themselves, what was this "nobody" doing in the Kuragins' sacred halls?

She was relieved when she and Brett were shown into a delightful parlour that looked like a summery gazebo decorated with greenery, and even a pair of leafy trees that would soon threaten the ceiling. In the shade of the sun-flecked gazebo was a chaise longue, with a coverlet in the Kuragin blue colours, obviously an invalid's chair.

Julie curtsied, then stayed a step behind Brett Athlone. Furtively eyeing the prince, Julie thought: *Poor man. Once he had everything and now he has nothing, not even his health. Princess Garnett ought to be here attending to him, letting him know he was sorely missed at the so-called New Palace.*

Prince Maximilian seemed to be a gracious host, even to a hired stenographer like Julie. He looked her over with a smile and greeted her indirectly, through the Counsul's son. "So this is my new stenographer. She does credit to the Palace Staff. But I daresay, you've found that out before this, my boy."

"Indeed, sir, from the first moment we met."

Considering that they had only met a few hours ago, Julie liked Brett Athlone's sense of humour.

The prince dropped onto his chaise longue. "Please," he ordered his guests gently to sit down. "I have a small but competent staff, and my housekeeper has probably heard by now that my guest – pardon, my guests, have arrived." He added on a note of apology, "We will call this an informal meeting. No work for today, Fräulein Jones. I am expecting the Princess Garnett early this evening. She is bound to want to fuss over me. We have been apart for too long. Aside from this stupid affliction that keeps me from the palace, there is her work for my re-election, as you know."

Athlone remarked, "The Reds were acting obnoxious around the main gates when we left."

Prince Maximilian sat up. "Surely, they will take care of my wife! This election will be a terrible blow to her." He settled back against the pillows. "Alexia will see to her comfort. A capable girl. Very like her mother."

This time Julie could not mistake the look Brett gave her. He needn't have bothered. She certainly wouldn't contradict His Highness. She envied Princess Alexia but never could believe the competent princess was in the least like her self-centred mother.

"Ah," the prince exclaimed. "Here is Frau Gerda Bergin. My good right hand. Far more competent than my tiresome valet, Biddicombe. Could you imagine? He is terrified of those foolish local Communists. Do you know, those very fellows who wore the hammer and sickle on their sleeves would go out of their way to express the hope that I would

128

win the election? Of course, it may have been their fear of my son-in-law who can be a ruthless devil. But still, it was amusing."

Prince Max's housekeeper, a dark youngish woman with a fleshy mouth and eyes that seemed heavily made-up, appeared in a black gown worn tight over her hips and bosom. A frightened kitchen girl followed with a heavily laden tray.

Julie was pleased and surprised when Brett Athlone lifted the tray from the girl's hands and set it on the round table for her. The housekeeper arranged everything, gave Prince Max a voluptuous smile when he thanked her, and the two women departed.

I wouldn't want to take orders from Frau Bergin, Julie thought, feeling sorry for the little slave who did all the work but got no thanks.

The prince began to talk about how dangerous it had been to call the election at this time. "It only split the party of the coalition – the Kuragins and the Elsbachs who have ruled this country for centuries. But young people persist in going their own way. If Stefan had waited until I was on my feet again, there might have been a different result. I am well loved in Lichtenbourg, you know. That is *entre nous*, my dear fellow." He gestured to Julie. "Do try everything, my dear. The bread is excellent. From a Viennese shop. The tea, of course, is English. There is an Hungarian assortment of little cakes, too. Excellent."

Julie felt that she was betraying her secret dream of Prince Stefan but she had certainly never enjoyed herself so much as she was doing at this minute. She knew she was only rehearsing for some imagined future, a far-off day when Princess Alexia divorced her unwanted husband, but meanwhile, she must keep learning everything she could so that she would be worthy of that great man and not disgrace herself.

Brett Athlone caught her licking her fingers after taking a bite out of the delicious but sticky little Hungarian cake. In her embarrassment she dropped what remained of the cake. Brett winked at her and licked his own fingers. He was really beginning to be quite nice. It was hard to believe she had only met him that day. If he would just keep those awful glasses off and look at her as he did now, with the twinkle that seemed very Irish to her, no matter what he claimed about his Spanish ancestors!

But even so, she was aware that from the beginning he had appeared to be sizing her up, studying her. It was as if he expected her to steal the silver. What had she done to him? She didn't even know him. But there were all those questions. And he seemed to know, or suspect things about her past. Things that verged on her childhood nightmares. Then, there was the Charity Hospital in London. Why was he so curious about Julie's connection with it?

She sat up straight at a sudden thought. These were the same things that Mr Chance questioned her about in Miravel. And Julie was certain that for some reason Mr Chance was her enemy because of them.

No matter. She picked out a less sticky sugared cake and began to eat it in a more dainty fashion.

The prince and the consul's son were discussing Tige Royle who seemed to be the patriarch of the Miravel Family and even the Kuragins. This Tige was very kind and loving to Princess Alexia, his great-granddaughter, and even to Prince Stefan, but perhaps less so to his closest relation, Princess Garnett. That was understandable, based on Julie's slight knowledge of her. But Tige Royle had one thing in common with Nick Chance. He was suspicious of

130

Julie. Thinking back, she decided he might have noticed her friendship with Prince Stefan and resented it for the sake of his great-granddaughter.

Maybe he thought the prince was too friendly to a former kitchen girl.

A distant sound cut in upon her disturbed thoughts. A curious mumbling, like many voices. Or a parade, with boots marching over cobblestones. And shouts.

She watched Brett Athlone and the prince. Brett appeared tense. Watchful, Prince Max saw this and reassured him calmly. "Kuragin followers, coming to serenade me. They didn't appreciate being thrown out by an Elsbach, with the Soviets waiting in the wings."

Julie watched Brett Athlone. He didn't look as if he believed this soothing explanation. "Yes, sir. But in case of trouble in the future, it would be wise to have your own troops at hand. I should think Prince Stefan would have ordered it done."

He seemed to have upset the prince who protested, "But it was my decision. I countered his order. A heavily armed detachment of guards would be the worst possible thing for my image. I was very firm about it to the Ober-Lieutenant. I cannot permit my own people to be frightened by my son-in-law's mistrust of human loyalty."

Even as he talked, Julie heard the rumble of noise and shouting as it drew closer. Not being the heroic type, she started to get out of her chair, rising in slow motion that threatened to turn to full flight any second. She could see that though Brett hadn't followed her example, he was aware of danger.

He touched the prince's arm. "Your Highness, these may be drunken Reds, celebrating their second place in the balloting."

Prince Max was unalterably opposed. "Very unlikely. However, my dear fellow, you have my permission to withdraw if you choose. As for me, my father, Franz Kuragin, would never have done so. I am my father's son."

Brett ignored this. To Julie's astonishment, he ordered her, "If they try to break in, go down the south staircase and turn to your right. Beyond the State Dining Hall is a corridor and then the kitchens. Remove your coat and wrap an apron around you, like one of the kitchen staff."

CHAPTER TWELVE

Brett had stolen the prince's royal prerogative from him. With some difficulty he started to get up from the chaise, then cried out and sank back, his fragile features twisted in pain. One hand was pressed against his breast. The other groped for Brett.

"Don't leave. I must stand when I – meet them."

"Certainly, sir. But you need someone. Your physician? Shall I call him?"

"No, no. Impossible. Chalgrin is in Vienna. And my valet is a poor excuse for a man. Don't involve him."

"But sir – "

"I have two specialists who visit me at regular intervals, but von Hartman is at his clinic, at the other end of the city. The other one – a poor creature – I dismissed last Sunday."

"Sir, don't upset yourself. I'm calling for reinforcements. Where the hell is your extension?"

The prince tried to speak but the effort cost him his breath and he pointed to his chaise. Brett looked around, puzzled, but Julie, who was trembling, got down on her knees and felt under the edge of the chaise longue. She held up the white French phone with its pre-war cradle.

Brett gave her a grateful nod and rattled the cradle of the phone. "Calling for His Highness, Prince Maximilian.

Send reinforcements. Good. We may need them." He set the phone on the table. "A detachment is on its way from the Chalet Barracks. They were ordered there as soon as the Chancellery gave out the election results."

"How could that happen?" the prince protested. "I had expressly forbidden any show of violence."

"It was ordered from the palace, sir."

The prince coughed, pressing his hand hard against his breastbone. "Stefan again." He grimaced. "Medicine. Ring for my valet. Stupid fellow can at least manage that."

Brett pressed the buzzer beside the prince's teacup. He had scarcely taken his hand off the buzzer when the door opened after a mere sketch of a knock. Frau Bergin burst into the room. "Highness. They are out there. Some with a Hammer and Sickle armband. Must be forty or fifty. Do the sentries have orders to shoot?"

"No!" The prince picked at Brett's sleeve. "No violence, remember, they will never forgive me. My reputation will be in shreds. Frau Bergin, my capsule."

The housekeeper bustled across the room, took a square inch silver case off the little white wicker bookstand and hurried to the prince while Brett poured water into a crystal goblet.

As the stricken man swallowed water after the capsule, Julie went to one of the long, sunny windows at the far end of the room and looked out from behind the old-fashioned lace curtains until Brett called to her.

"Don't let them see you."

She didn't need his order. Thirty or forty men and a sprinkling of women had crowded onto the steps, surrounding the single sentry who had challenged Brett. Obviously, the sentry didn't know whether or not to shoot at this close range. The sight of blood would set off a

134

mass attack. To Julie's eyes the men in the crowd were puzzling. They seemed so ordinary. Only two wore Soviet uniforms and full-skirted, belted coats. Even they might be phoney, wearing borrowed or stolen uniforms to impress the others by a fake connection with the Soviet Union. The Communist Party of Lichtenbourg made a great pretense of being free from "outside influence".

A few were waving their fists but Julie turned back to Brett. The prince, having taken his drug, was lying against the pillows, exhausted. His breathing sounded stertorous.

Brett came to join her at the opposite end of the room. "What are they saying?"

She guessed from his low voice that he wanted to hide anything alarming from the prince. "Just jeers. Somebody yelled that His Highness should join the People's Democratic Republic against the decadent Elsbach Regime." She pressed her nose against the curtain. "What filthy rats! As if His Highness could help the way the elections turned out."

Close beside her, Brett's voice was barely audible but she understood it. "That's it, he did nothing. No plans, no effort to promote industry and welfare. Vetoed every plan Stefan Elsbach put out. Living in a nighteenth century dream. I know for a fact that Tige Royle, the American tycoon, offered loans through a consortium. Stefan has several industries in the works, according to my father. The French show interest, and the Brits may do the same."

Prince Maximilian suddenly made himself heard over the noise outside. "In union is strength. My party could use them until a recall is complete, then we are strong enough to toss out both Stefan and the Reds. But with Stefan's party alone in power, I lose Lichtenbourg."

This leapt to Julie's attention: '*I* lose Lichtenbourg. *My* people. *My* Lichtenbourg.' He still thought of the little country as his private domain.

Something hurtled through the air. Brett dragged her away from the window but the soft, over-ripe tomato splattered against the glass and the weathered shutter.

"Come along to our side, Comrade Max," another young rioter yelled. "We'll do this to the mighty Prince Stefan."

A roar of laughter and applause was clearly audible to Prince Max and his guests, along with taunts and obscenities. Brett set Julie aside and went to the next window beyond the greenery that separated them from Prince Max's chaise longue. The window concealed a miniscule balcony. To Julie's horror he unlatched the French window and stepped out on the balcony. There was barely room for him but the unexpected sight of him gave the mob pause.

"What's the matter, Comrades?" he called down to them in German. "Bad winners? The British Consulate has orders to recognize the validity of the voting. You came in second. Want to spoil it all?"

The taunts aroused by his appearance led to questioning among the crowd. Those who did not wear the red bands exchanged arguments and opinions. Someone hidden in the crowd threw a beer stein at the consul's son, but he caught it deftly and waved it at them. "You can do better than that, Comrade. Go back and get it filled and I'll stand you all a round of Lichtenbourg's finest."

The laughter that began timorously had spread over the crowd and Julie knew he had won when he caught the stein. Someone yelled, "You too, Brit. Join the

Democratic People's Party. I'll drink with you. Who's to join us at Hummel's Bierstube?"

This invitation struck most of them as a far better way of celebrating over the sick man and his party. Also the Brits might even encourage their union, to prevent the intervention of the Soviets. Who could tell?

But Athlone called down to them, "I'll arrange it with Hummel now. Remember, that includes you all." A yell of approval went up. He pointed to one after the other of several in the group who wore red armbands or carried Soviet flags. "Yes. You're invited, Comrades."

More cheers. Julie rolled her eyes. Prince Maximilian evidently shared her thought. He remarked to the frowning housekeeper, "That will cost him a few pounds."

Frau Bergin added, "And pence too, Highness."

The prince chuckled, then coughed and put his handkerchief to his mouth.

Brett waited a couple of minutes before turning away and leaving the balcony. "Well, Your Highness, all I have to do now is keep my promise."

"What of His Highness's safety?" Frau Bergin wanted to know.

The prince said, "I shall be quite safe. Let him go. He must fulfill his promise. I believe I would have chosen a quieter way to calm them, but at all events, your method worked, Athlone."

Brett contradicted him politely. "Believe me, sir, I didn't count on my somewhat spendthrift offer until necessary. But now, the State Troops are arriving. That will hurry their exit. I don't think you will find your son-in-law remiss on many matters. He certainly got here fast. And it's up to me to keep my promise at Hummel's."

Prince Maximilian sat up in petulant anger. "Stefan

137

here? I will not see that man alone. He betrayed his wife and his country, and me, with this election. He is not welcome here."

Wondering how Prince Stefan would react to the sick man's anger, Julie pushed aside the lace curtain and looked out. The crowd below was still breaking up, but she was more interested in the reassuring sight of men in Lichtenbourg blue uniforms who had formed a semicircle around the south side of the drive. Prince Stefan, in a military peaked cap and a blue jacket without insignia, had been speaking to one of his officers. Then he started up the steps.

Julie turned away from the window and nodded to Brett's question: "Is he here?"

"Highness," the housekeeper began, "shall I send for the – " She broke off in confusion. "Would Your Highness prefer to be alone?"

The prince waved her away and the woman departed with several sharp looks at Brett Athlone, as though it might all be his fault.

The prince called to Brett. "Will you remain, my friend? It should make matters easier. I don't want a vulgar scene. This way, there should be more dignity."

"Of course, sir. If you wish."

Julie knew these men would hate her presence, and started past Brett to the door. He reached for her hand but she slipped past him. At the same time Prince Maximilian called across the room, "No. Let the girl remain. Her sort is probably used to scenes among the upper classes." He chuckled, a faint imitation of a laugh. "Not, certainly, among royalty. But stay, Miss – er – "

Her sort.

She felt her face burn with the sting of humiliation

138

she didn't often feel. Before she could decide to walk out with dignity, ignoring him, Brett Athlone answered Prince Max's unspoken question. He said coolly, "Yes. You refer to Miss Jones, Your Highness?"

His manner, more than his words, surprised Julie. Had he really understood or cared about her humiliation? Apparently so. She felt better. Before she could give him any sign of gratitude, Prince Stefan came into the suite with his usual long stride and a general, businesslike air, as if nothing untoward had happened. He had removed his cap, sticking it under his arm before he inclined his head slightly to his father-in-law.

"All serene now, I think, Max. They were just celebrating. Trying to remind Lichtenbourg of their own power."

The invalid prince was not so easily appeased. "Is this meant to be an heroic rescue? As you see, I am quite safe. I have enjoyed my tea with the British Consul's son, an old friend. You know Mr Brett Athlone, I believe."

"Certainly. I have known your father since before you were born, I imagine." Prince Stefan offered his hand to Brett who took it.

Brett was trying to follow Stefan's lead, treating this embarrassing meeting as a casual and friendly encounter. "Certainly, sir. It was you who obligingly put me onto the errand to the Chalet today, to deliver His Highness's charming new stenographer, Miss Jones."

Stefan turned to Julie and again held out his hand. His smile seemed genuine in spite of all that had occurred during the last few minutes in the streets. "Indeed, I know my friend Just Julie." He turned to Max to explain, "It was Miss Jones who saved me from an icy death on the road to Miravel, as I believe I told you."

139

"I know the place well," Prince Max put in with crushing indifference. "I believe my acquaintance with Shropshire precedes your own by some years."

Things were not proceeding well. Julie felt the warm pressure of Stefan's hand on hers and was sorry when he returned to more urgent matters.

"Max, I hope you don't think that business outside the Chalet was directed at you. It was obviously staged by the Red fringe who want the country to know their strength. I see no reflection on you in any way when troops are stationed here at the Chalet. It is a sign of your sovereignty, of respect."

"*Max*," the prince repeated with a dry laugh that was stifled by a cough. "Yes. I have descended to 'Max' very quickly. Since the voting ended at the Chancellery."

Julie saw Brett and Prince Stefan look at each other. The remark had been petulant and bitter. Julie was certain that the two men had been "Stefan" and "Max" for many years in their long relationship. She avoided everyone eyes, heartily wishing she had yielded to her first impulse and left the room before Prince Stefan arrived.

Stefan took a long breath. "Very well, Your Serene Highness. I merely want to point out to you that the Soviet Secretariat stationed in Lichtenbourg City was informed that the Chalet was unguarded at three o'clock today."

"Well?" The prince questioned.

"And they were informed by someone employed here at the Chalet," Stefan answered.

"Ridiculous. I suppose you have been monitoring my phone calls. Is there nothing you won't stoop to? You may as well know, I have personally chosen each of those who serve me. No one else would pay them the salaries I pay."

"The State pays."

To Julie, Prince Maximilian's reply sounded like something in one of those dry history books. The man obviously was not living in this century. "You forget. The State belongs to the Kuragins. It will come back to us at the next election. To me, in fact. Meanwhile, I need all the support I can get."

"Even Reds?" Prince Stefan asked. "What servants knew you were here alone?"

"I did not expect to be alone. I had asked General Athlone to visit, as he has promised to do. Meanwhile, his son is good enough to keep me company. Until my wife, Her Serene Highness, arrives this evening. There is no secret to that."

"In that case," Stefan said sharply, "Someone in this building had no confidence in your wife's arrival, with or without a bodyguard. You were lucky that the British Consul's son was here."

To everyone's astonishment, this set fire to Prince Maximilian. "How dare you insinuate that Garnett would desert me at a time like this!"

The two men did not seem to be aware of their audience. Max's fury caused Stefan to lose his temper at last. "Good God! Does your life mean nothing to you?"

A phone buzzed loudly and the prince answered. "Yes. I'll take the call . . . Alexia? Of course. I am quite safe. Do come. Your mother will be with you, I trust . . . I see.

No. I do understand. She should be present at the official announcements. For my sake. To show the Kuragin colours, so to speak. No. I really understand. Only a few minutes. I'll be expecting you both."

He cut the connection looking tired and drained. Stefan

started to say something. "Max, we will talk of this some – "

But Maximilian pulled himself together. "Well, you may go. Back to those friends of yours who forged this so-called election. But believe me, they won't include my daughter. Alexia is loyal to me."

Julie held her breath.

Prince Stefan asked with a touch of irony, "I have Your Serene Highness's permission to retire?"

"With all my heart, sir. My country, and certainly I, do not need your kind."

Everyone except Max was so embarrassed by this tirade that no more words were exchanged between the two princes, and Brett bowed to Max. "I believe I have overstayed my visit as well. If Your Highness has no further wish for Miss Jones's stenographic services at the moment, she too will retire." He opened the door to the hall without looking back.

Tiredly, Prince Max covered his eyes with the back of one hand. The other hand waved away his uncomfortable remaining guests.

Stefan waited momentarily for Julie while Brett bowed again to the unseeing Max and then escorted Julie in stately fashion to the door. Julie had never been more relieved than at this moment, to find herself leaving the room between the prince and Brett.

Stefan turned to them when the door was closed. He seemed to have gotten the best of his impatience and anger. "Sorry. I hope this business will go no further. His Highness had every reason to resent my visit."

"Oh, no, sir!" Julie protested but she was silenced by Brett's nudge. She coloured with embarrassment and was silent.

The little valet, Biddicombe, was waiting at the bottom of the staircase. Forgetting protocol, he rushed to Prince Stefan. "How is he, Your Highness?"

Stefan said gently, "I am going to bring back Herr Chalgrin from Vienna. Meanwhile, call Dr von Hartman and to the other specialist at the hospital. Tell them it is my order. No delays."

"Thank you, sir. Even though His Highness refuses to see the doctors?"

"Even so. But they must not use my name to His Highness."

"Excuse me, sir," Brett interrupted. "My little car is faster than yours. There isn't a car in Lichtenbourg that can beat it. Herr Chalgrin is my job. Those crowds of well-wishers at the palace deserve to see their champion. You can stop at the hospital while I'm bringing in Chalgrin."

"What of your promise to our Red friends?" Stefan asked.

"I'll charge it to my government. Good relations, you know."

Stefan looked back up the stairs, shook his head but then agreed with a rueful laugh. "I'll call Chalgrin in Vienna. Tell him you will meet him at the border. I know you won't fail His Highness."

"No, sir. For what it's worth, you have my word. I'll make it in no time."

After the last nerve-racking hour Julie felt both relief and pride in her companions. Trying not to bring them more trouble she curtsied to Prince Stefan, wishing him, "Good luck, sir," and to his companion, "Thanks for the ride, Mr Athlone."

Would she be going back to the palace tonight? She hoped so.

There was a tram to Kuragin Boulevard at the bottom of the Chalet hill. It would be easy enough to find her way from the boulevard up to the palace. She swung around and started to the doors which an usher was holding open with exemplary patience. She figured it was a reasonably graceful exit, and was surprised when the prince called to her. "You may as well be comfortable here instead of going back and forth until you are settled. I've spoken to Frau Bergin. I'd also like to have someone here that we can trust when my wife and her mother arrive. I'm not at all sure of Max's staff."

So she must remain here after all. Away from the palace. Still, Julie was anxious to be of service to him and agreed readily, but she let herself be a little flattered when Brett Athlone put in, "A pity. I'd hoped to drive Miss Jones back to the palace."

He might be mysterious sometimes, almost sinister in his prying into her life, but she had to admit he could be charming when he wanted to be.

Meanwhile, Stefan had put him in his place with the dry comment, "There's always tomorrow."

CHAPTER THIRTEEN

Out on the steps she watched both men as they were about to start off in different directions. The prince merely gave her a salute with two fingers to the bill of his cap, but before Brett Athlone headed for his white Porsche, he congratulated her. "Take care, Just Julie. This place doesn't strike me as very healthy in more ways than one. A word of advice. Don't trust anyone."

Whatever that meant.

She pretended to take his warning as a joke and waved to both men before going back up the steps into the Chalet.

Meanwhile, no one had told Julie what duties, privileges or rights she would have while she waited for the physicians and the invalid Prince Max's family. She doubted if her presence itself would be welcome to His Highness but if she didn't at least try to offer her help, Prince Max would very likely complain that she hadn't shown him the proper respect.

She sighed, straightened her skirt around, then brushed off her jacket, and started up the white and gold staircase. It occurred to her on the way up that the prince and his staff probably placed her among the servant staff. No use in antagonizing them unnecessarily. The prince had managed to upset them already.

She swung around and ran along the elegant old Reception Hall that paralleled the front of the Chalet. There were several full-length mirrors that would catch the light from the overhead chandeliers. She slowed a second or two, getting a quick flash of her figure in the mirrors. Nothing to equal Princess Alexia or her mother, but creditable. She slicked down her hair and hurried on.

Behind the south stairs she found another, much less impressive hall leading to the back of the building, the kitchen quarters and the narrow servants' stairs. The house was far quieter than Julie thought an ex-ruler's house would be. The only noise came from the kitchen where a surly voice complained while a great deal of pounding went on, probably the tenderizing of meat for the prince's dinner.

Julie grinned at the luck she had enjoyed while breaking her journey in Paris. Every café meal was delicious to her taste, brought up as she had been on the tough quality of meat and scarcity of vegetables in her girlhood after the war. And the cheap Paris prices! About two shillings-sixpence upstairs in the Rue de la Harpe on the Left Bank. Even in the Lido Arcade on the Champs Elysées there had been a memorable seven-layer cake and the *biftek-pommes frites*. Grand total around a half crown.

Looking back on those exciting two days, Julie compared herself with poor Prince Maximilian who, being a prince, probably couldn't be seen in such places, even when he was well.

There were a great many things to be said for her own identity, she decided as she hurried along the upper floor towards Prince Max's suite. At the last second, as she raised her hand to knock, she realized he was speaking to someone, probably on the phone. Best not to interrupt.

He certainly hadn't been feeling very good-natured a few minutes ago.

She waited. He was bound to end the call soon.

It was not a call. She was startled to hear another voice, low but spirited. Young male or a female? It was hard to tell.

"It is true. I swear. Test them."

An odd conversation. Test what?

Or "taste" them. Much more likely. Julie still had food on her mind. It could be food. *Not my affair*, she reminded herself, not for the first time in her life. Undoubtedly, someone was trying to persuade His Highness to eat a meal. Or take his medicine.

No matter. I'll wait him out. Or her, as the case may be.

Julie had always been an active girl and within two minutes or so she moved away from the door, strolling towards the white staircase but looking back in the hope of seeing the prince's visitor leave. By the time she reached the staircase, still glancing over her shoulder, she was surprised to see Biddicombe, the little English valet, at the bottom of the stairs, looking anxious and signalling to her. She rushed down and met him on the landing.

He asked abruptly, "What is his mood?"

She had to confess, "I don't know. I didn't knock. He was talking to someone."

"One of the staff, I suppose. At all events, they are always here."

"The doctors?" That wouldn't help the prince's mood.

"No. But he must be at his best. He would never forgive me if Princess Garnett saw him otherwise."

"The princess is here, already?"

That was sure to put him in a better mood

and maybe she could persuade him to receive his physicians.

"She is. His Highness so often asks to see her. And she's finally here. First time in over two weeks. Probably Princess Alexia's persuasion. She's very loyal to her father."

"Are they out of the car yet?" Julie asked.

"Just turning on the circle drive. We are informed by the gatekeeper so we may avoid any unpleasant scenes with the various political parties, or unfriendly newsmen. We take special care that none of the representatives of the foreign tabloids and their papers are seen by Prince Maximilian. Princess Garnett has always been, if I may say so, one of their prime targets."

From experience in many kitchens Julie was concerned with practical aspects of an unplanned visit. "I'd better tell the kitchen staff. Is it to be tea or dinner?"

"No, no. Not yet. Princess Garnett is a martini woman. Early habits, you know. She was very much a Twenties Belle. Never mind the kitchen. I'll go to prepare His Highness. Delay the ladies as long as you can."

He left her abruptly, taking the stairs two at a time with great speed for his skinny frame. She nodded without having the least idea what to do about "detaining" the ladies.

Julie wondered then to ring for the housekeeper or someone else who could notify the kitchen of the royal visitors but she saw one of the sentries trot up to the big black limousine as it stopped before the steps. Things would have to take their natural course.

She smoothed her hair again and walked out to the steps as sedately as was possible to one of her volatile nature. She was not in time to greet Alexia who got out of the back seat and started up the steps to Julie. The sentry and the chauffeur meanwhile were helping out the beautifully groomed Princess Garnett.

Alexia asked Julie, "How is my father? Has he seen a doctor today?"

"Not yet, Ma'am. Maybe Her Highness can persuade him. Excuse me. I think the Princess wants me."

With a sudden sharpness Alexia said, "Never mind my mother. She has all the help she needs. How is my father?"

Torn between the claims of the two princesses, Julie blurted out, "Better, Ma'am. He was talking with someone a few minutes ago. Very much himself."

"Thank God for that, after the election results and all."

Julie barely heard her. She had dealt with employers like Garnett before. They must receive attention at once to retain their self-esteem. It was perhaps their greatest need in life. She ran down the steps, curtsied and asked if she could oblige Her Highness.

"Yes, dear. I must see His Serene Highness at once. It's so dreadfully hard, continually running back and forth, especially today, so close to all the absurd celebrations I must attend tonight. For my husband's sake."

Julie was always surprised to hear the delusions of such women. Did Garnett Kuragin actually imagine she had been visiting her invalid husband at the Chalet continually? Day after day? Very likely, she did believe it.

Garnett waved away the chauffeur with the petulant, "Kurt, my boy, you are so clumsy. Will you never learn? Take a lesson from my dear old friend, Piotr Kallinen."

In Julie's eyes the stern, rifle-wielding sentry almost fawned on the princess. "Your Serene Highness remembers my name. It is a great honour. We have all missed Your Highness."

"Of course, I remember you, dear Piotr. Now, do let us get on to His Serene Highness. What a bore that he must be cooped up here all these weeks, just when he is so badly needed elsewhere. He might easily have won the election if only those tiresome doctors hadn't made so much out of his heart murmurs, or whatever they are. So – I must hold up the flag for both of us. Come, Alexia. Julie, that is your name; isn't it? Let us raise my poor husband's spirits."

Julie marched along behind the two princesses, with the sentry rushing ahead to swing both doors open for the ladies. No one paid much attention to her now, for which she was grateful. They might be thinking of so much else – surely, the health of Prince Maximilian – that they would not blame her if the arrangements were not completed for their pleasure as they visited the sick man.

Julie was relieved to see the little valet scuttle out of the prince's suite, bowing lavishly. He gave the real First Lady of Lichtenbourg a respectful nod, saving his flourishes for Princess Garnett. "He is waiting with great anticipation, Ma'am. Exceedingly anxious to see you. If I may say so, your appearance will be the brightest moment this old building has seen in many a day."

"Don't be silly," Garnett waved him away as she passed him and went in through the door he had opened. "It isn't as if I have stayed away of my own will . . . Here I am, Max, darling. I have been aching to see you but those tiresome managers of your campaign were so persistent. 'For his own good', they kept insisting. 'You are needed to bolster up the Kuragin Name. All this when I longed to be with you. We aren't through yet, you know."

After the prince's defeated and resentful attitude towards his son-in-law earlier in the day, Julie was puzzled over the sudden change in him now. He was so optimistic. Maybe he was trying to put on some kind of cheerful mood for his wife, but he seemed genuine. Since Alexia had gone into the room unnoticed, Julie stepped into the outer room with its greenery dappled by the setting sun and began to watch this scene with great interest. Royalty acted a good deal like so many of her other employers. The common denominator seemed to be what they thought of themselves and how the world accepted this self-evaluation. A nice arrangement if the world would cooperate.

"I must remember that," she told herself.

She felt in five minutes or so that something had to be done about seeing to Gin-and-It or whatever, and some hors d'oeuvres that would please the high-and-mighty Kuragin Royals. She was about to sneak out and order proper cocktail service when the efficient housekeeper appeared with her clumsy little shadow, the "slave". After Frau Bergin had arranged the interesting bits of fish and cheese and meat including what Julie was certain must be caviar on funny bits of black bread which must be pumpernickel, Frau Bergin was honoured by Princess Garnett with a personal thanks.

The housekeeper had placed before the princess her special American Martini, as the housekeeper explained, and it was obvious that the Twenties Belle had not changed her tastes. She sipped gracefully but her glass was often topped off by her attentive husband as he reached for the little carafe.

Was no one going to discuss the serious aspects of his illness? Princess Alexia, who might have mentioned it, sat there watching her mother and father behave like young lovers and vaguely smiled. The smile had sad edges to it, and clearly her mind was on their happiness, perhaps as opposed to her own. Her father teased his wife, tried to feed her a cracker spread with what the Reverend Tenby's wife had referred to as "a good liver paté". It didn't look appetizing but Garnett laughed and loved his attentions, only occasionally wiping her lips with her heavy damask napkin.

It was Frau Bergin who asked if Julie would care for a glass of Danish Schnapps, whatever that was. The glass was tiny and the liquid looked like water, but this belated invitation warned Julie that she had no business here observing the Royal Family reunion. Julie recovered her common sense, refused the Schnapps offer and after a hurried curtsy opened the hall door. In the doorway she reminded them all, "Please call me when I am needed."

No one stopped her, though Alexia thanked her and Garnett murmured, "Dear child. So obliging."

Somewhat deflated, Julie realized she didn't even know where her room would be in the Chalet, or indeed, if anyone had been to the rescue of her luggage from the New Palace to the Chalet. Before she could close the door behind her she heard the roar of a car motor out on the drive and knew another problem must be answered: Prince Max and his revulsion toward his physicians.

Alexia, who was not altogether wrapped up in her parents' romantic reunion, noticed Julie's nervous start. She got up, excused herself to her parents who did not hear her, and joined Julie in the hall.

"What is it?"

"Your husband – I mean His Highness, ordered the hospital doctors to attend your father. Your father refused."

"But they are here now." Alexia took a breath. "I'll see

what I can do. We can't have my father disturbed again. I might have known Stefan would botch things up. I hope it wasn't deliberate."

Julie protested, "Oh, no, Your Highness. Not Prince Stefan."

Without seeming to notice the girl's intrusion into family affairs, Alexia waved away her protests. "You know nothing whatever about the matter. I'll go and see them now. Don't mention the doctors to my parents."

"He's so much better now than he was half an hour ago, when Prince Stefan went out to bring the doctors. Maybe he won't need them."

Alexia shook her head. "I suppose it was to be expected. It was Stefan's visit that upset him."

Julie couldn't help reminding her, "Ma'am, we thought your father was quite ill before Prince Stefan came."

But the princess was already on her way down to urge caution on the physicians.

Julie was wondering if she should linger in the hall in case someone rang for her or just follow Alexia and hope for the best. She began to wish General Athlone's son was here. She was sure he could find a way that might get them out of this present impasse.

Alexia had already gone out to join the valet Biddicombe and the two sentries in warning the physicians when, to Julie's surprise, Princess Garnett opened the door of her husband's suite and beckoned to her with one slim forefinger. "Those two tiresome physicians are out on the drive with my son-in-law. Up to no good, as any fool can see. I want you to keep them away from His Serene Highness. Max must be kept comfortable and untroubled."

Julie remembered all too clearly how fragile and ill

Prince Max had been less than an hour earlier. "But if Your Highness is with him he should remain in this good mood."

"Impossible. I must return to the palace shortly. For his sake. There are so many things to be done before the celebrations."

"Celebrations?" Julie echoed faintly. What a word to use about the inaugural affairs of her husband's successful rival!

"Certainly. I must uphold the Kuragin name and remind them of my husband's place in this country's history."

"But His Highness was very ill today," Julie replied.

Princess Garnett looked back over her shoulder, an unexpected flash of concern revealing faint lines in her otherwise flawless face. "Well, at present, my darling Max has never been better. In fact, he insists he has a plan and many unsuspected friends who will be behind him when he makes his move. How is that for cheering one up? And his confidence certainly cheered me."

"But if Your Highness, you yourself, persuaded the prince to see the doctors, everyone would feel better, and he could more easily make his move, as you say. They would even find him a greater leader than before. Only you can do it. He will listen to you."

"That is certainly true. Max never listened to anyone but me. He used to say it was I who placed him in his great role as ruler of Lichtenbourg. I, mind you!"

Julie longed to repeat this wonderful statement of self-deception to Brett Athlone. He had a sense of humour and would certainly appreciate it. However, Julie could only repeat what was undoubtedly the truth. "You see, Ma'am? You will give him the very strength he needs for – whatever he has in mind." God knows what that was!

When her vanity was appealed to, there was no stopping Princess Garnett. She laughed, turned back to her husband's invalid suite, remarking as much to herself as to Julie, "With me beside him, my darling Max will see those ridiculous, troublemaking doctors. They can't tell me he is critically ill. Ridiculous. Not the virile man who held me in his arms a few minutes ago. And he is full of hope for the future. He has plans, he tells me. And has friends the stupid election officials at the Chancellery don't even know exist. Ties that should prove once and for all which man – Max or Stefan – is the better ruler. That should show the world."

Like a good servant, Julie could only say, "Yes, Ma'am," but it seemed terrible that the woman dismissed life and death matters for this dream which she had doubtlessly made up on the spur of the moment. Garnett Miravel Kuragin must have had a singularly sheltered life. Everyone seemed bent on protecting her from the pains and losses of life. Lucky little princess who could believe that nonsense.

Her Highness breathed deeply. "Perhaps I shouldn't have said anything. Just forget our little chat and I will go in and charm my dear prince. Leave it to me. I'll persuade him to see the dragons."

She swept off happily to do just that. With her luck she would probably succeed.

Julie went down to tell Alexia and Prince Max's physicians the good news. She suspected that the princess, at least, cared about her father's health. She cared so much that she had even been alienated from her husband on her father's behalf. This seemed strange to Julie who thought Prince Stefan was worth two of his father-in-law.

With these thoughts foremost she was a trifle shaken to meet Stefan the minute she heard voices in a large room decorated in Bavarian wintry brightness on the ground floor. She had walked in close upon her knock.

The two men talking to Alexia were not the blunt country physicians or busy London practitioners Julie was familiar with. Though one was tallish and the other a stout, little man, they were both formally dressed in tail-coats, a style flattering to the tall, young one but making the little fat man look like something out of Dickens.

Intimidated by them and preferring to deal with Stefan, Julie was relieved when the prince said, 'I hope you have good news. My wife seems to doubt that His Highness will see his physicians."

Alexia moved forward. Julie felt it would be wiser to address her. "Ma'am, Her Highness promised to persuade the prince. He is doing so well since she came. She says he even talks of having followers. For the next election, I think."

"Thank God," Alexia murmured. "Gentlemen, I'll take you to my father."

Stefan laughed shortly. "I should have thought of that. Garnett's charm will work when common sense fails."

Alexia accompanied the two physicians to the door. She stopped behind them, speaking to Stefan in a low voice. "It would be better if you stayed out of his sight for a little while. He is upset so easily. And they will be expecting you at the post-election hullabaloo at the palace."

Julie, whose presence the princess had forgotten, flushed with embarrassment for Stefan, but the prince was surprisingly cool. "Quite true. I hadn't thought of that. Musn't miss the hullabaloo." He bowed to her, held the door open and watched her leave with the two doctors. There was a moment of silence.

Suddenly, he slammed his fist against the door. Julie

was so startled she jumped and cried out. The sound of her cry and the rattle of the door under his impact brought him out of whatever mood possessed him. He touched Julie's hand. "Sorry. This has been a hectic day. Never mind that. I hope they've found you a comfortable room."

She knew this was no time to worry him over something he would consider a trifle. "Things being so busy now, I thought it would be better to think about that later, Sir."

She had been right. This was no time to trouble him over minor matters.

"Yes," he agreed, adding, "every order has to be given twice. But first things first. I'll speak to Frau Bergin again." He reached for the old-fashioned frayed bell-pull behind the edge of a tallboy while Julie waited in embarrassment.

Frau Bergin arrived so promptly Julie suspected she had been close by, possibly brought by the thud of his fist against the door. She knew the subject at once and gave Prince Stefan a smile along with a flutter of heavily mascaraed eyelashes. "Your Highness, Fräulein Jones will be placed in one of the little rooms on the upper floor. Very cheerful and bright. A view of the private ice rink and the little park beyond."

Stefan waved away details impatiently. "It sounds to me like an attic room."

"I believe, in the old days – " Frau Bergin began but Julie did not want the prince to regard her as a nuisance.

She interrupted eagerly, "I'd love it. It's my favourite kind of room. With a roof that slants and a little window that opens outwards."

Stefan smiled at her enthusiasm. He glanced at his watch, then shrugged. "Never mind. We'll see it before we decide. Which one, Gerda?"

The housekeeper explained nervously, "The one opposite

157

the small staircase. I can show Your Highness, but the doctors may ask for something, and I must be near at hand, unless you give me different orders."

"No. Certainly not. Wait near Prince Max's suite. I think I can still find the way up to the attic."

The housekeeper's full lips made a coy little *moué*. "A pity, sir. I had hoped that I could assist you. Personally."

But Stefan had already motioned to Julie and started across the hall with his purposeful stride. Julie looked back once. Frau Bergin looked definitely disappointed. Luckily, when she saw Julie she merely grinned. To Julie it was very much like someone who says, "Better luck next time" but Julie was happy to note that Prince Stefan didn't seem aware of her as a sexy female.

Julie was still surprised and feeling guilty at taking up his time when Stefan escorted her up a flight of steep, narrow stairs above Prince Max's floor to the room designated for her by the housekeeper.

Reaching over Julie's head, he pushed the door open and watched her duck under his arm and enter the tiny, whitewashed room with its sloping eaves overhead and relieved from stark simplicity by the casement window which opened on the view every bit as lovely as Frau Bergin had described it. The bed was narrow, little more than a cot, but no worse than most of the beds she had known in her lifetime, and this one need not be shared with other servants or homeless orphans.

Behind her, Stefan stared at it and pronounced a one-word verdict: "Awful!"

"It's not at all," she insisted.

"It's dark and dreary. Not a setting for someone who is all lightness and youth."

She was so worried over his possible displeasure that she paid little attention to his compliment. If he found her needs troublesome he might ship her somewhere else, even further away.

"It's my very own. I love it already. Look." She sat down on the edge of the bed and bounced. "It's got a mattress, a thick one, and these sheets and the blanket and the prettiest quilt."

He looked as if he found her enthusiasm incredible but he seemed touched by it anyway. "And a chest of drawers, of course. Put together by someone in a hurry. Probably a local lad, so we must be charitable. There may be a bathroom on this floor, but I wouldn't bet on it. And a loo, I devoutly hope."

"Please don't spoil it. The walls are all clean and white and look at those darling drapes," she replied.

No mistaking it. He did look relieved. He glanced at his watch again. "Anyway, we'll see how you and my father-in-law like each other. If you do, we can find you a nicer room."

"Oh, yes, sir. I know we will get on." She held out her hand. "I only wish everyone could be as happy as you've made me today."

He took her hand in his and she wondered excitedly if he would kiss her fingers. Instead, he drew her gently to him and with the fingers of his other hand, raised her chin. While her heartbeat appeared to make her whole body tremble, his lips touched hers and lingered, the warm flesh of his mouth leaving her breathless.

Then it was all over. He saw her wide-eyed surprise and lightly pinched her chin between his thumb and forefinger, murmuring huskily, "I'm not sorry, you know. But it was stupid of me. And wrong. A child like you."

159

"No, no. I'm twenty. Just about."

That made him laugh. "I know. Just Julie is Just Twenty. Or so. Then you understand my gratitude for your loyalty. Your kindness when I was feeling sorry for myself."

If he wanted to play it that way, she wouldn't disillusion him. But no matter what he said, she wasn't going to forget a single second of that kiss. He needed her. And she adored him, this wonderful, superior man – a real, live prince who had kissed her in a sweet and tender way.

When he patted her hand and left her, she saw the grim look harden his features when he went down the staircase to face the fickle, celebrating crowd at the New Palace.

He must know that they would be celebrating just as enthusiastically for his rivals if they had won the election.

CHAPTER FOURTEEN

While Garnett went to refresh her make-up and settle the stylish black hat and half-veil saucily on her head, a task she never left to maids or her lady-in-waiting, Princess Alexia assured her father that Garnett was desolate at not being able to remain with him.

"But, as you know, sir, Mother feels she owes it to you to make a good appearance in your name tonight. Maybe by the time of the Cathedral Service for the Inaugural you will be there yourself."

Prince Max accepted the excuse with a wistful smile and kissed his daughter goodbye. "My dear Garnett. How lovely she looked on the State Television coverage! Be certain to tell her how much I appreciate her devotion to the Kuragin cause. In a short time it will all count. I am not completely forgotten, my dear. I have friends in surprising places."

"I'm sure you have, sir." *Let him dream*, Alexia thought. He was happy then, especially as Garnett seemed to share his dream.

She left her parents to say their temporary good-byes in privacy and went out to wait for Garnett in the limousine. Presently, her mother came down the steps, escorted by her sleek blond chauffeur, Kurt, and two of the now four sentries who had been strung out like an operatic chorus across the steps of the Royal Chalet.

Alexia had felt the desolate silence of an invalid's quarters around the halls and behind closed doors inside the building. But at least, there was an abundance of armed soldiers, almost, yet not quite in sight. They were beyond every turn in the corridors that usually buzzed with gossip and domestic activity. The only normal action she had witnessed was the frightened little slave from the kitchen, rushing around to carry off the half-finished cocktail tray Alexia and Garnett had shared with Max. Many of the domestics had been in service to the Kuragin household, although kitchen girls were always being changed and this one looked like a scared rabbit, poor thing. She had taken an inordinate time cleaning up as well. She probably wouldn't last long. But there had always been hangers-on waiting to be received by Lichtenbourg's Prince Royal, Maximilian.

They had all gone now. Alexia knew she would find them flocking hopefully to Stefan's side. Sycophants to the end.

Her mother got into the limousine gracefully and thanked her eager escorts. "You will notify me at once if His Serene Highness should have a relapse. He seems well enough at the moment."

Prince Max's valet moved forward, obviously anxious to let the princess know that in spite of his unpopularity with his employer he was still a part of the royal household. "Prince Maximilian will do excellently after this visit from Your Serene Highness."

"Thank you, Biddicombe. You are a great comfort to my husband," Garnett flattered him.

Alexia envied her ability to win almost everyone in

162

the Kuragin employ. She wished she herself could be less concerned, less pessimistic over the future. If only Stefan . . .

There it was again and there seemed no way out. Things had gone too far, politically and personally. She then thought: *It must be wonderful to be loved all one's life, as Garnett has been. First by her studious father, Lord David Miravel, and then, almost from her birth by her boyhood idol, Prince Max, future ruler of Lichtenbourg.*

It had not happened to Alexia. Little of this devotion remained for the single child of Max and Garnett who was practically raised by her vigorous great-grandfather, Tige Royle, and his busy, active connections in California.

The drive back to the palace was hampered by celebrants, many of them drunk. Garnett found this a shocking expression of their anxiety to be rid of Prince Max. She reminded Alexia firmly, "Your father was the greatest ruler Lichtenbourg ever had. But he was forced to steer a cautious course between our little country and the Nazis. Now, we are surrounded by those nasty Soviet connections. Of course, they may be useful, temporarily. Anything that would be a barrier to Stefan and his crowd."

Alexia shrugged. Stefan, of course, had stepped in when necessary. She knew his worth. In her more honest moments she wondered if her resentment was based on her fear – no, her knowledge, that he had married her solely with this goal in mind. That realization shattered her love and trust in him.

Eventually, in order to get back into the palace without being hailed by the crowd at the gates for all the wrong reasons, the chauffeur drove on to the secluded upper gates of the Royal Gardens and came down to the east face of the palace.

From the noise of the Royal Lichtenbourg Band playing its loudest in the big front reception hall, both women knew they were late for their duties and hurried up to their respective suites to shower and dress.

Alexia always felt a great deal of tension when she was with her mother and was relieved to reach her own apartments alone.

Miss Hoschna, her volatile Hungarian dresser, trained at Dior's in Paris, met her with clasped hands, as if in prayer, and the veiled reproof: "Your Serene Highness is so much asked for. The telephone rings all the afternoon."

"Yes, yes. While I shower, please get out my blue Dior." On her way to the bathroom she added, "And the red oriental scarf Cousin Dan sent me from Japan."

"Blue and red! But Ma'am, those aren't the colours of His Serene Highness. I mean to say – not the Elsbachs."

"I want everyone to see my Kuragin colours."

Miss Hoschna knew better than to argue. She put the gold lamé back into its wrappings in the long wardrobe, only permitting herself a "tsk-tsk" of disapproval.

When Alexia emerged from her dressing room she found that her two ladies-in-waiting, no longer expecting her, had long since joined the noisy excitement below the great front staircase in the Reception Hall and Ballroom.

She was about to descend the stairs unattended when a man's hand touched her shoulder and she found herself being escorted down the marble stairs by the British Consul's son, Brett Athlone. She smiled her thanks but he shook his head, saying firmly, "I got back from Vienna just in time. Someone ought to show such a lovely lady the courtesy she deserves."

Her first reaction was resentment at his obvious slur against her husband, but a second thought made her say instead, "Manners and breeding. Pretty rare, these days. You remind me of your father."

She wondered why he frowned and found herself studying him. He was a good-looking young man who females were attracted to. Maybe, like so many others of this generation he felt there was something old-fashioned, even effeminate, about good manners. She hoped not. But then, he gave her a grin that was extremely effective.

"Poor Dad. He's been trying to make a gentleman out of me since he and his lovely wife first adopted me."

"Oh, I see. I beg your pardon."

"Not at all. I was lucky. I could have been blown up by General Franco and his merry men."

"Good heavens! You were adopted during the Spanish Civil War? Are you Spanish?"

He shrugged. "Probably not. If my investigations are on the money, my mother was definitely . . ." He stopped, added, "Not Spanish. Incidentally, your father is now in good hands. Prince Stefan sent me to get Herr Chalgrin."

"That was good of you. But you were speaking of your natural parents. Do you really want to find them? General Athlone seems very fond of you."

"I'm very fond of him. I just have this irresistible urge to find the woman who dumped me into strange hands at the moment of my birth."

Alexia was startled and disturbed by what sounded like some kind of vendetta against his natural mother.

"But she might have been ill. Or died. Are you sure there weren't extenuating circumstances? Some valid reason why she couldn't rescue you when the fighting broke out?"

"Yes. I'd say there were excellent reasons. Ah! Here we are. May I escort you to the champagne? These military bands are liable to deafen us before His Serene Highness takes his oath, or whatever he does."

She said grimly, "His Serene Highness will take the oath first at a private ceremony here in the palace, then publicly in the Cathedral in ten days. Very formal. Very heartfelt."

He laughed but his hand tightened on her arm, almost as though in sympathy. "Well, Your Highness, you and I are one bitter couple; aren't we? Just remember, I'm in your corner. More than you know."

She felt uncomfortable but thanked him as they passed the Royal Band in its freshly pressed but faded Elsbach colours. Brett Athlone headed her towards the two great rooms that opened into each other, the Small Reception Hall and Banquet Room currently cleared for dancing under the sparkling chandeliers. Some private drinking seemed to be going on in the ballroom beyond. This opened onto the Royal Gardens beyond.

Alexia didn't know whether she was relieved or sorry when her husband came up to her, under the eyes of half the glittering, chattering crowd, and offered her one of his two glasses of champagne. He looked tired, or maybe just annoyed at his surroundings, but his eyes had that warm, caring look she had always loved. "I know they're a noisy lot. You needn't stay long." She warmed under his gaze. "Only I've missed you."

She pulled herself together and accepted the glass.

"Thank you, Stefan. Where is my mother? Does she actually intend to see Father tonight?"

She wondered at the definite interest shown by Brett Athlone at their conversation which had been in German. The muscles of his hand tightened as he freed her arm. With a kind of brightness that did not sound like the man she was beginning to know, Brett remarked to Stefan, "I don't see the Fair Lady. Is she around? Such a charmer!"

"She's somewhere about. Sorry." Stefan offered the extra glass of champagne. "Here. Take mine. I haven't touched it." His light-humoured apology was pleasant and Alexia was surprised when Brett refused it and started away.

"No, thanks. Just thought I'd be lucky enough to win a dance from Her Highness."

Both Stefan and Alexia looked after him as he made his way through the crowd.

"Now, what was that all about?" Stefan wanted to know.

Alexia was still troubled. "I don't know. He's nice enough but somehow, I don't trust him. I keep thinking he means – " She smiled and shrugged off her uneasiness. "Silly. Why would he mean us harm? He did stop the riot around the Chalet today. Maybe he's a riot agitator."

Stefan laughed. "I doubt it. Shall we dance?"

His touch still excited her but she managed to say calmly, "Why not?" and set the glass on the tray of a passing footman.

In the warmth and strength of her husband's arms Alexia let her feelings drift back to the troubled and yet glorious days when she had persuaded herself of Prince Stefan von Elsbach's genuine love. A love for her, not the future, not the tiny principality that the Kuragins and Elsbachs had fought over for six hundred years.

The orchestra in a far alcove was playing a Lehar waltz and in spite of the half-drunken state of many palace guests they had swung into the dance as if they were at the old Vienna Hofburg Palace. A little too much swinging and dipping but as Stefan remarked, "I'm surprised they can stay on their feet at all. They must have rushed here direct from Hummel's Beer Garden."

Her mood had lightened and the knowledge evidently pleased him. "Shall we show them how it's done?"

"I'd love to," she replied. In his arms she felt ready for any challenge.

Almost immediately, they were noticed and the floor began to clear. Alexia knew they were objects of great interest and gossip but didn't care. It seemed so long since she had felt this exhilaration.

Stefan swung her around the far end of the ballroom, smiling as he looked down at her face which she knew must reveal her love for him. Some of the dancers had begun to take the centre of the floor again and Stefan remarked without undue emphasis, "I see the general's son has found a young partner. Amazing woman."

Over his shoulder Alexia saw Brett Athlone dancing with Garnett. The princess managed to look more beautiful than ever since the visit to her husband. Her hair was piled high, doing full justice to the celebrated emeralds in her tiara. Emeralds also adorned her ears, her richly displayed décolletage, and the one arm draped over young Athlone's shoulder.

Alexia admitted, "I don't know how she does it, but I wish I had inherited it."

He held her close. "I don't."

She hoped his remark was a compliment, but he was watching her mother and the consul's son. He looked thoughtful, or was he perhaps jealous of Brett Athlone?

She didn't take this suspicion too seriously. He had never shown any sexual interest in her mother before. He seldom troubled to hide his contempt of Garnett.

Garnett found some remark of Brett Athlone's amusing. She laughed and at the same time dropped her emerald satin evening bag. Athlone stooped to pick it up, causing other dancers behind them to whirl out of their way.

Stefan said, "Athlone seems to know how to charm the lady."

But Alexia knew her mother better. "Don't judge by her smile. Whatever else she is, Mother is never clumsy. She was startled. I wonder why."

"I didn't know anyone could shake that glitter of hers. But I grant you, he seems to have done so. What the devil did he say? Not a proposition, surely. She must be long used to that."

Experience had given Alexia some skill at reading her mother's countenance, though it still appeared to be wrinkle-free. There was a tightness around her full lips. *As if the smile were pasted on*, Alexia thought, and she puzzled over what she had sensed about the young man's interest in Lichtenbourg's Royal Family. She said aloud, "Could he be a Communist? Or a Neo-Nazi? He's something, I don't know what. He has such an odd effect on us."

"Us?"

"Mother and me. And he certainly controlled that gang of rioters at the Chalet today, from what I hear."

"For which he deserves our thanks."

At that minute the princess, accepting the arm of her escort, left the floor, but she limped noticeably, though her laughing remark to Brett Athlone seemed to dismiss her problems.

Stefan manoeuvered Alexia off the floor. They joined the other pair at one of the aged gilt chairs, near a footman from whom Athlone took a champagne glass and offered it to Garnett.

The princess delighted in the attention she had caused. Gazing up over her glass as she drank, she had never looked more sparkling. "What a flutter over nothing. I do beg everyone's pardon. Herr Athlone – may I call you Brett? – was amusing me with stories of his travels and I made a misstep. I think I broke the strap of my shoe."

They all looked down at her perfectly formed ankle. The gold strap with its little emerald-studded buckle was still intact, for which Garnett murmured her relief.

"No harm, apparently," Stefan murmured. "I know Her Highness will excuse us if we continue the dance."

The dancers were in disarray, a few standing around, others having left the floor as three footmen rushed from various stations in the ballroom to rescue the princess. Alexia heard Brett Athlone's apology received with her mother's usual allure. As Alexia went into Stefan's arms again, she said, "May I make a catty statement?"

"Please do. It might cut some of this phoney atmosphere."

"The strap of her shoe wasn't broken."

"So I noticed." He was studying the various dancers who had followed his example and continued the dance. "What does that tell you, Miss Sherlock Holmes?"

"I'm dead serious, darling."

He swung her around past the big double doors to the Reception Hall, squeezing her hand while he looked at her with all the old, remembered warmth. "I know you are. So am I." He then asked, "Would I upset protocol if I kissed you for that, my darling?"

Unfortunately, before she could give him the obvious answer, a slight stir of excitement from the open doors of the great hall caught her attention. She groaned. "Oh, no. Fräulein Steig wants you. She's giving a message to the footman. Can't business wait for you, even tonight?"

He glanced around, seeing the chunky, efficient Number One Exchange operator whose large face told him and Alexia nothing as usual. "Damn! I can't guess whether it's important or not. I certainly don't want to talk to some drunken constituent at this hour."

Alexia released herself reluctantly. "Better go. Affairs of State wait for no prince. Maybe the Soviets and the Americans have declared war."

"Good God! What an idea. Well, I'd better find out." He signalled to the ancient Secretary of the Royal Council, Count Thallin, now a nobleman without a job. He was being succeeded by the Russian-born Colonel Grigori Vukhasin, representing the party that came in second in the elections.

Having left Alexia in the safe hands of the old count, Stefan strolled off to receive Fräulein Steig's clear, heavily inked telephone message from the footman. Alexia watched him go and then remembered the matter that concerned her even more than her mother and certainly more than it concerned her husband. She went after him anxiously. "Stefan, could it be about my father? Maybe he has had a relapse. I must know."

171

He was taking the folded message from the footman and said, "Probably not. But here it is."

He let her read the message as he read it. She appreciated his gesture. He was not usually so indiscreet.

To His Serene Highness, Prince Stefan von Elsbach.

> From Julie Jones.
> Private.
> Two gentlemen are here. You know them.
> They mention you. It is not politics. I can't say
> any more. Please come to the tram line below
> the Chalet. I'll wait where the tram turns.

At the end of the note Fräulein Steig had written:

'She sounds excited, sir. Very breathy and frightened.'

"Fraulein Steig is a good judge of voices," Stefan said.

"But Miss Jones is an enterprising little minx," Alexia murmured and then frowned at her own remark. "I'm sorry. Do you think it is genuine?"

She knew from Stefan's expression that he, at least, took it seriously. "Julie is loyal. That I'll swear. What I don't understand is who they could be. Not Reds, I take it. That would certainly be political. I'll have to go, of course."

Alexia was beginning to fear the real danger. "It is Father. Why doesn't she say so? It's Father who is in danger."

"I doubt it, but we can't risk it," he replied. "It seems to be a matter of some urgency. Would you present my

172

excuses to that noisy crowd? I'll have to make this a pretty cautious business. It has all the earmarks of a Soviet trap, but if it isn't political, what other secrets have they uncovered?"

"Whoever *they* are. Oh, Stefan, I know it's Father. I'll get a coat."

He seemed to guess that arguing with her would only take precious time. "If you must, darling, but for God's sake, borrow one. We haven't much time. Just don't take one of your mother's dazzlers. Need I remind you, we've got to be inconspicuous. And as for your part in this Mata Hari business, you go no further than the end of the tram line, until we find out what it's about."

She understood and being well versed in palace intrigues, walked calmly to the lift used only the Royals. Two of the younger revellers embracing in the shadows beyond the little newly polished lift cage, watched her with some curiosity but did not break from their embrace, and resumed kissing when she stepped into the lift, nodding to the male operator. Alexia was amused, and a little envious, to see how the girl's hands wandered seductively over the hips of her partner.

Alexia stepped off at the upper floor and went to her apartments. Miss Hoschna was asleep in the slipper chair. Alexia woke her when she tugged an old sport coat out of the outdoor wear closet. She opened her eyes, saw Alexia's coat and screamed at this horrible choice, but Alexia waved her to silence, belted the coat and gave her the explanation. "I'm walking in the gardens with my husband. All very romantic and proper."

She certainly relieved the Hungarian dresser who had been known to give up positions where her ladies dressed like normal human beings. "In such case, Madame, you make a wise decision. Love before all, even in such a coat. May your night be happy, Your Highness."

"I doubt that. Unfortunately, it isn't likely to be tonight, at least."

She left a puzzled dresser behind her as she stuck her head out, looked up and down the hall and then went out on the run.

CHAPTER FIFTEEN

As the long afternoon shadows merged into what Julie found to be a romantic blue dusk, she went down to superintend the arrival of her luggage from the New Palace. The two suitcases, a vanity case and a matching hat box came in a limousine with the royal crest.

Their means of arrival impressed her more, she suspected, than they impressed the footman who lifted her bags out and gave the royal chauffeur a casual salute of dismissal. Then he leapt up the long front steps, two at a time and set them down in a pile in front of Julie. In an unexpectedly cocky way he said in fair English, "Ask me prettily and I'll take them up for you, Fraulein Jones."

He was not ugly enough even to be interesting and she was immediately put off by his bulbous lips, and the way his eyes looked her over from head to foot, as if he himself were so gorgeous he had a right to regard her as a girl on the slave block. His expression verged on contempt but with a smirk she found more offensive than his contempt.

She guessed what he thought. He had heard gossip about Prince Stefan's concern for her comfort. Or he had seen the prince's gentle treatment of her and probably suspected the worst. Such gossip did not promise anything good for her future. Her instinct was to tell him off haughtily but that had never brought her good results.

She brushed aside his insolence, becoming casual but impatient. "Don't be silly. It won't be the first time I've carried my baggage. If you are willing to help me, fine. If not, I've got to be going. There are stairs to climb."

For a few seconds they stood there looking at each other. He gave in first, with a fleshy grin. "As the GI's say, 'here goes nothing'."

She laughed at his version of American slang but this made no impression on him. He hoisted one case under his arm and took the other three by their straps. "After you, Fräulein."

He let her go ahead of him and followed her up each flight of service stairs until they came out in the attic corridor under its low ceiling. When he had set her cases down in her room and turned to go, he stopped in the open doorway.

With the leer that made her think of a slavering canine he put her in her place. "Except the legs, Fräulein, I think, what is the attraction for His Highness? May be, because he is not a man for the ladies. Too ambitious."

She held onto her pride and indignation for her own and especially Prince Stefan's sake until she had closed the door, which she did with only a moderate slam. But she seethed.

His Highness probably thought nothing of insults, especially if they weren't true. She, on the other hand, had nothing but her own character and she would show the world just how high Miss Julie Jones could rise some day.

It was while she was unpacking and hanging things in the long, thin clothes press that she resented his comment about her looks. All these nice clothes she had bought in Paris and had been so proud of meant nothing to creatures like the footman. Maybe, even when she finally overcame that awful business of having no parents, she would still be treated like a whore who was lost among decent people.

She threw a few more things around, wrinkling the red Dotted Swiss of Princess Garnett's that Miss Alexia had given her. She picked it up, smoothed it out, and began to wonder where the nearest bathroom or washroom might be. The dress ought to be ironed out with her hands if all else failed. But she still wouldn't look the way the Royals looked when they wore clothes.

It was hard to discover that she had been wrong all her life. It wasn't how you acted, or what you accomplished in life. It must be who your ancestors were. That was a thought she still found hard to accept. But, judging by her own experiences, it was probably true.

After she had her wardrobe in order she felt a little better. Her looks had been insulted before. They would be again. Meanwhile, she thought she looked quite special in the Dotted Swiss after she had found the bathroom, the toilet and basin, and cleaned up. She was also pleased with the long mirror on the wall opposite the toilet which revealed her entire body in the new gown when she stood on the toilet seat. It was a bit girlish, but who cared? As that idiot footman had said: "What is your attraction, Fräulein?" It was hardly possible that her legs would get her by. So the answer was the same as it had always been: hard work and cleverness. No one had better say she didn't learn!

When she was too hungry to put it off any longer, she went down to the kitchen quarters to find out where she was expected to eat her dinner. Or her supper, as the case might be.

Thank heaven, the fancy chef who served only Prince Maximilian was gone for the day and a tiny Frenchwoman of uncertain age and temper bustled around preparing for the rest of the staff. It was easy enough to do a few favours for the little woman, reaching for things, moving about. All the things that made Madame Dubois furious when she was forced to do them herself.

"The pace," she told Julie sharply in English, which was much more understandable than her German or Hungarian, "all must be in readiness. Then comes the feast. Not before."

Julie set down the heated plates for her. "Yes, Ma'am. Mrs Tenby, the vicar's wife, told me that."

The little woman looked up with the pinched nose and bright, wild eyes of a vixen fox. "A vicar's wife. Well enough. Now I, Miss Jones, I was cook to the curé, the priest of our village. Yes. The First Cook. There was another to help me at harvest time, the blessing and all of that."

Julie let her eyes grow wide with admiration. "Madame, you were First Cook for a priest? How splendid! You ought to be the prince's chef here."

Madame looked over her shoulder and then confided, "Me, I am of that opinion. A clumsy fellow, the chef. Drinks vodka. It is bad enough to be a *Boche*. But to drink vodka?" Her boney shoulders shrugged. "What can one expect? Now, sit down and eat your *cassoulet*. Vite!"

"Yes, Ma'am."

It was just about as good as the unforgettable *Boeuf Bourgignonne* in the Paris café. All the worries and trouble of the day seemed to fade.

By the time the staff had eaten dinner in their dining room with its ski lodge decor and a few trophies, Julie found her relations with Madame Dubois showed a gratifying little tinge of warmth. Madame was no Mrs Skinner, but still, a woman who could cook like that was entitled to be a bit cranky.

Since Julie had nothing to do and was dismissed in her autocratic way by Madame Dubois, she was still too excited over her first day in Lichtenbourg to go to bed quite yet. She walked out the door and headed around the ice rink, now covered for the summer. Beyond was a woody little path leading down to a busy thoroughfare and the end of a tram line.

It was very dark at this hour, except for the tiny estate lights that bordered the path, and the woods apparently part of the royal property, looked like something from a Grimm's fairy tale; one of the more sinister ones. She stood there hesitating, wondering if it was worth taking this trail, just to come out on a typical, dull street whose traffic had begun to slacken off now. There was a parking lot which opened onto the street and backed on the royal property. There must be a locked fence somewhere between the property and the lot, but she could see a big car as it pulled in and for a minute before the lights went out, Julie saw two men, one getting out, the other at the wheel.

A funny place to park. Few shops were open at this hour on the street. Even the two car blue tram that had reached the end of the line seemed empty of passengers. Julie stepped back towards the covered rink, wondering if the two men could be on their way to visit Prince Maximilian for some reason. She didn't want to seem to be spying. But if she started up to the Chalet she would certainly be seen. She was behind the trunk of a tree, thankful that she was so thin, so she just escaped

179

being silhouetted against the deep, velvety darkness by the little lights strung along the path.

The man who had been driving the car looked like a stranger at first, then she realized he was General Sir George Athlone who had given her a ride from the train station that morning. Not surprising. She remembered that someone had mentioned he would be visiting Prince Max soon.

The presence of the other man, older, with a mane of white hair and a strong, weathered face, was even more familiar to Julie. What was the American tycoon, "Tiger" Royle doing here without having paid his daughter and son-in-law a visit at the New Palace? And if he had actually stopped by the palace to see them, why had he come across town to see Maximilian, without Stefan?

With her sympathies entirely in Stefan's corner Julie hoped this didn't signify that Tige Royle's influence had switched to Prince Max. She waited quietly for them to pass but they appeared to be in the middle of a serious discussion and according to Tige, they wanted to settle something before entering the Chalet.

"Best be careful what we say and don't say to him; don't you agree, General?"

He stopped with one foot on the tile border where two steps would take the skater down to the ice in late fall and winter. General Athlone stopped beside him. They were looking thoughtfully towards a dark little clump of trees across from the rink. Café tables and chairs were in place between the trees where Prince Maximilian and his visitors probably sat during "Blue Hour" cocktails.

The general agreed with Tige's cautionary advice. "Absolutely. He is in a bad way, as you doubtless know."

"Poor devil." Tige glanced over at the Chalet's kitchen and pantry walls. "Although, in the long run, it is Stefan who would be the target of the Commies. You know the routine: 'sabotaged the story. Snapped at the chance to add *serene* to his royal title'. That sort of thing."

"Afraid so. Naturally, nothing is definite or even known for a certainty yet, my boy has his own ideas. I won't go into them now. They are pretty far-fetched. But he's not at all sure about anything." He slapped his thigh expressively. "Jove, I wish the old woman in London hadn't died, left everything in an uproar."

It was very mysterious. Julie almost held her breath for fear they would hear her.

Tige burst out suddenly, "I'd like to shake the truth out of my granddaughter. Shake Garnett 'til her teeth rattled."

"Quite true, old fellow, I must admit. First things first however. And it would be sure to get back to Elsbach before we're ready. If we ever can be ready."

"Too damned bad," Tige said as they walked on. "I think he'd have made a good ruler."

"All too true. Damn! I hope His Highness still has some of that excellent old port left in the cellars here." He rubbed his hands. "This mountain air carries a chill at night."

They were out of hearing now, making their way into the chalet by the garden door that opened into the servants' hall. A minute later they were inside the building.

Julie waited cautiously until she was sure the men were not liable to pop back out on the doorstep. Then she slipped out of the heavy shadows and across to peer in at the kitchen windows. No one seemed to be in the long room; so she came in quietly and crossed the long, narrow kitchen, much calmer than she felt. She took care to arm herself with an end piece of strudel that would be re-heated for those of the staff who satisfied themselves with a sweet breakfast.

Armed with her excuse, if she should be caught wandering around the chalet at two hours before midnight, Julie sauntered along the servants' corridor towards the handsome old reception hall that filled the entire front of the house and faced the steps. She looked out at the circular drive and saw only the sentries, beefed up now to six with rifles at the ready, and over beyond the south side of the drive, tiny flickering lights that she guessed were cigarettes of the hidden soldiers who guarded Prince Max.

It seemed rather stupid to have all the guards in front when Julie had seen two men get into the house from the wood and the covered ice rink. Tige Royle, being who he was, probably had a key for the big gate above the parking lot. All the same, she couldn't imagine calling the guards out in front of the chalet to save Prince Max if his two mysterious visitors made trouble for him. She had a strong suspicion that Tige Royle and Sir George Athlone with his British government connections could buy and sell this little country.

What were the Englishman and the American up to? Obviously, some action against the legally elected ruler of an independent country.

Still, it was nice to know the soldiers were Prince Stefan's men and would – she hoped – be loyal to him if the necessity arose.

The hall still seemed deserted. She thought it would do no harm to find out if the two secretive gentlemen were planning something with Prince Max. Judging by this afternoon's painful scene between the two princes, Maximilian might fall in with any crooked schemes of the rich and powerful Tige Royle. Apparently, the American wasn't called "The Tiger" for nothing.

She started back to the servants' stairs but was stopped by the clink of glasses and Sir George's jolly, booming voice. "Still the best port north of Lisbon, Your Highness. Don't know how you do it."

"One has ways, my friend," Prince Max replied in his gentle voice.

Julie realized the three men were here on the ground floor, probably in the little panelled bar that opened off the reception hall and close enough to Julie to give her a fright.

Common sense told her to move back into the deeper shadows of the servants' hall behind the wide south staircase, but she realized that only Sir George would be audible from there; so she waited. She did wonder if this secret business was bad enough, or earthshaking enough, for men like Athlone and Royle to silence any witnesses.

Perhaps not. They certainly approached their subject in a gingerly way. Tige said appreciatively, "I had some damned good, full-bodied port in – where was it? Not Andalusia but to the north and centre. Little town, hardly more than a village, outside Madrid. Just passing through. Happened to stop off during one of those crazy Spanish dinner hours at midnight."

Julie wished they would change the subject and stop harping on about Spain. Hot as it might be in parts of Spain, as she had been told, the subject always made her shiver and this hall was none too warm.

Sir George then put in, "Fascinating country, Spain. Haven't been there lately, of course."

"Franco? Came out of the Big One pretty well," the

prince said. He sounded languid, not too interested. Poor man. They shouldn't be keeping him up.

For some reason they persisted in milking the subject of Spain. Tige Royle kept at it. "Been there recently, Max? I know my granddaughter was crazy about it. You and Garnett were there on your honeymoon; weren't you?"

"Yes. Wonderful days. They treated us very well. Proper protocol and all that. Meant a great deal to Her Highness."

There was a definite change in Tige's voice as he said quickly, "Didn't I get a card from you two at that beach in Malaga? I seem to remember Garnett wanted to go across to Tangiers and you were under the weather or something."

"North Africa was not the place for my wife, my dear fellow. Certainly not in the Twenties with the French Protectorates all torn up by Riffs and such people. She came to realize it, of course."

"Yes. Very likely. Let's see. There were other times though. In the mid-Thirties, wasn't it? Just before the start of the Spanish Civil War."

"What? Tige, you are getting old. When we were there on our honeymoon, Alfonzo was still king. Nice, fellow. Treated us with the old-fashioned courtesy to be expected. A parade and a superb reception. Garnett was very fond of the family, particularly Queen Ena. English blood, naturally."

Sir George slapped his knee and burst out, "I'm like Tige here. Could have sworn we met Princess Garnett in Seville sometime during the Thirties. The Feria, you know. I couldn't understand why she didn't make the ride. All those gorgeous females would have been eclipsed. Magnificent horsewoman, I always thought. Still is, come to think of it. We met last autumn, riding to the Hungarian

184

border. Came back to the city together. She was a guest of the Albas in Spain in the Thirties some time; wasn't she? But I'm like Tige. Brains are slipping with age."

Prince Max was apparently stirred by the pictures his visitors conjured up of his beloved wife. His voice sounded stronger. "She is still the outstanding beauty of Europe. As much today as ever, as you will see when I get back to running things and she has her proper place again. I do remember, now you mention it, that she was forced to make official visits without me in most of the Thirties. Things were very tight here. The Führer breathing down our necks."

"Still, I could have sworn – " Sir George began but someone coughed and Sir George broke off with an embarrassed laugh. "Well, I certainly am rambling tonight. All your fault, Your Highness."

"Oh?"

"Your excellent port, you know."

Someone laughed softly. Julie thought it must be the prince. She had begun to feel relieved at the way the conversation had avoided any mention of Prince Stefan except Maximilian's talk of returning to power. Her arms were cold and she felt stiff all over. It had been a very full day and even her volatile, active body was a little tired. She was about to edge away to the back staircase when Tige spoke into the little silence that had lasted a minute or so.

"A pity you never had sons, Max. I wouldn't match my favourite, Alexia, with anyone but I suppose you were too busy for the family responsibilities. Lucky for me and my flock in San Francisco that you were. I can safely tell you, that little girl was the brightest light in our lives."

"On the contrary, Tige. A small family was not my

idea at all. But it would have been bad for Garnett. She might never have survived another miscarriage. She had one early in our marriage, you remember."

Sir George pursued the subject rapidly. "So now, there is our friend Stefan. Good fellow, but perhaps a little ambitious?"

"A little!" the prince exclaimed with sudden, unexpected sharpness.

But Tige interrupted. "Well now, I wouldn't go that far. It's just a matter of blood lines, as far as I'm concerned. I don't want any member of my own family to be going through life without his heritage."

"What on earth are you talking about?" the prince asked, growing more querulous as the two men seemed to overlook him in the line of succession. "After all is said, gentlemen, I am the true and God-given ruler of my country."

Both men spoke at once, trying to reassure him, but invariably they got back to Spain.

Julie shivered and quietly made her way back into the servants' hall. There was a telephone connection in the reception hall and there must be many scattered about the chalet but she might be caught in one of those rooms by a servant and have no excuse. Still, she must take a chance. There would very likely be a telephone on the prince's own floor, on one of those delicate stands that were set along the hall.

She heard Stefan's name again as she left the hall in mousy silence but too much time had been lost while she eavesdropped like a Cold War spy. She reached the hall above where one lamp glowed beside the door of Prince Maximilian's empty suite, and another across the hall cast a pleasant gleam over the ebony stand which held a swanky, special order black and gold French telephone.

186

It would be too easy to see her here but she had to take the chance.

To avoid troubling Max with unnecessary calls during his convalescence, outside calls to and from the Chalet went through the switchboard at the New Palace. Julie thought that ought to make it easier to get through. Surely, Prince Stefan would know that it must be something important if it came from the Chalet.

With one hand on the French phone she looked around, saw nothing moving in the silent night and tried to compose her message. Suppose no one believed her? Suppose they didn't consider it important. But she would still have done her share. It wasn't life and death matters concerning Julie Jones. Only Prince Stefan, and maybe his country, would lose.

Pulling herself together, she asked for the palace operator.

A woman answered with no-nonsense tones and speaking in the always intimidating German language.

Julie burst out in a scared voice, "I'm calling from the Royal Chalet. It's important. For His Serene Highness personally."

The woman's voice switched at once to Julie's English. "His Highness, Prince Maximilian, has he had an attack? Have the physicians been called? Are they prepared at the Chalet? Alarms must be sent out at once!"

"No, no. Prince Maximilian is with guests. But His Serene Highness ought to know. It seems to be a secret meeting."

"*Gott in Himmel*! The rumours are true. He makes a deal with the People's Party. The Communists."

"Not politics. Please tell him to meet Miss Jones at the end of the tram lines, by the parking lot below the Chalet grounds." She thought of it as the only place where they might not be seen from the Chalet. Unless, of course, someone was sneaking around the closed skating rink as Julie had been.

The operator was puzzled but she knew panic when she heard it. "*Ja.* Yes. Understood. I will notify Prince Stefan at once. Will you speak to him over the telephone?"

Julie scarcely heard her. Voices intruded from the foot of the main staircase. Two servants were accompanying Prince Maximilian who complained that they took the steps too slowly. "I am not a cripple, you know. Tige, will you please tell them in that assertive voice of yours that they are not nursing an invalid?"

Surely, it couldn't be good for a man with serious heart trouble to be climbing steps at midnight, after the unnerving quarrels and events of the day? But although Sir George protested that they should not have intruded, Tige said nothing and the prince ignored him. They must think the subject was important or, surely, they wouldn't have risked all this activity.

Julie was thankful that General Athlone and Mr Royle had to follow at the prince's slow pace. It gave her a few seconds to spin away from the phone to the narrow service stairs at the far end of the hall.

It was not comforting to hear Tige Royle ask after a moment's silence, "What was that? Sounded like mice scampering in the walls."

Sir George chuckled. "By Jove, the place has mice. You should protest to your son-in-law, Your Highness."

High on the staircase, Julie knelt on a stair, peering down between the bannisters. The men had reached the hall near the prince's suite. Tige, who seemed to notice everything, strolled to the telephone on its stand.

"Interesting. Your mice are sure well-trained, Max. They can operate these dang French phones. That's more'n I can do, half the time."

While Maximilian and his two aides moved slowly to his suite the prince called back to his guests, "I imagine my servants are very like others. They save a few pennies by using their master's phone."

Tige looked around the hall slowly. Julie was sure he must see right through her, near the top of the next flight of stairs, but luckily he couldn't see her in the dark. He shrugged, replaced the receiver and went to join Sir George who was apologizing for having put the prince's maids to so much trouble.

"I don't sleep well, gentlemen," the prince told them. "If I should have something to say to you in the next hour I will let you know. Meanwhile, sandwiches and a nightcap will be sent up to your rooms. I trust you will be comfortable. I am grateful for your visit, particularly as, in Tige's case, it came before you paid your so-called official visit to my son-in-law. I can only hope this signifies that your sympathies, and perhaps you assistance at some future time are with me."

Julie thanked what ever angels stood guard over her, and when the prince had gone into his suite with his aides, Sir George yawned widely. "Well, Tige, it looks like a long night for us. And I was looking forward to a little sleep."

"I doubt if he has any idea what we're talking about," Tige complained. "We've still got a long way to go if we are going to get to the bottom of this."

They went on together to the room assigned to one of them, apparently for more private talk.

Julie crept down and took the service stairs to the kitchen

quarters. She didn't look forward to going down that dark path to the street with the trams below, but she knew she owed it to Prince Stefan who had given her this post. She felt like his secret agent, very much the movie heroine.

She was a good deal surprised, and not a little startled when she slipped out to the ice rink and started down the path under the tiny, decorative lights, and found her arm seized out of the darkness. A male voice challenged her in German.

Common sense told her that this had to be one of the soldiers on guard, but his grip was hard and she could only hope he would understand English, as he did, luckily.

"I work for His Highness, Prince Maximilian, sir. I am off duty. His Highness has gone to bed, and I am to meet my gentleman friend in the Kuragin Square. This may be the last tram of the night. Could I be excused, please? I mean, *bitte*?"

The soldier stepped out under the light and looked her over. "I know you. You were with General Athlone's son today."

"Yes, sir. Please, I must catch the tram."

He studied her up and down. Obviously, she didn't look dangerous, although one thing troubled him. He was a rough-looking man but he had rather kind eyes, she thought.

"Aren't you cold? I would never let my daughter run around at this hour, and with no warm coat or wrapping."

She shivered realistically. "I was in such a hurry, sir."

He sighed and let her go. She felt his grip, but that merely signified that he was a good man at his job.

"Love, these days, it is not as it was in my youth. I went after the girls. Not the other way around."

"Oh, but Oscar is so charming!" Oscar? She had never known an Oscar in her life. She only hoped the name was German. Or at least, Lichtenbourger.

"Well, you may go. Best of luck with your Oscar." He turned back toward the Chalet, just looking around once to mutter: "Oscar!" and then went on.

She wanted to laugh in her relief, but was too tense at the moment to find anything funny.

The path would have been interesting in the daytime. Halfway down there was a bench and a water fountain, certainly too romantic for her imaginary "Oscar", but very nice for someone more interesting. She couldn't see Prince Stefan sitting here talking to his faithful spy, Just Julie, but it might suit someone with a casually romantic air. Like Brett Athlone. She supposed he would take practically any girl here if he chose to. He didn't look like a one-woman man.

She came out on the parking lot after one last hurdle. The big gates and the high wire fence that extended quite a distance parallel to the street were opened by the key she found in plain sight about ten feet up the path, hanging from a post. She was about to ask herself why the guards were in such a location when she sensed that she was being watched. The street guard gazed in at her between the tangled old wires of the fence. "I have a call about you, Fräulein Jones. You may use the key for the gentleman friend."

This one was much younger than the other, and conscious of his position, but he made no trouble and had a kind of likeable, scared look, as if he hoped he was doing the right thing.

The tram would stop about half a block further; so she walked along the dirt pavement, glancing every second or two towards the heart of the city from which Prince Stefan ought to appear.

It got colder as the minutes passed. She glanced back at the young guard wishing she had his heavy blue coat. He seemed to watch her furtively, but was far from menacing. As the time passed, she grew more grateful for his presence. She didn't like the look of various passers-by, almost all men and not the kind she liked to think of encountering on dark streets. Some still wore the old, faded uniforms worn by the Reich during the late war. At least, there weren't any swastikas. She had seen those lightning slashes of the SS somewhere in her early childhood, so early she couldn't remember where it had been. Not in the Blitz, surely, or in the Buzz Bomb days. Somewhere.

A church tower tolled nearby but she couldn't see it at this hour. When, after a very long time, at least an hour, a short, stocky man stopped by her, rubbing the hard, rough material of his coat sleeve against her bare arm, she gave up and went back to the young guard who was looking at his wrist-watch, probably checking the time until his watch was over.

"I think I have to go back in now, sir. May I?"

For the first time he looked as if her affairs might be as important as his job. "He didn't come? Too bad. He has bad taste, that one. Here is the key."

"Thank you. I mean, *danke schon.*"

He put two fingers to the bill of his cap. "A pleasure, Fräulein. But remember. Oscar has a heart."

She was halfway up the path, hugging her cold arms when she realized what the kind blond boy had said.

Dear Oscar. Nice boy. So there really were Oscars in Lichtenbourg.

Meanwhile, she began to be terrified that since she hadn't seen Prince Stefan, would he call the Chalet tonight or tomorrow and let them find out by accident that she had betrayed whatever they were up to?

It was all very disillusioning.

CHAPTER SIXTEEN

The streets around the New Palace were still crowded with celebrants, although Alexia made out a few malcontents on the edges of the crowd.

She regretted that only the People's Democratic Party, not her father's Kuragin Volunteers showed any signs of dissatisfaction with the results of the election. She certainly didn't want Stalin's boys breathing down Lichtenbourg's rather small neck. It would be like the Hitler Days all over again.

Torches lit up the scene as Stefan, driving one of the staff cars, a German Mercedes, navy blue and not too obtrusive, pulled into the Kuragin Square and headed down the street, following the tram lines towards the suburbs.

In spite of their recent differences, especially what she regarded as his usurpation of her father's position, she felt a closeness tonight that they had missed for months. She knew that in an emotional sense it was her fault, and for the moment she banished her deep sense of loss, her mistrust of his emotions.

He must have noticed it. He reached out one hand and touched her thigh which was covered by the old sports coat she wore. Coat or no coat, however, she felt the strength of that hand and remembered all the glorious hours of excitement she had enjoyed in his arms.

It was terrible to think that only sex held them together. But surely, that was better than ambition and plain, lazy tolerance, which held so many other people in high places together.

She looked over at him. He was frowning at the street ahead, avoiding a double tram as it rattled by in the opposite direction, but he seemed receptive. His hand squeezed her flesh and he smiled. She said, "Do you think there will be any trouble from the others, the ones who lost the election?"

"I hope you don't mean Max. I'm doing all I can to preserve the things he cares for, the honours and bowing and scraping. You know how he and Garnett are."

She bit her lip. "No. I meant the Soviet fringe."

"They can't do anything without joining Max and he isn't that big a fool." She bristled, but he added, "Politically speaking. I know he loves this country. He wouldn't knowingly sell it out. But unknowingly?"

"Now, how could he do that?"

"I hear they're putting pressure on him. I can't help feeling this business tonight is all about it."

"Your friend Julie says no."

"She's a good girl. Loyal, I think. But she may not understand what was going on. I'll make you a little wager, one of the men was old Grigori Vukhasin, our new Lichtenbourg citizen and Vice-Chancellor of Lichtenbourg."

"Joseph Stalin's good left hand?"

He nodded. She agreed that he might be right but reminded him, "You put a great deal of faith in that girl. There was something going on at Miravel that seemed odd. I wouldn't be surprised if Nick Chance had sent her over here."

He pulled up sharp to avoid a shouting youth in shirt-sleeves and a red star armband. Having driven around him impatiently, Stefan asked, "What the devil has Nick Chance to do with it? I don't think she even likes the fellow. She seemed afraid of him, I thought."

"For heaven's sake, don't be defensive about her."

"I'm not being defensive. I'm only saying – " He broke off. "I don't know what I was saying. I should have let Klaus do the driving. These toy lights are a poor excuse for city lighting."

She couldn't help reminding him, "You now have more weight than anyone in Lichtenbourg. Have them taken out and replaced by decent city lights."

She huddled deeper into the collar of her coat. "I wish I could be sure these mysterious night calls haven't something to do with Father's health. He was doing so well after Mother visited him. I don't think that girl knows what she is talking about most of the time." She gave him a side-glance. "I suspect her one interest in life is you."

He surprised her by grinning. "I'm not out to rob the cradle. By God, you *are* jealous. That's a happy sign."

"The election has done wonders for your conceit."

Although he laughed at this they had nothing more to say until they reached the Boulevard Franz Kuragin, named after Lichtenbourg's martyred hero. As they stopped for cross-traffic, which consisted of one ancient tumbrel, heaped high with bright green, red and gold vegetables, a sharp chunk of street cobblestone was hurled through the two open windows, just missing their heads.

Alexia screamed, feeling the cold dread that had always

haunted her at the thought of what had happened to other Middle-European royalty in the days since the First World War. The sound of her scream, and perhaps even more, the way her body was trembling, infuriated Stefan. He got out of the car, swung around the bonnet and stalked after the men who backed away and began to scatter under the trees that lined the side of the street. As Alexia could see from the car as she opened her side and started after him to stop him from what might be a trap, the men who had fled were older. The boy who had thrown the piece of cobblestone was about sixteen and had become entangled in his own skinny legs, falling flat on the cobbles.

Alexia threw the car door open, calling to Stefan, "Don't! The ones who put him up to it are gone. Wait."

By this time Stefan had collared the boy and was pulling him to his feet. Even to Alexia the boy looked frightened, his pale blue eyes wide, his eyelids batting and blinking. He kept insisting in German, "Not me, sir. They said it was for the Cause. The people. I didn't know a lady was there. Please, sir. Please don't put me in prison. My father is a tax-collector. He hates the Reds. He will kill me."

To Alexia's relief this struck Stefan as funny. All they needed for a first-class scandal, and on election night, was for the Prince Royal to provoke a scene in public, attacking a boy of sixteen. It might help Alexia's father, but surely, not this prince. And the Red Party would love it.

The boy was still snivelling when he heard Stefan's laugh and recovered, wiping his running nose on his bare arm. "Did the lady get hurt, sir? I could pay. I only have a few schillings with me but they're yours, sir."

Stefan shook him with rough good-humour. "You'll pay for committing a public nuisance, and a good price it should be. With labour, shall we say?"

"Labour, sir? I'm good with my hands. Just don't tell my father I was with the Reds. Please."

"Very well. This row of trees along the path sheds badly. Suppose you get a broomstick and clean up this area. But don't you think your friends ought to share the payment? Funny friends they are. Running off and leaving you to face the music."

The boy, who had obviously been to Yankee cinemas with GI's, understood the expression and looked around, seeing no one in sight to defend him except the lady from the elegant car and this militant stranger who didn't look too dangerous, after all. "Must I go to the police?" he asked nervously.

"Perhaps not. But how can I be sure you will appear tomorrow with your broomstick?"

The boy looked over his shoulder again. No help there. "If you just wouldn't tell my father, I could give you my address, so you'll know I'm telling the truth, and then report here early in the morning. With a broomstick."

Alexia caught the suppressed humour in Stefan's voice as he asked her in a magisterial way, "What do you say, my dear? Can we trust this young man?"

She moved closer, lowering her voice. "We have witnesses. That chauffeured black car behind you. The Old Bear."

Both Stefan and the boy turned to stare at the dark car. The boy's eyes brightened. Though Alexia couldn't see any signs of the boy's recent comrades, she knew he must have recognized the General Secretary of the People's Democratic Party, Grigori Vukhasin, who had lowered the rear window of the car and was studying the scene. His hat brim might shadow his heavy face but the milky light of the street lamps lingered on the

198

unmistakable jowls and flat nose of the government's new vice-chancellor, second only to Prince Stefan in power.

Seeing that he had been recognized, Vukhasin gave the little group a flippant wave of the hand, leaned forward, said something to his poker-faced chauffeur, and climbed out of the car with the difficulty of a heavy man.

Stefan muttered to Alexia, "I think the balloon just went up."

The boy's hopes, which had been rising, faded rapidly when Stefan collared him again and pulled him along to greet the celebrated ex-Russian. "Good evening, Grigori. I'm surprised to see you out here in the suburbs like any good democratic citizen. You will be glad to report at the council meeting tomorrow that we are at last cleaning up the streets. This young patriot has volunteered to lead us in the task."

It was difficult for Alexia to imagine Grigori Vukhasin as sympathetic but before greeting her, the Old Bear asked gruffly in his accented German, "This is true, young Comrade? Surely, the Herr Chancellor has not used his capitalistic influence to make you a wage slave of his system."

Seeing rescue offered to him the boy burst out, "It was the gentleman, Comrade. Not me."

Alexia drew in her breath sharply at this view of the case and Vukhasin glanced over at her. Two of his steel false teeth seemed to gleam at her. Before she could straighten out the boy's story, Stefan spoke, more in sorrow than in anger. "Grigori, you have alarmed him. He is afraid of his father. The only thing we can do is tell his father the story. Perhaps he will see the matter as a patriotic duty. Let's be off. Shall I take the boy home in our car and leave the matter with his father?"

That set the boy into a panic. "No, sir. If you please, I did not ask the General Secretary of the Party to interfere." He lowered his shaken voice. "Father will kill me."

Stefan looked at Vukhasin, remarking *sotto voce*, "I'm afraid, old friend, you are not popular with one of my constituents."

The Old Bear grinned. "As you say, better luck next time. Now, I must be getting home. My wife is like the boy's father. She is the law in the Vukhasin family." He whispered, "Hush! That is between the two of us."

Stefan laughed and watched the older man make his way back to his car. The chauffeur who had been leaning back against the car with one hand on his pistol, dropped his hand and hurried to help Vukhasin into the car. They drove off with a spurt and a roar, drawing after them a small string of other cars, bicycles and skooters for whom the show was over.

"Now, young man," Stefan got back to his case. "What is your address and your father's name. Where is he employed, and what is his full name? His work card." He thought this over. "And another adult as reference for your honesty." He got out a small leather notebook and took down the information probably not at all sure he would ever see the boy again. But at least, Alexia thought, he might throw a scare into the boy. Stefan's instincts were usually correct. He had been a brilliant aid to Maximilian when the latter was ill or otherwise undecided. If only he hadn't been so ambitious!

When Stefan had his information given reluctantly by the boy, Willy Krantz, he got back into the car and asked if Alexia was comfortable, squeezed her hand, and started off. But seeing her frown, he assured her, "The boy is of no importance, darling. And I think we set back one of the Old Bear's little games. He probably put that gang up to the trick. They scattered so fast you'd think they'd been warned. With me shaking young Willy, the Party would have had evidence of my brutality. I'd be on the cover of every Communist rag in Europe. Not to mention the States."

"I wasn't thinking of that. It was something else. Does it occur to you that Vukhasin's estate is further up in the mountains, not anywhere near this street. Remember how hard it was for the chauffeur to climb that last estate road to what he called his 'Capitalist Dacha'?"

"You mean, his presence was due to something besides a propaganda trick? Of course, the business with the young toughs may have been a pleasant little coincidence for him." He looked at her. "In which case, you know where he was going."

She rushed to deny what he hadn't spoken aloud. Certainly, her sick father would not countenance a visit from the head of the Communist People's Democratic Party, and on the night of the election.

"Besides, he is undoubtedly asleep by this time. After that awful scene between you and Father today," Alexia replied.

He was silent for a minute. Then he asked with a quiet menace that she found uncomfortable, "How did you hear about that? Not Julie Jones, surely? Or Brett Athlone? His father is close to Max."

"One of the servants. It was all over the Chalet. Even in the kitchen. They probably listen at keyholes."

He said nothing more but she knew he was far from dismissing the matter. They drove on until the street narrowed and she could see ahead of the tram route, a darker area, heavily wooded on the right side where high fences separated the path from the Royal Estates. She was reasonably sure that her father hadn't seen Vukhasin tonight and it would be good to have this night pilgrimage at an end. She had gone because she and Stefan had been so close at the celebration and she sensed his love for her had not completely died. At first, it had seemed possible that her father was suffering from a relapse, but the palace operator had made it clear that this wasn't the problem.

Alexia was beginning to suspect that the entire trip had been some sort of ploy by the ubiquitous Julie Jones to see Stefan again, at night and alone. Whatever she might suspect her husband of, she doubted very much if he would yield to the blandishments of a girl more than young enough to be his daughter.

"Here we are," Stefan said and pulled up beside the path where a young soldier in uniform marched slowly back and forth, looking stiff but tired as the shadow of the woods fell across him.

He recognized Stefan at once and stood to attention, looking worried but ready. Stefan brushed aside formalities. "Sorry to interfere with your duties. Have you passed anyone through this gate tonight?"

Hearing her husband's question, Alexia had expected hesitation, perhaps an attempt on the part of the soldier, but he replied at once, with precision. "Yes, sir. Three visitors."

"Had they been turned away from the front entrance?"

"I cannot say, Highness. The two gentlemen are frequent visitors. Often from this gate. Less formality, sir. Prince Maximilian always gave orders for their admission." He broke off.

"Yes? Was there something different this time?"

Oh, Lord! Alexia thought. *He is going to mention Gregori Vukhasin.*

"Not with the gentlemen. They are friends, I believe, but I have not seen them arrive together previously. General Sir George Athlone occasionally visits with his son, and sometimes alone. The young Herr Athlone works out of the British Consulate. He acquires information for his government, I have been told."

Stefan turned to Alexia. "Spying, I suppose. There are more spies than honest citizens in Europe today." To the guard he asked, "Who were the other two you passed through?"

"A young female named Jones. She is from the Foreign Secretariat. Prince Maximilian dictates to her, I am told. She waited here for a gentleman, but he failed to arrive. She returned to the chalet twenty minutes ago."

Anxiously, Alexia leaned out the window of the car. "Who was the man with General Athlone?" She was sure the bad news would come now. The new vice-chancellor, Gregori Vukhasin.

The young soldier blinked at sight of her. "Forgive me, Highness. I thought you knew it was your relation, the American gentleman, Herr Royle."

Alexia and Stefan stared at each other. She had a feeling that he was as surprised as she had been. He said, "What the devil?"

She knew that her great-grandfather always visited the New Palace first. It was expected of him, and many times his visits concerned important money deals. Stefan must think Tige Royle had sneaked in here secretly, and to visit her father, with some sort of betrayal in mind. It wasn't like Tige, and she couldn't believe he actually wanted to give her father more support in his efforts to restore his position.

Stefan must be thinking she too had betrayed him.

"I knew nothing about it," she said in a low voice, ashamed that their relationship which had been her whole world, should come to this suspicion on his part. He must think her very devious since he knew how bitterly she had resented his taking over from Maximilian. What more natural than that she should use Tige to accomplish her own and her father's goal?

But it wasn't true. Even now, she would never sell out the man she loved, and use her powerful great-grandfather to act behind his back. "Are you going in to confront them?" she asked, knowing such excitement might kill her father.

His mouth twisted a little, as if he were changing his mind about whatever had had been ready to say. "I'm afraid it wouldn't accomplish anything except to further antagonize Tige and possibly the British Government. It's more than likely they met on their way to pay their condolences to Max and it's no more than that."

She touched his hand, closing her fingers around one of his. "Thank you, darling. You may have saved Father's life."

He laughed shortly. "And the Old Bear did not show up. We are filled with good luck. At least, we know our friend Julie Jones was on my side. She tried to warn me. That is certainly why she called."

She settled herself as he thanked the young soldier and got back into the car. He said nothing to her as he turned the car and started home.

Our friend Julie, she thought, for the first time envying a girl like Julie Jones who had a lifetime ahead and the initiative to go after whatever she wanted. She had certainly climbed rapidly in the last month or so.

Lucky young Julie. She could probably get anything she wanted, though she would hardly aspire to the absurdity of a crown.

Alexia sat up. Or would she?

CHAPTER SEVENTEEN

For the first time in her life Julie awoke to the unobtrusive, hollow sound of knuckles on her door and the plaintive cry: "The breakfast, Fräulein Jones."

Julie pulled her wits together, remembered where she was, and called out, "Come in. I mean, *herein*."

The shy girl from the kitchen came tiptoeing in and asked in her breathy voice, "Will it be the dressing table, Fräulein Jones?"

She pronounced the name "Jones" with two syllables, which amused Julie but not so much as the girl's reference to the old wooden shelves covered by a curtain of some heavy, flowered cotton material as a "dressing table". It wasn't that she hadn't ever used a dresser like this. Quite the contrary. But no one ever flattered the poor, useful piece of furniture with such a title.

Julie thanked her but wondered who had schooled the pallid, watery-eyed girl in her job. Poor thing. She was probably older than Julie but she wasn't the most skillful girl in the world. She seemed almost feeble-minded and always with the scared rabbit manner.

She scuttled out of the room and Julie pulled her straight chair up to the "dressing table" and sat down to enjoy an especially appetizing breakfast. There were eggs and a big polish sausage, plus potatoes fried in the

German style, with a raisin sugar bun and coffee with snowy mounds of what proved to be whipped cream. Even dear, kind-hearted Mrs Tenby's household didn't eat like this.

It was also the first time she had ever had a tray brought to her, except once when she was hanging curtains for an actress at Drury Lane and fell off the ladder. She hadn't minded the broken wrist so much. Everyone made a great fuss over her, but she minded the actress telling everyone that Julie had been nipping the actress's gin, which wasn't at all true. She didn't even like gin without something nice in it to change the taste.

While she ate she considered the events of the previous night. It disappointed her that Prince Stefan hadn't paid any attention to her warning. It showed how little he cared when people like her tried to help him. Unless of course, the palace operator had never given him the message. She brightened at this possibility. Maybe the woman thought he was too busy greeting his victorious friends to leave them during a party.

Still, she comforted her bruised feelings with the thought: *It's his loss. Not mine.*

She had two very glamorous Italian nightgowns given to Mrs Tenby by the heirs of an elegant old lady who had died at Elder Home. They were a silky nylon material and except for being too short, fitted Julie reasonably well. The hems, which she let down, were almost non-existent, but people would have to get very close to Julie, and on their knees, to discover this.

When Julie was dressing for whatever the day would bring, the kitchen girl shuffled back to get her breakfast tray. Her watery eyes generally looked as if they saw very little, but now her eyelids flickered with surprise as she passed Julie's violet-sprigged nightgown thrown across the bed.

Julie grinned to herself and went on dressing with renewed confidence. As the kitchen girl was leaving with the tray, Julie asked, "Are the gentlemen gone yet?" She didn't want to come upon them accidentally this morning. If Prince Stefan hadn't contacted the Chalet, or if he had telephoned and not mentioned Julie, she might not be suspected of anything devious.

She didn't care about Sir George, one way or the other, but the great Tige Royle frightened her. She had a feeling that he could buy whole countries if he wanted to and he could destroy one woman of no family or attachments, like Julie, with the greatest of ease.

"The gentlemen?" the girl repeated vaguely. "There was a telephone call for His Prince Maximilian from the offices of Herr Vukhasin. Frau Bergin, the housekeeper, took the call and referred it to His Highness."

"No, no. I meant someone else." She had almost committed a more serious breach of confidence than her call to Prince Stefan last night.

"Who else, Fräulein Jones?" the girl asked with unexpected persistence.

"I thought maybe the Princess Garnett might have joined her husband. He was much better yesterday after her visit."

By the time she had finished this explanation the kitchen girl was at the door, pushed it open wider with her foot, and went out carrying the tray. She wasn't interested in Princess Garnett. That was plain.

After breakfast Julie took a sponge bath, using the big pitcher and basin her her room. There wasn't a great deal of choice in her wardrobe but she liked what she had;

so she chose the red voile Dotted Swiss dress and spent some time with mascara and a delicate eye shadow.

Reasonably satisfied with what she saw in the unframed mirror on the wall, she opened the door. Seeing no one in the hall and hearing only a maid humming as she cleaned the servants' rooms, Julie went down the service stairs to the reception hall on the ground floor where she was waylaid by the persistent footman she had met and disliked the previous day. He had just given orders to a taxi driver whose cab waited in the semi-circle at the foot of the steps and came back, apparently to escort someone from the Chalet. She backed away from him. She didn't like his manner.

Even Julie's meagre knowledge of aristocrats told her that people who visited Prince Maximilian either came in limousines or their own cars. This person must be unusually democratic.

She had her answer when a voice with a strong accent of the American West interrupted the footman's first words to Julie. "That my cab?"

"It is, Herr Royle."

"Good. Tell him to keep his pants on. I'll be out in a minute."

The footman blinked but bowed and went out to relay the message.

Julie felt Tige Royle's power as she had felt it in Miravel, but here, in this alien country, he seemed slightly sinister.

"Well now, if it isn't our little friend Just Julie! Been here long?"

"No, sir. Not long."

"But you sleep here now."

What was he hinting at? She wanted very much to

ask but managed to behave in what she considered an adult fashion. "Yes, sir. Prince Maximilian has a great deal of correspondence to answer. I think I'm considered one of the staff. On the Upper Floor. Frau Bergin arranged it."

"And not Stefan? The new Serene Highness?"

She insisted, "Frau Bergin found the room for me." That at least was true.

The footman shifted his position, moving nearer to hear the rest of the conversation. But Tige apparently had eyes in the back of his head. He motioned the eavesdropper away. "You, Heinrich, isn't it? Wait for me at the taxi."

The fellow looked disappointed but retreated after a knowing leer at Julie.

She wished she could follow him, especially with Tige staring at her in that stern, magisterial way, as he asked, "Were you here last night?"

"I was told to stay here at the Royal Chalet. I slept in my room on the top floor. With my door locked."

He smiled for the first time. "Very wise of you." He looked her over. "You look very pretty this morning. You have good taste. Where were you going now? To the telephone?"

She was frightened but angry as well. "His Highness hasn't called for me yet. I will take my orders from him, as you must know."

He nodded, but he was thoughtful. She wondered if he could destroy this new life for her. Why would he do such a thing? That business with Sir George must be awfully important.

She hoped she didn't look the way she felt. Cringing.

Her whole body stiffened with pride. "I think your taxi is waiting, sir."

Before he could react to this, Frau Bergin, the house-keeper, called to her from the service hall. "Miss Jones, His Highness would like you to bring up the mail the palace delivered last evening." She saw Tige Royle then and preened herself handsomely. "Oh, do I interrupt you, Herr Royle?"

"Quite all right, Miss. I won't keep the young lady. Let her have Max's stuff."

But while Frau Bergin handed Julie an armful of mail and packages, much of it decorated with the seals of various countries, Tige eyed the armful with interest.

When the housekeeper had retreated reluctantly, vanishing into one of the reception hall rooms, Tige said, "Excuse me," and pulled out several tabloids from under the pile. They all seemed to be from Italy or France and one from West Germany.

Julie didn't see how she could stop him. She had no authority, but she ventured, "If His Highness asks for those foreign magazines what should I say?"

He was riffling through one of them. He didn't find the scandalous, long-lens pictures of famous people very enjoyable. She wondered why he bothered. Then he came to a double-page spread in a well-known Italian scandal sheet and his mouth set angrily. One of the pictures was of a woman in a shocking new bikini bathing suit and another also clearly Princess Garnett in a stunning evening gown whose neckline just missed exhibiting her nipples. It was all very well to resent the stunning pictures but other women of Garnett's class were exhibited. It must be the articles he objected to.

He hesitated and then stared hard at Julie. She told

herself anyone else would have wilted under that stare, but outwardly she managed to remain expressionless, like a good, mechanical servant.

"Miss Jones, I've never trusted you. You're a minx and a climber," he said quickly.

She flushed but kept her temper and her silence.

"I've got nothing against climbers. I've been one myself occasionally. But betrayal is something I won't put up with. I can make things awfully unpleasant for meddling little girls."

I could kick him on the shinbone, she reminded herself, and felt better at the thought.

"Now, I must trust you," he went on. "Do we understand each other?" She nodded. "Good. This filth shouldn't be seen by a good and sincere man who adores his wife. A man who is dying, moreover. I'll take them with me, tear them up and personally burn them. I want you to say nothing to His Highness about these tabloids. Everyone who cares about him at all keeps them from him. But he has enemies too."

There was some merit in his order.

She wanted to say "OK I'll do it," but this was all concerning a Lichtenbourg prince, so she said carefully, "I'll remember, sir. I saw His Highness when Princess Garnett came to visit him yesterday. He felt much better. Ever so."

"Yes. My granddaughter has one gift in that line," Tige agreed, rather negatively, Julie thought. "But if I can count on you, I'll be on my way. Don't let me down."

"No, sir."

She watched him go down the steps and get into the taxi beside the driver. This seemed odd but probably was a habit in the United States where people acted less formally. There was a curious, anachronistic freedom in all Tige Royle's movements and actions. Like some nineteenth century cowboy in a twentieth century world. But she was exceedingly relieved to see the taxi drive away.

Heinrich, the footman, came back up the steps, called to her in the doorway in German, something supposedly seductive. She didn't need any more enemies, but he was the kind of persistent Romeo who had to be dealt with. She brushed him aside with the reminder, "His Highness asked for his mail. Please move. You are in my way."

He stepped aside but taunted her, "Stepping up in the world, aren't we? Now, it is the ex-ruler of Lichtenbourg you are after. Clever little girl. But me, I can wait for Old Max's left-overs."

She'd had just about enough from Tige Royle. Now, this revolting creature was treating her in an even more contemptuous way. She swung around in a rage and slapped him across his smug, powdered jaw.

The action made her drop most of Prince Max's mail but Heinrich, with his lip curling, merely stood there watching her pick up the letters and packages. He didn't even leave when she started up the stairs. She was still bitter over his humiliating assumption and wondered why neither he nor Tige Royle could accept her as the lady she wanted to be.

Anyway, Prince Maximilian was glad to see her. The little valet, Biddicombe, was fussing around, making him comfortable in that bed-sitting room which was almost barricaded from the rest of the long room and the world itself by pots of foliage, plants and leafy ferns.

After her tentative knock, Biddicombe let her in and was told with the prince's gentle indifference.

"You may go, Biddicombe. If I need you, I will ring for you."

The little man, looking crushed, bowed his way out.

"He always fusses over me so," the prince explained, seeing how she watched the little man's dejected departure. Then the prince smiled. He was looking very handsome this morning, with more colour. He wore his blue uniform with grace and elegance, the jacket open at the neck, for the day was warm, even for summer.

"Now then, Miss Jones, shall we get down to this tiresome business of correspondence?"

She had set the mail on the little wicker table beside his chaise longue and was looking around, wondering what to do for a pen or pencil. Despite her claim to experience in that line, it had never occurred to her until this minute that this equipment was essential.

Luckily for her, the prince must be used to incompetent social secretaries. "You will find equipment in the centre drawer of that desk." He waved a delicate hand towards a wicker desk against a far wall. A bust of Garnett Miravel Kuragin dominated that half of the room from its marble pedestal beside the desk.

Remembering just two of the pictures in the tabloids, showing Garnett in the loving company of several males, Julie wondered at Maximilian's devotion to her. But there were hints last night from Sir George and Tige Royle, and she realized that this devoted husband either didn't believe the evidence in any scandal magazines he might accidentally see, or he considered that his wife was merely a loving substitute for his own presence at foreign official gatherings.

She hoped this kind, uxorious husband would never find out the truth. It would be too cruel.

214

Julie located a pad and several sharpened pencils and returned to the prince. It looked as if she must write on her knees, the way so many better trained professional stenographers were forced to do. It wasn't a pretty prospect, but then, neither was Julie's rudimentary shorthand.

Prince Max picked up the top letters, looked them over and tossed them aside with the remark, "Official business. Let Stefan handle this sort of thing. A fiend for detail, my son-in-law." He ripped what appeared to be a soft, bulky package. Seeing it, Julie jumped and cried, "Don't!"

He laughed at her concern. "My dear child, do you think it will blow up? All of this mail goes through the palace mail room."

Feeling like a fool, she sat down again, slowly, on a stool she had pulled up. Meanwhile, the prince opened the package and drew out a hand-knitted wool muffler of Kuragin blue, with his Royal Family's insignia woven in.

Julie gasped. "It's lovely. Your Highness must have very loyal followers."

"Yes. I may safely say my people do adore me." He leaned forward, holding the muffler out toward her. "This is only one more proof that if I hadn't suffered a slight illness, which I assure you, is practically cured, I would never have been defeated in the elections. God knows what lies Stefan spread about me. I had a very enlightening conversation with the new vice-chancellor this morning. He said they would be honouring me at a banquet in two weeks. He asked me if I would appear to receive an award. I, a born royalist! It was amusing. I hated to refuse. But it was so absurd."

"What a compliment, though, sir. Communists presenting an award to Your Highness."

A slight wrinkle appeared between his eyes. "Not precisely that. It was as a peacemaker between the parties. It seems a number of influential members in the party are leaning a bit towards forming a Socialist-Democratic People's Party. They would throw their votes and the party's vote, to the Kuragin supporters. In exchange for leniency, or perhaps an understanding." He leaned back, dreaming of a glorious future. "It has incredible scope. The sort of thing Garnett, Her Serene Highness, always encouraged. To avoid future wars by an understanding between the parties. Co-existence, in fact."

Having already summed up the prince's character, Julie thought: *If you believe that, you'll believe anything.* Others might be able to carry it out, but Prince Maximilian sounded far too naïve and gullible. Poor man.

"Well, enough of that for the moment." He looked across the table at her. It was nothing like the stare of Tige Royle which could scare her. But she saw the dreamer's hope in his gentle eyes. "You realize, Miss Jones, that I would never consider such a thing, and certainly not appear at their precious banquet."

"Of course not, sir. But Your Highness appears to be extraordinarily popular. It must be flattering to be pursued even by opposition parties."

"Gratifying, not flattering," he corrected her. "We will send a note to Herr Vukhasin, thanking him for his kind interest, and send similar notes to these others."

He looked over the letters, separating the typical messages of regret from other matters and a few gifts, handmade like the muffler. "The gifts deserve a particular

216

note of thanks, suitable but never forgetting who I am. We must not appear to be soliciting sympathy."

"No, indeed."

She was relieved over the preponderance of form letters, which cut down her use of shorthand, but even the dictation of the form letters tired the prince. He dismissed her half an hour later, telling her she would find a typewriter in the bar off the Reception Hall.

She bowed herself out with armfuls of mail. On most of the envelopes were notations for her guidance. If all her work was this easy, she would certainly have nothing to complain about, except boredom.

Downstairs in the oak-panelled American type bar with its bar stools and leather-cushioned chairs, she finally located an ancient Underwood manual typewriter. It was hidden on the bottom shelf of the zinc-covered bar, beside a number of half-empty liqueurs. After some effort she got the machine out and placed it on a burn-scarred little cocktail table where she began her job. The cocktail table was too low but she hadn't expected much better.

Although her hand stung from the slap she had given the footman, her typing skill came back after several ruined sheets of the prince's thick, creamy paper. It seemed likely that he would always retain the title usually borne only by the reigning monarch: "His Serene Highness, the Prince Royal of Lichtenbourg."

Meanwhile, the Chalet was so quiet that the clatter of her typewriter must be heard all over the building. No one interrupted her and she finished before noon, rather proud of herself.

"Quite a nice piece of work if I do say so," she congratulated herself as she stacked everything up neatly.

A voice in the doorway teased her, "Aren't we satisfied with ourselves today!"

She knew that teasing voice very well after her first day in Lichtenbourg.

CHAPTER EIGHTEEN

Alexia awoke suddenly after a troubled sleep. She hadn't gotten to bed until after two when many of the election guests departed pell-mell to complete their celebration at a favourite French Cellar Bar. She doubted if Stefan had gone with them but she had no way of knowing; since she had not slept with him after he decided to call the election for a new reigning chancellor against her father.

As soon as she had reached the palace she telephoned her father and heard his voice, gentle as usual but understandably irritated at having his sleep interrupted.

Yes. He was feeling quite well. Why would she think otherwise? This was followed by his anxious question: "Is your mother well? Has anything happened to her? You musn't withhold the truth from me."

So much for my concern, Alexia thought, trying not to feel hurt.

"I'm sorry for disturbing you, Father." Knowing his sensitivity to his title, she corrected herself, "Sir, I'll let you get back to sleep. I hope your visitors didn't tire you out."

"My visitors?" He laughed softly. "My dear, you flatter me. A reigning monarch who has been betrayed has no friends. I'll say good-night now, my dear, and try to rest for a few hours."

She had murmured, "Good-night, Sir," and put the phone back.

Had her father lied, or didn't he consider Tige and General Athlone as "visitors"? Yes, probably he had evaded the subject by telling himself friends were not, properly speaking, mere visitors.

Sleep was an effort after that, but the evening had been wearing and she finally closed her eyes. Her sleep was filled with short snatches of dark dreams. When she was awakened before dawn by a sound in her sitting room, she was still shaking off a nightmare. For an instant she wondered if she was faced with the danger that had haunted European Royals in the past.

An assassin.

She lay very still but silently reached into the drawer of her dressing table. Long ago on a camping trip into the High Sierras with Tige Royle's nephew and his wife, she had been taught to handle a rifle. As an added thought, Chris had given her an Italian Baretta which was supposedly "very light". She hadn't found it so, but she knew how to use the gun in her dressing table, if the fatal necessity arose.

Her fingers were still feeling carefully for the Baretta when a tall figure appeared in her doorway, outlined by the first pre-dawn light, leaving her with the horrified thought that she had almost shot her husband. "Stefan! Good God! You might have said something. I almost shot you."

She heard his deep-voiced laugh, a chuckle, she had always called it. He said, "I'm not worried, sweetheart. You are a notoriously bad shot."

She turned on the lamp and moved over in bed, leaving a space for him to sit down. He accepted this as a token that he was not unwelcome and took the place she offered. His strong fingers closed on her hand which she had hastily withdrawn from the gun. He raised her fingers to his lips and then let them go. "How cold your fingers are! Do I dare boast that I could warm them?"

She had been about to ask, "Has something happened?" but common sense told her he wouldn't be talking about warming her hands if he had come to tell her about some calamity.

"You look tired, darling," she said instead and noting that he was still wearing his dress-shirt and trousers, she added, "have you gotten any sleep at all?"

"Some other time. I kept thinking about how domestic it had been to drive around the dark city with you. It always seemed highly erotic in some way."

He studied her face for a few seconds. "Did you have memories too?"

She wanted to say, "Of course, I did, and I wanted you so," but she felt so much better, so confident and happy, that she challenged him teasingly, "Why don't you put your memories to the test? Or are you afraid?"

She held out her arm. He came to her and laughed again when she tried to undress him. Together they ripped off his shirt. Studs and buttons rolled over into the trough of the mattress made by their bodies.

They had waited so long. As he reminded her when his lips had touched the soft flesh between her breasts, "If you only knew, darling, how hungry I've been for you." He lingered over each of her breasts, as if he would satisfy that long hunger like a child. Her body throbbed with her longing for him until she knew she would scream if her passion was not satisfied. In his own way, and with his own hunger, she felt that he was devouring her body.

At the peak of her craving they joined and she held that part of him deep in the warm cavern of her body. They had once boasted to each other that they could stay linked in a fiery orgasm that no one could match.

The old passion remained. They were both breathless when their heartbeats slowed and they could laugh at each other as they regained their breath.

He spoke low with a languor not common to his firm and commanding nature. "The world finally righted itself."

She lay with her head against the muscles and flesh of his shoulder. "I thought it would never stop turning." She considered this. "You know, darling, I never wanted it to."

He gave a long sigh of contentment. "It's good to be home again. God! I was tired. Tired of the fight and the bickering and the underhanded deals with this job."

She felt a twinge of guilt, wanting to tell him about her father's lie, but afraid to. A sudden quarrel now, or even a confrontation, could kill Max. Stefan coaxed her out of fear by asking in a businesslike way: "Do you take in boarders, Frau von Elsbach?"

Falling into his mood, she said, "Not recently, but I have been known to make exceptions."

He turned over, kissed one of her full, rounded breasts, and in two minutes was asleep with his cheek against her breast. She would like to have remained here forever but eventually, she too was asleep. The nightmares receded into the back of her consciousness.

When she awoke the summer sun was shining and she was alone. He must have moved very quietly when he got up. He hadn't disturbed her.

Her maid brought her tea and her dresser, Miss

222

Hoschna, was ready with the carefully organized looseleaf binder that revealed her wardrobe with swatches of each material where possible, and all additions up to date.

She had never been interested in clothes, except as they might please her husband, but she knew how important they were in what Garnett called "our profession", and what Stefan often referred to as "the business".

"What a thrill, Your Highness," Hoschna said, babbling with enthusiasm. "That wonderful man, Mr Royle, arrived very early. Such a great person! One knows at once that he can command nations."

To Hoschna's surprise Alexia's reaction was less than enthusiastic. "How nice!"

She had never believed Tige Royle could be so devious until last night, along with her father's reticence to mention him on the phone. They must be up to something. She had been surprised last night that Stefan accepted his secret visit to her father so easily, but she was worried too. It wasn't like Stefan.

The dresser pursued the subject while taking out a girlish summer dress of sky blue. "Monsieur Royle, he loves to see you in this colour."

On her way to the bathroom for a very quick shower, Alexia reminded her, "I am not a teenager, Hoschna. Give me the red and black suit with the harlequin blouse."

"Oh, but Madame!"

"Do it."

The dresser and the maid exchanged eye-rolling looks. Her Serene Highness was in one of her moods. As Alexia was aware, there had been a lot of them lately, since the break with Stefan.

When she came out of her apartments, she almost ran

223

into a flustered young footman who was hurrying to find an unopened bottle of Bourbon.

Alexia knew who that was for. "Herr Royle, naturally."

"Yes, Highness. They are in His Serene Highness's study. His Highness stressed that Herr Royle must have the best. He was very firm. Nearly snapped my head."

This didn't promise a pleasant meeting.

She wanted to run to her husband's study, to try and play down the damage of a quarrel between the two men. But at this hour the halls were full of servants hurrying about on morning chores. Half of Lichtenbourg was sleeping off the previous day's celebrations in this building.

She went down to the Great Hall and crossed it with her usual calm, unobtrusive air, not even interrupting the three cleaning women at their work. She had always been proud of that unobtrusive air. For too many years her mother's flamboyance had humiliated and embarrassed and sometimes disgusted her. Garnett was a powerful role model to be avoided.

She hesitated as the old-fashioned latch went down under her hand. She hadn't intended to eavesdrop and didn't like the idea any better when she heard Tige say, "Nothing to it, actually. We pitied the poor devil. Having everything taken from him just at the moment when he must know he is dying. We paid our respects very briefly and left. It was late, so I stayed at the consulate until an hour ago."

Stefan's deep voice could make him sound as dangerous as Tige at times. "You surprise me. I wonder why I thought you and General Athlone, of all people, would have had something more to discuss with my wife's father. But I suppose, considering His Highness's condition . . ."

"Just so."

Alexia came in, closing the door.

The study had belonged to Prince Max but she tried not to think of that. Stefan had done her father's work for so long. Not that it was an excuse for usurping his title and breaking his heart but she tried not to think of that. It was a useful room, well-lit and modern, with the two long, vertical walls lined with books and two portraits of Alexia displayed, one against the books and one on his desk. The elaborately cushioned throne chair that had belonged to Max was now gone and Stefan had moved in a modern desk chair which Tige was sitting in now while Stefan perched on the corner of the big, well-worn oak desk.

Tige saw Alexia first and was obviously grateful for her presence. He blew her a kiss and got up briefly, though it was Stefan who came to her, explaining, "I sent someone for you, darling, but you seem to have anticipated him."

He kissed her cheek and she gripped his hand tightly while he led her to a chair between her great-grandfather and himself. He perched himself again on the corner of the desk.

Tige leaned over and likewise kissed her cheek.

She assured him, "You were so unexpected, otherwise, Stefan and I would have driven you over to the Chalet. Does Mother know you've arrived?"

Tige glanced at Stefan who said, "Good God, no. Not yet. I intended that we should have a little chat first."

Tige grinned. "If my granddaughter was here, she'd be all over the place. I'll get to her later, with presents to be sure of my welcome. So! You're all moved in and comfortable."

Stefan seemed to know Tige better than Alexia did. He waited through what the other two found to be an uncomfortable pause and then said, "I do think, Tige, you owe us a little more of an explanation. We're all delighted when you drop in. There's nobody more welcome. But I keep thinking there is something on your mind. We might play a little game of international politics, but surely, we know each other well enough for the truth."

Tige studied his fingernails, got out an old steel file his daughter had given him over fifty years ago, and worked on the cuticle of his powerful thumb. He spoke without looking up. He wasn't usually afraid to look a man in the face; certainly not Stefan whom he had always admired, but he was definitely choosing his words now. "What do you know about my granddaughter and Spain?"

Stefan was so surprised he got off the edge of the desk and stared at him, then at Alexia. She shook her head, as confused as he was.

He said finally, "Garnett and Spain? Nothing what-soever. She was at Miravel recently. But you know that. She stopped for a couple of weeks in London beforehand." He glanced at Alexia again. "What did she do there? Shopping, I thought. At least, the bills all came here."

"She is a little extravagant," Alexia apologized. "You know that, of course, Grandfather. Tige."

Her great-grandfather had been 'Tige' to the world, including his family, since long before she was born, but his age made the name seem disrespectful to Alexia.

"What's all this about?" Stefan asked. "How does it

concern us? Or is it Lichtenbourg that her peccadilloes threaten?"

Tige pulled out of his wallet a much-folded piece of paper and handed it over to Stefan. Alexia looked at it over his shoulder. It was the top quarter page of a tabloid sheet showing Garnett Kuragin's glorious and young figure draped in a beach towel that covered her right breast and thigh. Her pubic area was shadowed by the dangling arm of her dark bronze beachboy companion. The sun spotlighted her large, milky left breast, her rib cage and leg. Her escort had his other arm around her neck in a proprietary way.

Alexia felt nauseated, not at the nakedness of her mother, who was probably very much in style at some private beach in Southern Europe, but because she seemed to enjoy providing perfect ammunition for her husband's political enemies.

Stefan returned the picture to Tige who folded and put it back in his wallet.

The writing under the picture had been torn off and Stefan said, "Rather an old picture; isn't it? Even Garnett can't look like that at fifty-six; can she? What is the point of this?"

Tige shrugged. "If our – my calculations are right, she was in her early thirties at the time. Anyway, it's an old picture the Italian bunch dug up from its files."

Alexia wanted to be rid of the whole disgusting business and she couldn't see why Tige made such a production out of an ancient picture. "I hope you aren't going to sue them. That would only give more attention to the picture." After swallowing hard she added, "And others like it."

"If you are concerned that this sort of thing happened

recently," Stefan put in, "It didn't. Alexia has been with her ever since they made their trip to Britain. And I assure you, before that she was here in Lichtenbourg."

Alexia nodded, anxious to change the subject. "Mother and Father have taken their vacations together when things were calm enough, since the war. Because of Father's health."

Stefan was watching Tige's face which told Alexia nothing, but apparently Stefan read more in those ruddy, still powerful features. "I don't see what this is all about, Tige. Does it matter now, after all these years? Is that beachboy character trying to blackmail her or something?"

"Nothing like that. And so far as I can see, Garnett knows nothing about this either. It was just something that came up recently. A friend of mine showed it to me."

Alexia felt a prick of uneasiness when Stefan said, "That wouldn't be George Athlone, would it?"

Athlone's connection with Tige and Prince Max last night could be alarming. Alexia was glad Stefan cared enough to remind Tige, "I hope you didn't discuss this with Max. If he thought Garnett capable of this, especially now, it could kill him."

Tige shook his head. "No. It was something else entirely. That is, the general wanted to express his sympathy over Max's illness and his election loss. Something like that. I say, folks, can I go and wash up? Maybe get a bite to eat. I'm starved."

As Stefan pressed one of the new buttons on the desk and looked as though he would accompany him, Tige added, "Don't trouble. You've got lots to do. I know my little old cubbyhole. Two floors up and to the right."

Stefan couldn't hide his impatience. "Tige, you know

perfectly well there's a suite waiting for you just above us here."

"Not my style. Take it easy now, folks."

An eager young male in livery appeared in the doorway, bowed and took Tige's old-fashioned valise.

Tige moved forward, after him, then turned, slapped his forehead and said, "I'd forget my head if it wasn't fastened on."

He reached into one of his trouser pockets and pulled out an envelope full of scrawls. "Here's what I want to see you about when you have a minute. We've got a couple of live-wires lined up to headquarters in Lichtenbourg. Presuming they get a tax break. Reckon you've heard of Eban-Albrecht Gesellschaft. They're clean, politically speaking. Big steel boys. And Parfumerie Français. That speaks for itself. They want to call one of their new sassy nosegays 'Garnett'. I said I'd leave that up to you."

He gave a flippant wave to Stefan, handing him the envelope, then pinched Alexia's cheek and was gone, leaving Stefan and Alexia to stare at each other, in considerable doubt.

When the door had closed Stefan went over and closed it again, securely. Then he asked Alexia, "Well, sweetheart, laying aside his little business postscript here, what do you make of that?"

She shook her head. "I could almost think he was – "

"Lying?"

"No! Leaving out something."

"Lying by omission."

He shifted around the objects on his desk, took up a ballpoint pen and compared the point with an old fountain pen that Max had left behind.

Alexia asked nervously, "Can't we forget all this

229

intrigue for a little while and just accept the odd way people act?"

He didn't seem to hear her. He was still frowning. "Why do I get the feeling that he has a good deal more on his mind than French and German industries?"

She didn't know and didn't want to argue. She wished Tige hadn't come. It put a rift of some kind between her and Stefan.

It didn't make her any happier when he asked himself thoughtfully, "I wonder if that wily little Julie – you know – Just Julie – has found out anything about this business between Tige and Athlone and Max? It would explain her telephone call last night."

Alexia wished they were still warmly together in her bed, in each other's arms, and Just Julie was far, far away. Preferably back in Britain.

CHAPTER NINETEEN

Julie thought: *I don't need Brett Athlone's sarcasm.*

She wanted to be annoyed, partly because of his father who, in her opinion, had behaved very underhandedly last night, along with everyone's hero but hers, Tige Royle.

On the other hand, when she swung around and saw Brett Athlone in the doorway looking so high-spirited and good-natured, she found it hard to keep up the resentment which had started with Prince Stefan's indifference when she tried to help him last night. It had seemed until now, and might still be true, that she was in a strange, foreign place without a single friend she could count on.

Maybe this mischievous fellow might cheer her up. In the light of day he brought more into her life than anything that had happened since Prince Stefan left her here.

However, she drew herself up and said with a challenging air, "Well, it really was a good job and I did it quicker than I thought I would." He looked like a man who would enjoy the truth, so she confessed, "I'm not really very good at shorthand. But my typing is quite average. Maybe better."

"I'm sure it is. I'll bet you make yourself good at everything."

The old annoyance was beginning. He knew how to

get a rise out of her without reflecting that his own life had obviously not forced him to consider the paths to success when few were open to him.

She reminded him, "We don't all get by on our charm, you know."

"I'm sure you could."

"Don't be funny." The moment after she said it, she realized that he seemed to be sincere. The idea made her stare at him like an idiot with her mouth open.

He started into the room. "You must know you have more charm than the law allows. Drop that infernal machine and come along."

She had been lifting the typewriter and wondered what she would do if she really did drop the heavy machine. Luckily, he played the gentleman, took it from her and set it on top of the bar.

She felt that she was entitled to know where he was going and what he was up to but didn't want to press her luck. He might not be the romantic, mysterious, unreachable man of her dreams, but he made life seem full of fun and she had no objection to that.

"I'd better get a jacket," she said as he took her arm. No need in telling him she had only one jacket, the one that went with her green suit, and its shade would clash with the white-dotted red dress.

He said, "Don't be coy. This is July. Who are you covering up from?"

She let it go at that.

It wasn't until they were getting into his white Porsche that she realized she hadn't made any excuses to Prince Max, and worse, hadn't delivered the letters for his signature or his seal.

Out in the drive her companion surprised her again by

coming around and helping her into the car. Men in her experience considered courtesy to have gone out long ago with the Great War. This attention made her feel regal and elegant, the way Prince Stefan had made her feel. Only she wasn't in awe of Brett Athlone. Above all, she felt a nonchalant indifference to her job.

She couldn't recall ever feeling like this before. Satisfaction in her work was to have been the key to her future success. It was the only weapon she had, and it had never played her false until now. She hesitated and he asked, "Well, what did you forget?"

"The mail. His Highness has to sign it."

Brett took this easily enough. "Forget it. The minute you left the bar someone, probably that nosey parker, Gerda Bergin, looked in. She always does."

"What's a nosey parker?" Not that it mattered. How easy it was to live as he did, immune to many of the civilized little chores, like one's job!

"Never mind. You're going to enjoy yourself for once without thinking of getting ahead and working your b – " He laughed. "I've been associating with too many Yanks lately. I'll rephrase that. Just because you are an orphan, that doesn't mean you have to keep busy all the time."

"Why not, for heaven's sake?"

"Because you give the rest of us orphans too much to live up to. We're not all fiends for work."

He had started the engine but was looking behind him at a car pulling into the semi-circular drive. She followed his gaze. 'Who is it? Somebody important?" Then she shivered and grabbed his arm on the wheel. "Not Mr Royle? Or your father?"

"Good Lord!" He turned his attention from the oncoming Lichtenbourg state car to Julie. "What's the old man done now? I didn't know he had the power to scare anybody, including the enemy."

"He was here last night with Tige Royle. They talked to Prince Maximilian."

He didn't look at all pleased. "Oh, they did; did they? Can't keep their mouths shut until they have a few facts, damn it! Did they mention any names? I hope they didn't upset Old Max."

She asked herself if she could trust him. But just because he happened to be charming on occasion didn't mean he was trustworthy. "I don't know. I don't go listening at keyholes, if that is what you mean."

He tried to soothe her ruffled feathers. "OK, OK. I just thought they might have said something to you. They definitely scared you. I can see that." He broke off and pointed to the car behind them. "How do you like that? It's our esteemed new chancellor and the Serene Highness. Shall I just ignore them and go on?"

Excited by the thought of seeing Prince Stefan, she looked out of the open window, then remembered that stenographers don't go around waving at reigning princes and she stuck her head back in. If he had thought her call last night was important, he wouldn't wait until noon today to find out her message.

She took a breath, raised her chin proudly and said, "It's none of my affair. If you have any business with him, help yourself."

Brett slapped the wheel, definitely pleased. "That's good enough for me," and zoomed out around the drive, passing the prince with a wave that was a half-salute.

The summer day had a slow, still quality that was unlike any Julie had been used to in England. She wasn't surprised when Brett sniffed the air pleasurably as they headed down towards a cross-street. Here they had to wait for a rattling double tram-car to pass and he said, "When I was pretty small, before Lady Athlone came along, we had a day now and then that was like this. It's odd, because we're in a higher altitude here, but it does make me think of quiet, peaceful days and nights, me running and playing with kids a good deal older than I was, children of the village. They were all hell-bent to form a *corrida*."

She had been thinking. This was the street where she was going to tell Prince Stefan something he should know, and he didn't think it was important enough to bother with. So it served him right if he never found out what those men were talking about.

Brett took her inattention reasonably well. "You aren't listening to my fabulous memoirs. I've got to find a new approach."

"No. I really beg your pardon. You were old enough to remember things before you were adopted?"

He looked at her. "You said you were taken to England. But you don't recall anything that happened to you in Spain?"

"I was never in Spain," she snapped, not for the first time. "Could we talk about something else?"

"Well, just suppose your future depended on your remembering those early days. Maybe you were actually a millionaire's child, lost in some weird way. Maybe a whole estate awaits you if you can just own up to those early memories. Ever think about that?"

She laughed and jeered at once. "I know. Gypsies kidnapped me. I happened to work with a fortune-telling gypsy when I was awfully young, and she wouldn't kidnap a fly. She drank a bit too much vino, but she told great fortunes, exciting ones."

"What did she tell you?"

"Who cares?" She stared out at the busy street scene.

"Tell me," Brett insisted.

He was oddly persistent for a carefree young man on his first date with her. Or was this a date? Maybe it was something else, a probing, prying thing. She didn't want him to turn out like Tige Royle and General Athlone. She wouldn't trust them as far as she could throw them.

"Magda was a gypsy. That's all. She escaped from some place in southern Hungary. The Nazis were rounding them up for – You know."

"I know."

"And she said I was *gaio*, I think it was. Did you know they consider their race older than ours and much wiser?"

"It wouldn't take much to be that. What did she predict for you?"

She thought back to her early memories of Magda who had lost all her family, even her mother and sister, at Dachau. "Magda was so bitter against the Nazis that she was even angry at my fortune."

"Why? You weren't a Nazi, even a baby one. Or *were* you? What else did she say?"

"She said I would be very close to a great future, and I would speak German, too. You see, I do, just like she said. But the crystal didn't say if I got the great fortune or not, though she did tell me not to bathe."

"Not to what?"

"Well, you see they rub themselves with bear's grease. Their whole bodies. She said it was very good for the flesh or something. It gave her an odd smell."

236

He laughed. "I can believe that. But she didn't say beware of Spanish guitars?"

She was happy to say, "She never mentioned Spain. Where are we going?"

"I thought we'd drive to the border. I didn't know you had Hungarian acquaintances, but that should make it more interesting to look through the Iron Curtain."

She sat up anxiously. "My passport!"

"Just to this little border, not much as borders go."

Whatever else Julie had forgotten, she vividly recalled Magda's gutteral voice when she spoke of the crimes against her people in Hungary. Still, Julie had always thought Hungary would be fascinating and exotic, but not without a passport.

At the Franz Kuragin Boulevard crossing Brett saw a lanky boy with stringy hair picking up fallen treelimbs and other debris from the pavement which had deteriorated into a dirt path. A lorry moved slowly beside him and the driver got out now and then to remove the bundles of twigs.

Brett remarked, "At least Stefan is getting the place made liveable. It may even be a respectably clean city by the time he's through."

They crossed Lichtenbourg city in a southward direction, the street narrowing after the suburbs until it became little more than a country byway, generally following what had been, before the war, the famous Arlberg Orient Express tracks. Julie had travelled to Lichtenbourg on the post-war version of the train and since she had nothing to compare it with, she had still found it glamorous.

Once they reached the outskirts of the city, there were fields and clumps of dry looking trees around them and she saw soldiers either exercising or patrolling the road along the field paths. All of the soldiers looked sinister to Julie who had heard the tales of life behind the Iron Curtain.

It was a little embarrassing however, to exclaim with a shudder: "Look! Russian soldiers," and have Brett say with some amusement, "Sorry. Those are Lichtenbourgers still in their winter gear. You see ahead, on the skyline? Those will be Hungarian. Or Russian, as the case may be."

She felt like holding onto the seat but managed to pretend an imperious calm she was far from feeling. The Porsche had stopped zooming along when they reached this field area where the road was badly in need of repairing. Obviously, nothing had been done since before the war. She wondered if this and other conditions were responsible for Maximilian's defeat by the more active regime of Stefan von Elsbach.

What she assumed must be the border zone was barricaded by crossing bars she had seen from the train yesterday. There were signs in German and another, remarkably difficult looking one, which she assumed must be Hungarian.

The crossing bar was the goal for two sets of soldiers who marched to the bar, swung around and marched away again.

"But when the Hungarians march away they have their backs to the border," Julie noted.

"Not necessarily." Brett pointed out the ancient shack on the Hungarian side of the wired fence that separated the two countries at this point. The shack looked as if it had been there since the beginning of time. It appeared to have had two rooms once, and a roof of obviously combustible straw. At least, the roof had burned leaving only a hole through which a brick chimney stuck out at one end of the shack. The bricks looked badly faded, or the mortar was worn away by heavy weather.

Brett explained, "Two guards in there. Fully armed. And two more about a quarter of a mile down the road where the watch tower is. To get a little revenge on the Russkies, Lichtenbourg put in all those bushes hugging the fence on our side. They smell to high heaven and when the wind is right, which it pretty often is, the odour is carried across the fields to the Russian guards."

Julie laughed and clapped her hands. "That's my sort of revenge."

Brett slowed down and finally stopped to ask one of the marching Lichtenbourg pair, "What have you done with our friendly Cossack neighbours today?"

One of the Lichtenbourgers kept up his march but the other pushed the bill of his cap back and grinned at Julie. To Brett he asked something in the Lichtenbourg-German patois. Brett, perhaps for Julie's sake, replied in English, which the guard apparently understood. "Miss Jones is a friend of the family. I have the pleasure of driving her around. Anything worth seeing today?"

Julie gave the guard a big smile and he became voluble with regret. He even spoke English, with a heavy but understandable accent. "It is forbidden for civilians to be here at this time. Riots in Budapest. Some try to escape by this road. Not so much guarded as the Wien Highway."

Brett was slowly backing the car. "What has happened?"

"A puny fellow is being questioned by the Russians in that – what you call 'shack'. If he crossed here and had no papers, we would challenge and then perhaps, who knows? But the fool ran from their challenge. We are reinforced shortly."

Brett nodded. "And civilians are much better out of the way."

"Just so. It is good sense to stay away from the line of fire. Please leave the zone. You understand?"

"Perfectly. I'm no hero. Thanks, friend."

Brett studied the road behind him, seeing two jeeps full of soldiers rattling along on the rutted country road. They were coming at high speed, almost side by side, as though one tried to race the other to the point of action. Brett pulled further back to the side of the road but a ditch ran along just behind the wheels and even at this period in summer there was water sluggishly flowing between dead rushes and weeds.

He pulled forward to keep the rear wheels from the crumbling edge of the ditch which looked to be something over three feet deep. The water was the least of the problem. Only inches covered the bottom of the ditch.

Brett muttered, "Taking you here wasn't the brightest decision I've ever made. Damn! It's usually quiet as a pond. The only ones who cross here are peasant farmers with crops to sell in the Lichtenbourg open market. It's about the only free enterprise they get, poor devils."

Her eyes sparkled. "I don't mind, I mean about coming here. It's something to brag about, as soon as we get back to safety."

"Ah, yes. Famous last words."

She looked at him quickly but he grinned and besides, she trusted that the two jeep drivers knew what they were doing. Meanwhile, Brett moved forward and having left several feet between the car wheels and the ditch, he was about to turn around when the jeeps spurted forward and came to a halt forming a barrier across the road.

"What's this?" Brett asked of no one in particular. "World War Three?"

Julie tensed suddenly as she realized how far the actions of these men might go. They leaped out of the jeeps, with their eyes glued to the events on the other side of the fence and their rifles slung off their shoulders.

Two soldiers in Russian uniforms with side arms came out of the shack. Between them was a thin, unheroic figure looking like a caricature of a middle-aged school master. He squinted at the early afternoon light and appeared completely harmless.

Brett said, "Good God, what next? Here." She knew better than to struggle when he pulled her down on the seat and changed places with her. "Now, open the door. If things get going, drop into that ditch. The ditch and the car in front of it will protect you. But don't stay too close to the car. Understand?"

"What about you?"

He ignored that. After opening the door a few inches she crouched on the floor of the car but raised herself up several times to peek through the windscreen and to see what was going on. Brett remained where he was, looking behind him and out across the field that bordered the left side of the road. Julie guessed that he was wondering if he could drive across that field, avoiding the bottleneck of the jeeps, before violence blew up in everyone's face.

If it did come to shooting, the white Porsche would be passing behind the Lichtenbourgers and in the direct line of fire. It wouldn't need more than one hit at the fuel tank to put a blazing end to the car and its occupants.

Julie felt for him in his dilemma. She put a hand out in a gingerly way and touched his tense knuckles with the tips of her fingers. It was not her habit. Long ago she had found that physical demonstrations of friendship or understanding could be taken the wrong way, even with women.

Several of the older girls in a bombed out, temporary morgue after the Buzz Bombs had reminded her, "They'll use you more. They pick the ones that's willing. They'll use you like a meek old horse."

It had been true, but she kept the reputation for "willing hands" in order to advance herself. It worked.

With Brett Athlone it was different. She felt his plight and knew he blamed himself, but she wanted him to understand that she had been glad to come on this trip, even if it should turn out to be dangerous.

In any case, Brett appreciated the gesture and understood it. He looked away from the scene across the border fence long enough to give her a smile that she felt was genuine. "Thank you, love. I really was an idiot. But thanks."

She didn't take the North Country "love" too seriously but she warmed to it.

The Lichtenbourgers were shouting orders but Julie heard nothing from the Hungarian side. She raised her head, beginning to think this whole episode was a false alarm. The man would be taken back to Budapest, or the village he came from, and everything at this bucolic border would get back to normal.

At that instant the thin, docile-looking man broke from his captors and dove for the ground under the barrier

242

crossing bar. He wriggled through to the Lichtenbourg side. For several seconds the Russians did nothing. One of them glanced at the other. But the rifles swung up.

One of the Hungarians gave them an order to stop. Beside Julie, Brett said, "They are saying 'The other side will surrender him. If he has no papers, they must.'"

Before he finished speaking, the rifles went off, much more noisy and violent than Julie had remembered. Some things had been deliberately blocked out since the nightmare times, long, long ago.

She closed her eyes, pressed her hands tightly against her ears. Brett watched her, then reached over to her and touched her hair, smoothing it gently. She felt the touch but was too stiff with terrified memories to notice it.

He raised up and looked out over through the windscreen. "By God, they're doing it. Shooting at the poor devil."

She opened her eyes, peeked out through the dust stirred up with the reverberating noise of more shots. One shot struck the road close to the car. Dust whirled by full of dirt and pebbles. She felt the door beside her open under the pressure of her body and she tumbled out, down into the ditch. The debris-filled water felt warm through her pretty Dotted Swiss dress and she thought: *I've ruined it. I don't have any others I can use for nice afternoons.*

Several return shots were fired from the Lichtenbourg soldiers. But they were still taking care. They out numbered the Hungarian side and a fusillade of their shots might well start World War Three.

The thin "schoolmaster" who was their prey, scrambled over the dry grass and across the ground, avoiding the Lichtenbourg soldiers, half of whom were on one knee with rifles ready, but only two shots had been fired from their side and these were directed inches from the feet of the Russian soldiers. The Hungarian guards remained stationary, looking as if they would fire but careful not to do anything provocative.

Shots had been fired sporadically by the Russians, slowing to a pause and then one shot. The running man shrieked, swayed, and tumbled into the ditch. He slithered toward Julie just as Brett threw himself out of Julie's side of the car. He was still on the edge of the ditch when the wounded man reached Julie, his fingers groping for her, his eyes wide, scarcely more than the eyeballs showing.

Instinctively trying to avoid his eyes, Julie drew him closer but her grip on his shirt was not strong enough. The cheap material of his shirt, which had stuck to the wound on his back, tore away. At the same time his dying body collapsed over her, saturating her with a warm, thick moisture. She knew that pungent stench of blood from her earliest nightmares and began to scream.

There were no more shots. There should have been. Most of the children in her nightmare were dead already, or disembowelled, armless and legless, with blood and urine where the dying lay. But there had to be more screaming rockets overhead, a grenade exploding upon the dead.

She had lost her voice in the terror and now heard other sounds, a kind of moaning.

Brett pulled the corpse off her body. "You're all right, love. It's over, Julie! It's all over."

Brett kicked the car door open and lifted her light body into the front seat. Then he yelled something at the Russian soldiers across the barrier. They paid no attention. They turned heel and began to march back in good order, past the nervous Hungarian guards towards the watch tower a quarter of a mile away.

The hideous combination odours, evocative of her earliest terrors, went with her into the car and she began to shiver. When the Lichtenbourgers came up to assess the damage, drag the dead man away and sternly reprimand Brett for making a sightseeing trip out of the border area, one of the Lichtenbourgers reached in and patted Julie's bloody hand.

She knew he had said something kind and soothing but she was shivering and hiccuping too much to reply. A part of her mind was still back in the Spain of long ago.

Brett took his reprimand without making excuses. He merely gave his name and address at the consulate and agreed to testify when the matter came up for investigation. He had one arm around Julie, holding her against his body so she wouldn't sink down to the floor of the car. With the other hand he started the engine and waited for one of the jeeps which was in the process of being moved.

CHAPTER TWENTY

At a little farm on the edge of the wasted fields near the border Brett got two beer steins. One, the farmer's wife obliging if puzzled, filled with water. The other, she explained, was "Good Lichtenbourg beer".

The sight of clean water roused Julie from her huddled silence. While he watched Julie drink some of the water, Brett said with a bracing air of confidence, "Frau Kupperman is going to help you get those stains out. You'll feel better then."

Julie roused herself at the prospect of being clean again, especially the flesh of her arms and throat. She was taken to the chicken yard behind the little house and as she had hoped, washed away some of the horror with the blood stains. Her dress was another matter but together she and Frau Kupperman scrubbed the neck and top of the bodice.

"Ah, you're in luck it's summer, Fräulein Jones," the woman pointed out. "On your warm body it will be dry before you reach the Boulevard Kuragin."

Julie thanked her in a hoarse voice, secretly horrified for fear she had screamed a lot. When the two women returned to Brett she asked him about this, but he insisted it wasn't so. "Only once or twice. It was

246

enough to make me scream, believe me. But you had the worst case of hiccups I've ever heard. Here, try the beer."

She didn't usually like beer but today, anything tasted good that would wet her parched throat. Besides, it made her feel better. This foaming stuff, tasting like bitter champagne, was a world away from the unthinkable, the nightmare time of her childhood.

Stout, good-hearted Frau Kupperman acted insulted at the money Brett offered but managed to overcome her better nature and take it with many thanks. "You were lucky to get such a show," she congratulated Brett. "We haven't had any shootings on this border for months. I suppose it's the trouble brewing there. I have a cousin in Budapest. She says things are getting worse and worse. Well, *auf Wiedersehen*."

They drove on into the city, their backs turned to the crime of the border. After some minutes and a silence between Julie and Brett, he asked, "Feel better?"

They were on the Bahnhofstrasse in front of the ornate, glass-roofed railway station.

She had a headache that threaded its way across her forehead above her eyes, and her insides felt like pounded meat, but she couldn't bear that he should know this. "I'm much better. Isn't it funny? Here is the railway station where your father offered me a ride. He was very gallant." She put on a painfully bright smile when he looked at her. "I didn't like you at all. I never did know why you were so awful."

She thought the lineaments in his face tightened. He didn't grin at her and tease or insult her, as she expected.

He then replied, "I didn't know you then. I thought

247

you were someone quite different, out to make a fantastic killing."

She thought that over. "Well, in a way, I am. I'll show everybody. I'll rise on my very own work, so high you'll have to bow and scrape to me when we meet."

He put one warm hand on hers which were still trembling, in spite of all her efforts.

"All right. I believe you. I just thought you wanted to do it the easy way." He felt the stiff, shocked resistance in her body and laughed. "Not that way, you little idiot. I meant, by some legal shenanigans. Never mind, they are wrong. And I'm the most wrong of them all, because I started it."

Her head ached too much for her to pursue this ridiculous babble of his, but she was more puzzled than ever at his weird talk. And who were "they"? His father? Who else? And what did they have to do with Julie?

She began to feel uneasy again, remembering suddenly, the strange little conversation with Nick Chance at Miravel. Whatever this mystery was, Mr Chance seemed to have some interest in it. Curiously enough, he had seemed adamant that she shouldn't believe it. Why, for heaven's sake!

"Still scared?" he asked her on a gently teasing note. "They can't hurt you now. I know what it is. You've ruined your pretty dress."

She looked down. The tight-fitting bodice was dry now but stiff after the scrubbing. The low neck of the dress had meant that her neck and an inch of her breasts were all stained. The terrible stains had been lighter on her flesh than she had remembered, rather like watery blood.

"It's not that." It was partly that hideous re-enactment

248

of an old nightmare, but she didn't say so. She wanted to lock it away as it had been before they drove to that obscure crossing. "It's the idea of facing all those people I ran away from at the Royal Chalet."

Thank God for Frau Kupperman, the stains were barely visible now.

"Oh, that. I'll simply tell them I kidnapped you."

She heard herself giggling before recalling that Mrs Tenby had warned her very nicely, *Men hate giggling, my dear.*

They were nearing the end of the tram line where she had waited for Prince Stefan last night and she would soon be making her excuses. If only it could be postponed a little while until she thought up a really terrific excuse.

Maybe Brett Athlone was reading her mind. "I meant to take you to lunch."

"Like this? They'd throw me out."

"Not with my jacket on. We'll eat out on the pavement. Then you won't smell like a slaughterhouse. Here, take the jacket."

She put on the corduroy jacket but thought his remark was a cruel, insensitive thing to say, unfair to the dead man, but men had a way of bringing these truths out in the open. It might be a psychological cure.

He went on, "Leave it to me." He swung the car around and headed away from the Royal Chalet grounds toward the Austrian border.

Before she could protest he promised, "Not another border crossing. Just a Danish pavement café. All the things little girls like: those tiny sandwiches just right for a starvation diet, and the best pastries in the world. Well, we'll see."

She looked back anxiously, still wondering what she would use as an excuse when they finally went back to the Chalet, but it was plain that Brett knew what he was doing.

Sitting at the little table for two on the *terasse* which occupied most of the pavement, Julie found the little Danske Café all he had predicted, especially the pastries. These were so delicious he ordered two of her favourites for her, big, round, custard-filled pastries. Then she could only eat one. She was determined to save it. In her experience you never knew at what time you'd be free for another meal. She wrapped it in her handkerchief but it could still be seen, a crass reminder that not enough food was served at the Royal Chalet.

A pair of young women had just left the table beside them, dropping a famous Italian tabloid weekly under their table. Brett reached down and got the entire magazine. "Here. This ought to disguise the stuff, although, I grant you, the inner contents are better than the covering."

She looked over his arm at the double page spread of photos, all of prominent people, mostly European cinema stars who appeared regularly on the beaches of Cannes and Venice and appeared glamorously at the night showings of critically acclaimed films.

"Well, well, well," Brett said. Like most people, he mingled his contempt with a human curiosity. Julie remembered Prince Maximilian and her instructions that he should not see any pictures of his wife in these rags.

"Don't use that double page. It might have something the prince shouldn't see."

He tore out the double page and threw it down again,

remarking at the same time, "If I were dying, this sort of thing might liven me up."

"Not if it were your wife whom you adored."

"No. You're right as usual. OK, here you are. All wrapped up in trash, so you can hide the awful crime of a custard pastry."

The time had come. No more excuses. She suggested one more hope of not being seen as she came in. "Maybe we could slip through the path from the tram street."

He agreed but added, "Julie, you were a born conspirator. Consider it done."

Lunch had done its usual repair job on Julie and by the time she and Brett reached the garden door of the Royal Chalet her pride and sternly built-up self-confidence were at least outwardly restored. Above all, she wanted to make her companion forget the appalling weakness she had shown at the border.

Brett opened the door into the service hall. "Here we are. Home again. As good as new."

Are we, she wondered . . . *But I've moved backward. For a few minutes today I was that haunted child again. Helpless. And I'm not helpless. I never will be again. I must prove it to myself. I'll start with you.*

"Will you do me a great favour, Mr Athlone?"

His hand slipped off the door. "Brett," he corrected her. "But certainly. Sounds serious."

"Not really." She was fairly sure she looked easy and confident. "Let me make my excuses alone." She offered his jacket to him.

He frowned and then surprised her by patting her arm, almost as if – a nasty thought – he pitied her.

"I wouldn't interfere for the world, love. You do that.

If anything goes wrong, and you need a backup, just remember your old pal Brett."

While she watched him he stepped back onto the little pebbled path among the rapidly maturing vegetables. She closed the door and went into the great reception hall and on to His Highness's bar.

She didn't know whether to be relieved or otherwise when she looked in and found Prince Maximilian's dictated notes and letters gone, the typewriter moved away from the top of the bar, and the furniture replaced in exactly the spots where she had found them.

It was hard to know what to do now. She was an employee of the Foreign Office Secretarial Staff; so the woman who was the housekeeper here, her usual employer, would not be involved. Strictly speaking, Prince Maximilian was her employer at the Royal Chalet, just as Count Thallin von and zu "something-or-other" was her direct employer at the New Palace.

She wished she hadn't seen Prince Stefan today. That would be an exceedingly awkward moment to explain. Had he come today to find out about her telephone call last night? Painful thought. She couldn't very well call and ask what his business had been. She hoped he would believe she hadn't seen him.

There was still no one in the great reception hall, although it was well into the afternoon. She hurried up the service staircase, figuring that as soon as she changed her clothes, she might as well bite the bullet and face the inevitable.

Prince Maximilian must be the first one on her list.

Her room had been carefully made up, for which she was relieved. In some houses where she had worked, and especially in institutions, she was expected to make her

252

own bed and clean her room. Today she had forgotten which might be a mark against her.

She unwrapped the scandalous tabloid magazine and threw it into the waste-paper basket, leaving the pastry wrapped in her handkerchief, in the wash basin with a scarf over it. She hoped at this altitude, which was chill when the sun went down, that the pastry wouldn't dry out before she could eat it this evening. Even in a princely home her motto was preparedness. You never knew whether you would have three meals tomorrow.

She wore her grass green suit to fulfill her next obligation, the interview with Prince Maximilian. She went down to the prince's little enclave on the elegant lower floor and knocked before she heard voices in the suite. She hesitated after knocking but the door was opened by the kitchen girl, looking bedraggled as ever and carrying two big baskets of debris from shedding flowers, plants, and the *Lichtenbourger Presse*.

The kitchen girl ducked out around Julie and shuffled down the hall. Meanwhile, Julie saw that His Highness had been listening to a 'Voice of America' broadcast. Apparently, that was the voice she had heard. She curtsied and waited for him to snap off the radio which he did as if it had burned him. "Nasty stuff. Mostly lies, glorifying my successor."

Julie was surprised but hardly in a position to protest. At last, he gave her his attention, prefacing it with his pleasant smile. "Miss Jones. I meant to thank you for the work you did today. But I've been so busy." He sighed. "One cannot conceive the matters that pile up, things my son-in-law is unable to handle. Social matters of enormous import. It was through social relationships that my reign was so successful."

"Yes, sir," she replied dutifully. She was wondering why he bothered to hear the propaganda which, like the BBC, hoped to reeducate those people behind Mr Churchill's 'Iron Curtain'.

He leaned forward from the chaise longue. "Do be seated. I am going to rattle off a few ideas and you must give me your opinion of their strength."

"Their strength. Yes, Your Highness."

Before sitting down she reached for a shorthand notebook and pencil on the shelf above two long rows of leather-covered books that seemed to be handwritten journals. On the spine of each expensive black book was a year and below that, running vertically, a name in gold: "MAXIMILIAN II".

She hadn't known there was one before him in the hazy past of Lichtenbourg history. Hoping he wouldn't talk fast enough to cause her trouble with her less than perfect shorthand, she realized shortly that she had nothing to worry about on that score.

He appeared to be making a speech on paper to Colonel Grigori Vukhasin in which he agreed that the People's Democratic Party had much in common with the Kuragin supporters, an autocratic party devoted to the restoration of supreme power in the hands of Maximilian, Hereditary Prince Royal of Lichtenbourg.

By the time she got that written down, and it wasn't difficult, she was secretly shocked by its naïveté and worse, its downright treason against the legally constituted power now ruling the Principality.

While jotting all this down she wondered how she could warn somebody. Prince Stefan, obviously. But she had tried that before. She was not at all sure where Brett Athlone's sympathies lay, and that left no

254

one she could trust. Certainly, neither of the princesses, Garnett or Alexia, would do. They probably agreed with Prince Max.

His dictation went on, shocking her by its treachery and the man's ignorant trust in Comrade Colonel Vukhasin. Everybody knew the colonel was a humorous, sly man, clever and devious but exceedingly popular with the rank and file of hardworking men in the blue-collar, the unemployed, and the would-be intellectual crowd.

Much to her relief, the prince decided reluctantly, "Naturally, I can't attend the banquet they are holding in a couple of weeks but many of my supporters will be there. Think of it, my dear, with our influence, we can fool that sly fox, Vukhasin, into supporting us."

"But after you win, sir?" she ventured. "It might be like having a – a bear by the tail." She had read that somewhere, but he hadn't. He appreciated it.

He laughed softly. "Well, child, we must make allowances for your innocence in politics. I can certainly handle the Old Bear. You see, I was responsible for eliminating the red tape and bringing him in as a citizen. A grateful citizen, I may add."

"But Your Highness, suppose he thinks you are just using him until you return to power. Or the other way around. Suppose he uses your party."

He shook his head. "Let's say I have a spy in the Old Bear's camp. Aside from Vukhasin's debt to me, I have evidence of his secret dealings with me that would not set well with the Kremlin. I am not a fool, Miss Jones."

Unless, of course, the Kremlin knew all about those "secret dealings". Maybe Colonel Vukhasin had orders to make a tentative deal with Maximilian. But Julie could go no further in the matter, and if she betrayed him to Prince Stefan, she would be a despicable spy.

Prince Stefan must learn himself. She hadn't figured out how. She still didn't understand what Mr Royle and General Athlone were up to. Whatever it was, Brett knew something about that too, but he and his father could hardly be involved in the Communist business with Colonel Vukhasin. None of their conversation with Maximilian had touched on that.

She was relieved when she was dismissed with instructions to give back the letter to Colonel Vukhasin to him. He would see that it got to its destination.

Julie left his suite with her head whirling. She went down to the little panelled bar and typed her letters, doing a fair job, allowing for a few mistakes. It wasn't the easiest thing she had ever done. She ached in what seemed to be every bone in her body. The mental shock of what she had seen earlier was beginning to recede under all those devious matters circling around Prince Maximilian, but physically, she felt that she had seen better days.

She stood up, shook herself like a wet terrier, and took the finished correspondence up the service stairs, after passing two maids busy dusting the ground floor's famed *torchère*, the buhlwork cabinet, and other treasures. The women ignored her but exchanged glances. She did not doubt that they had been gossiping about her. What shocking scandal they could find would undoubtedly be news to her.

She had just stepped out onto the corridor, headed towards Maximilian's suite when she was startled by the appearance of a dark figure in the shadows. Tall and imposing, he barred her way. She would have cried out in her surprise but Prince Stefan put a hand over her mouth. It was a firm clasp, as was his other hand on her arm but she had no doubt there was a good reason for his secrecy.

In his low-pitched voice he said, "We will go to your room."

With difficulty she nodded and they went up the service stairs to the rooms under the eaves with his hand still on her arm. At least, he had removed the other hand from her mouth which felt dry as cotton.

By the time they reached her room she was ready for anything. Maybe he thought she was working secretly for his father-in-law. Or maybe he even thought she was a Communist. On the other hand, there was always a possibility he wanted to find out what had actually happened at the border today.

She watched him bolt the door, once they were inside her room. He motioned for her to sit down. She backed up in confusion and fell onto the bed. Her muscles hadn't gotten any better since the unfortunate Hungarian had fallen onto her today.

Prince Stefan pulled out the only chair in the room, turned it around with the straight back in front of her and straddled the chair, resting his hands on the curving top of the back. "Now, Julie, I've spent a very unpleasant day in my first meeting of the Royal Council, wondering what is going on around me."

"I – I've just finished some letters, Your Highness."

Beginning to shake, she cupped one of her hands in the other to hide them. Her letters dictated by Prince Max fell to the floor and he reached over, picking them up. She held one hand out for them and grew more uneasy as he riffled through them.

His eyebrows raised as he came across the letter to Colonel Vukhasin and then went on to read the other envelopes. She braced herself to explain as simply as possible. She didn't want another quarrel between Max and Stefan that might give Prince Max a deadly attack, and she was caught off-guard when Stefan remarked in an unexpectedly friendly voice, "According to Radio Lichtenbourg, the British Consul's son and a female companion were in what they call 'an incident' at a Hungarian Border Crossing."

"About that," she began, then asked in surprise, "How did you know it was me?"

He smiled for the first time. "Mental telepathy? You see, they described his companion as 'young, honey-haired, very thin, and employed in the Foreign Secretariat'."

There was little in that description to argue with.

"That's me, all right. You see, it was around noon and I thought I'd be back before I was missed."

"All that is important only if it becomes an international crisis, which is unlikely. I received the news in Council at the same time the vice-chancellor heard it. Frankly, neither of us wants to bring it to international attention, war commissions, et cetera."

He glanced over the letters in his hand. They were easy enough to read. None would be folded until Prince Maximilian had signed them and they were closed with his Kuragin-Lichtenbourg seal.

Stefan nodded, not nearly so angry or shocked as Julie expected. He handed them to her. "Was it this little toying with the Russian Bear that upset you last night?"

"No. Mr Royle and General Athlone talked about something quite different, Your Highness."

"A plain 'sir' will be quite enough. Now then, what else could it be that unites the aristocratic Athlone and the very democratic Tige Royle in such secrecy? And with my indiscreet father-in-law, of all people."

She tried to put the weird, rambling conversation together in as few words as possible. "They kept asking if Prince Max was in – you know – Spain in the early Thirties. They seemed positive Princess Garnett was there several times."

He grimaced and studied his fingers as if he expected to find the answer there. While he was thinking over this puzzler she broke in abruptly, "He seemed to know about it when he talked to me today. Mr Brett, I mean. In fact, he always questions me about Spain. And today, when the poor dead man fell against me, it made me think of that awful time. As if I'd been there."

He raised his head. "What awful time?"

"But I wasn't there! I was born in England somewhere. I've read about Spain. That's all."

"I see. That explains young Athlone's pursuit of you." He reached for her cold fingers and squeezed them gently. "Not that there aren't other reasons."

She reddened and murmured, "Thank you."

He shrugged. "However, this doesn't explain all this secrecy from me. I have nothing to say about Spain and whether Max or Garnett were there. In fact, Garnett was there frequently during the early Thirties. Max was stuck here making botched-up deals with Hitler's National Socialists, and the rest of the Council was trying to walk a tightrope."

She felt very wise when she made the observation, "It's like His Highness and the Democratic People's Party."

"I'm afraid it is." He got up. "All right. Take the

letters to be signed and let him do what he likes with them. I've no doubt Grigori will give me a hint or two later. He likes to butter his bread on both sides."

She thought of Prince Max's naïve belief in his own destiny and in his beloved wife. "Poor man."

He looked at her. "You mean Max? Yes, I'd say that." He reached over, slapped her hands in a friendly way, and started to the door. Before unbolting it he glanced back. "I am a good deal more puzzled by this Spanish business and how it can affect Lichtenbourg."

"They are not keeping it a secret from Lichtenbourg, but from you, sir. I heard them mention your name."

He shook his head in what she took to be a total lack of comprehension, then added, "Thank you. I knew I could trust you the minute I laid eyes on you that night on the Miravel Road. Take time out for enjoyment. See young Athlone if you like."

"You've been very kind, sir. I'll never forget it."

"Thank you and goodbye for now, Just Julie."

He was gone then. The corridor looked shadowy with dusk when Julie went to the door and looked after him. She was about to start down towards Prince Max's floor, to give him the typed letters when she saw a door at the far end of the corridor close quietly.

She had no doubt that someone, servant, or otherwise, knew about Stefan's visit to her, though no one could have heard the conversation through that heavy door.

At least, she had made up her mind that she knew where her loyalty lay. It had always been with the man who made her trip to Lichtenbourg possible, and had defended her at every turn. She thought back. He even defended her against Nick Chance's harrassing attacks at Miravel.

Spain again. Mr Chance, as well as the good Reverend Tenby, knew something about the matter. How could it all possibly be connected?

No matter. There was her work to be done now, and the first thing was a return of Prince Max's letters.

CHAPTER TWENTY-ONE

Behaving like a spy didn't prove to be as shameful as she had expected. Prince Stefan had practically asked her to be on his side, so it was clear that he needed her. Besides, he was right and the others were clearly wrong. There was always the possibility of a steady job and at least a friendly contact with Prince Stefan, plus occasional rises in salary.

Still, it would have been a lonely life and often dreary, without the frequent visits of Brett Athlone. Julie had grown up suspicious of unexpected windfalls that came without her contrivance. But after Brett had popped in three or four times, taking her to little pavement cafés or simply teasing and chatting with her in the back garden of the Chalet, she began to accept him and almost, though never quite, dismissing her suspicion that he had ulterior motives. Whatever those motives might have been, they were not sexual. He kissed her cheek once or twice, and several times, with exaggeration, kissed her fingers, but he hadn't gone further, so far. Maybe she didn't tempt him that way.

All in all, her job and her salary should be her top consideration, and most of the time they were.

The first time she received her week's salary was a great moment. She had to go to the New Palace and the Foreign Secretariat Offices to receive it and Brett, very kindly drove her there. But she was paid more per week than for any work she had ever done.

Prince Maximilian's sweeping great signature, a work of art in itself, on the voucher for her first paycheque made her feel a twinge of shame that she might be forced to betray his secret dealings with the Communist Party or the curious business with Mr Royle and General Athlone. However, Prince Stefan had asked nothing about his father-in-law. She was much relieved, and confined her attention to anything the Athlones or Tige Royle might say about the topic of Spain. So far, this subject had not been discussed anywhere near her, unless the two men assumed that Prince Max knew no more than they had elicited from him.

Almost every day Princess Alexia came to visit her father. Several times, to the prince's delight, his wife came along too, driven by her hard-faced good-looking chauffeur, Kurt, and seeming so glad to see Prince Max, it was hard to believe otherwise.

A week later Julie was asked to relieve the staff at the New Palace in filling out invitations to the cathedral service where Stefan would take the oath of his high office. On this occasion Prince Stefan sent a special car for her. Nevertheless, at the Palace he took the time to speak with her outside the stenographic pool that morning, and to wish her well. He asked her no questions about Prince Max and politics, for which she was grateful, and she volunteered nothing.

Once or twice Brett had teased her about Spain but immediately changed the subject when she became defensive. No one had mentioned "Spain" except that she filled out the engraved invitation to Generalissimo

Francisco Franco and the Senora Franco for the cathedral service. Brett Athlone happened by at lunchtime and found the Franco invitation of considerable interest.

"Do you feel anything, good or bad, I mean, when you write to the Generalissimo and all those grandees?"

Hiding her annoyance, Julie looked at him, wide-eyed. "Why should I? I don't even know those people. What do you think I am, some Spanish grandee who wants to hide her background?"

"Even if you think it's a fabulous background?" Brett wanted to know.

"Luckily, you will never know."

He had one hand pressed against the wall beside her. Then his thumb caressed her cheek lightly. He began again. "Come to lunch with me?"

She was amused and thrilled by the sensual effect of his touch but she reminded him, "That depends on the last time you took me."

"What? You don't like Danish pastry?"

There was a particular excitement that she had never known before in his teasing and his trim young body. She enjoyed his light-hearted ways and found them even more attractive when he revealed a serious side and seemed to care what happened to her.

Even his teasing about what he imagined were her dreams of fame and fortune, in Spain, of all places, had a deeper sincerity. They might have intrigued her if they had been centred in some other country.

She said, "I have to be back in an hour to finish addressing the envelopes."

"Oh, to be in France," he sighed elaborately. "They have two hour lunches. If I promise to get you back in an hour?" He looked beyond the wall panel to the spacious hall. "I see I'll have to. Your dragon-angel is watching us."

She swung around, knocking aside his arm, and saw Prince Stefan watching them with a look that was a half-smile and a half-frown.

She curtsied, although he brushed that aside with a quick gesture. She had wondered uncomfortably if he was jealous over Brett's attentions but it seemed that he was concerned over something else entirely.

"Hello there, Athlone," Stefan called out. And then, to Julie, "I hope our friend here isn't asking you about Spain again."

To her surprise Brett asked, "Is there some reason I should ask her, Sir?"

Stefan smiled. It was a tight smile that did not reach his eyes. "Who am I to say? You might ask your father."

"My father?"

"Did I say *father*? I meant General Athlone, of course." The prince was moving away. Over his shoulder he added, "Doesn't he have interests of one sort or another in Spain?"

When the prince was out of hearing, Brett muttered, "That's an odd one. What the devil was he driving at? My father has discussed this problem of ours with Tige Royle, but I didn't think His Highness knew about it. Not yet, at any rate."

Knowing a little more about it than Brett supposed she did, Julie said, "There is something else I wondered about. His Highness was surprised, and so was I when he called Sir George 'your father' and you reacted so sharply."

He seemed perplexed. Maybe he was. "It wasn't because he called Sir George my father. I was just

265

taken unawares by his mention of Sir George. I often think of him as my father, of course. And Lady Athlone was the dearest mother any child could ask for. Are we going to that lunch?"

She looked down at the little gold children's wrist watch that her friend and employer, Mrs Tenby had given her at the Annual Christmas Auction. Mrs Tenby had paid two pounds to the Church Fund for it, actually apologizing to Julie because it was a little girl's watch. It was Julie's most precious possession.

"I can't now. The hour is half gone."

He looked disappointed, which gave her both pleasure and satisfaction. "Well then, why don't I come for you when you are finished for the day? I'll take you to a café I know of, I think you'll like it. And then I promise to escort you home to the Chalet like a respectable suitor."

She laughed at that, wondering what would happen if she took him seriously. "I'd love to go. You don't even have to play me up like that, so long as you stop teasing me about places I've never been to. Can you really be here when I've done with the envelopes and all?"

"Oh, certainly. I've got powers I haven't even used yet."

She was still laughing when he leaned over and kissed her right on the mouth before she could close it. She almost bit him, more or less by accident. Still amused, she was especially pleased when he accepted this unromantic end to his gesture by calling her a witch and pretending she had taken a piece out of his lip.

"Never mind," he said finally. "I forgive you. I'll get my own back. But next time, I'll see that you hold still."

He strolled along the big hall and turned once to wave as she was going into the stenographic pool full of typewriter desks.

Fräulein Stieb, likewise returning from her lunch break, saw Brett Athlone's figure and remarked in her businesslike way, "Make the most of your time, Fräulein Jones. Any of those foolish girls you work with would be happy to take your place."

It was a nice thought. Julie went back into the ill-lit room with its noisy manual typewriters clattering away, but her thoughts were on her recent encounter. She hoped she hadn't hurt Brett's lip. He might need it again sometime. She had been kissed before by young and older men, who annoyed her by their attempts to commit further sexual familiarities, but they left her with nothing but disgust or boredom toward them. Prince Stefan, of course, had been different, but he was so far above her in station that she couldn't take that seriously, wonderful as it was.

On the other hand, there was Brett Athlone. She refused to believe he was far above her in station or any other way. And his touch was definitely thrilling. She put her forefinger to her lips. Yes, Brett was different.

Prince Stefan, coming from his daily Council meeting, stopped in to thank the women who had worked hard on the invitations by hand, and the other paperwork involved in his inauguration.

The women, most of them older than Stefan, were properly thrilled, although it did not escape them that His Highness exchanged a few words with the new "foreigner" in a low voice before leaving.

"Have a great evening, Julie. I needn't offer any

267

fatherly advice. I'm willing to wager you can handle a dozen fellows like Athlone."

She was pleased enough by his good wishes, but then, he took her hand. She didn't know whether he would shake it or kiss it, but was reasonably satisfied when he gently let her fingers go and left the room.

Almost every female in the room stared at her, some of them giving each other knowing glances. Julie knew that gossip like this might be disastrous, on the heels of his election. Princess Alexia ought to know better than to spend all her time with her father. She ought to spend at least a little time in her husband's company. Worst of all, her father was so unappreciative. His whole life was woven around Princess Garnett.

Julie hadn't taken dictation from him for two weeks without realizing that even his dealings with the People's Democratic People's Party and Colonel Vukhasin were motivated by the dream of setting up his wife again in her role as Her Serene Highness, the First Lady of Lichtenbourg.

Julie was relieved when the aged Count Thallin came in, pointed his cane at the clock on the wall, and dismissed them all. No one needed to be told twice.

Along the busy hall outside the stenographic room several males waited, two or three leaning casually against the wall and smoking cigarettes while others sauntered along, and all tried to look as if they belonged there. Julie understood them perfectly. She had often tried to look as if she belonged somewhere which was far too elegant for a kitchen girl or an upstairs maid called "Julie Jones". They knew. People always knew.

She wondered if Julie Jones would ever be able to walk among the middle class, let alone the aristocrats, without standing out like what her Chicago friend had called so aptly, "a sore thumb".

Maybe it's my clothes, she thought. I'm still wearing my stupid green suit. On the other hand Brett Athlone really liked her. She was almost sure of that now. And he knew what she was. What made it even more logical, he himself was an orphan. He wasn't born an aristocrat. Maybe that was why she had been attracted to him, and he to her.

Brett wasn't anywhere in sight now. Of course, she could hardly expect him to be waiting for her in the hall of a palace, like all those other males waiting for the stenographic crew.

She started away from Fräulein Stieb's little cubbyhole and headed towards the smaller staircase for domestic staff, where Princess Alexia had taken her that first day, almost two weeks ago. It occurred to Julie as she walked past the several couples who were meeting and planning romantic evenings ahead of them, that she always knew her place. A cynical observation, but true.

Naturally, this didn't apply to Brett Athlone after all. He had a beginning no better than hers, but he had made people believe he was a member of that aristocratic class. No matter. She was probably too old to change. She did not turn around for the running steps along the floor until she heard her name being called: "Julie. Hi, Julie! Wait!"

She stopped in the middle of the hall and waited. Brett had cared enough to parade her name through the long, echoing hall. This morning he had kissed her and given her a genuine thrill of delight. Now, he called her name before all these Lichtenbourgers, not caring whether he embarrassed himself or not.

Orphan meet orphan. There was a bond stronger even then sex between them. He took her hands as if to hold her there. She laughed at his breathless state and at his complaint: "You didn't wait. You just marched off, independent as the Devil. Have you got a better offer? Or aren't you hungry?"

She thought his effort on her behalf deserved an honest reply. "It wasn't that at all. I just thought you might have been joking about dinner."

He shook both her hands. His hair was still unruly from the summer breeze outside and he did look as if he had been running.

"I never joke about my dinner. Come along, back this way. My car is parked just inside those big, ugly front gates facing on the Boulevard. Unless, of course, you want to walk across town to the Tokay Café.

He tucked her right hand inside his arm and walked back through the interested crowd to the impressive staircase already lit by a glittering chandelier overhead.

He bent his head to hear her whisper, "I don't know if I'm allowed to use these stairs."

"Why not, for God's sake? The building belongs to the people, and you can't find any more 'peoply' people than two orphans."

He did understand. He recognized that special bond between them and wasn't ashamed of it.

His flamboyant white Porsche was parked as he had said, just inside the gates and a Lichtenbourg Palace guard was standing there beside it, trying to read some sort of identification.

"Now, you've done it," Julie teased him, but as she might have expected, he merely shrugged and did not increase his steps.

270

"Business with the Palace from the British Consulate," he explained breezily to the guard who hesitated, looked up at the grey façade of the New Palace and then gave in.

He saluted Brett, smiled and said something in the Lichtenbourg patois which made Brett laugh.

"Not at all," he said. "This is my Aunt Julie. Can't you tell by the family resemblance?"

She had probably been insulted, but she didn't care.

"Tokay. I know that word," she told Brett as they drove out the lofty gates of the New Palace like royalty.

"The owners are Hungarian. But they've got gypsies working for them. Playing their fiddles and Russian balalaikas. Things like that." He looked over at her. "I thought you might like it. Remind you of that friend you worked for who told you to beware of baths. I'm glad she didn't tell you to be beware of fire. *Tokay*, that is."

She felt festive and daring. "I don't care if she had. *Tokay*. That's wine; isn't it? You know, that's funny, Magda didn't drink wine. She drank cognac. A lot of it." Julie thought back. "She was nice, though. Abrupt and scarey at times, but I liked her. She was real. Like the Tenbys."

He zoomed down the slope of the Boulevard to Cathedral Square which turned out to be a circle. "Doesn't sound like a vicar."

"No, I mean, Magda and Mrs Tenby never said things they didn't mean."

He thought that over and surprised her with the quiet boast, "You ought to like me then. But sometimes I get the feeling you don't believe me."

She was pleased but didn't say so.

271

He was still trying to get her to admit she put him in a class with the Tenbys and Magda, the fortune teller, when they reached the Hungarian restaurant. This was southwest of the railway station in the direction of the Hungarian border. It was not imposing but the permanent tables were beginning to fill up with dark, exciting people who didn't look Nordic like so many Lichtenbourgers.

The location of the restaurant made Julie nervous and she began to look around for help in case the Russian border guards started shooting. Fortunately, none were in sight, though she could hear instruments being strummed and remembered the passionate excitement of Magda's playing. When Julie had shown fear because the music reminded her of plaintive instruments in her nightmares, Magda had scoffed at her.

"This is balalaika. No guitar. Balalaika plays for long ago sadness of my people in Russia. And for me. I lose them all when they go to Hungary. All lost to the cursed Nazis." She had glared at Julie, her black eyes like coals burning in a campfire and Julie had backed up, wondering if Magda would give her the evil curse she saved for Hitler and all *gaje*. Magda had laughed at Julie's fright and when Julie explained, Magda pointed to the girl's palm. "You think fire in my eyes is danger? No, little *gajo*. Not fire you must watch. Maybe fire in the eyes."

Julie told this to Brett who was amused but teased her, "I don't think you followed her advice about bathing. You smell of perfume. Something subtle." He pretended to sniff over her head. "I like it."

She found this an exciting compliment and almost forgot their proximity to danger. She had often ordered for herself when she was out with boys her age, but those amounted to beans or ham sandwiches. Here in this little nest of exciting Hungarians, all of whom looked like gypsies, she asked Brett to order.

"Fair enough. I think we'll start with that old reliable *Gulyas*. *Tokay* is a little rich for a starter, but let's take a chance. Then a very rich and sticky Hungarian pastry. I know you like them."

She flushed, remembering the day she ate sticky pastry in Prince Max's presence and licked her fingers. But Brett had done the same thing.

A swarthy man in costume, complete with gold earrings and a bright red kerchief of cotton around his head, was going from table to table playing the large stringed instrument like an overgrown mandolin that Magda had called a balalaika. Julie looked away, avoiding the gypsy's eyes but he came over anyway.

Brett gave him a silver Lichtenbourg schilling, one with the handsome profile of Maximilian II on one side and the Lichtenbourg-Kuragin Eagle on the other. Thus encouraged, the gypsy began to play a Russian lament. Julie shrank away from the table, trying not to cringe, but Brett put one hand over hers, closing his long fingers around hers.

"Just give it a chance, love. It's beautiful. Very like the first musical sounds I remember as a baby."

She shuddered and then broke in to ask him over the music, "Were you actually born in Spain?"

"Actually and positively. In a village south of Madrid. Place run by an English group, mostly women. My mother – I mean Lady Athlone – was the mainspring of the whole business, finding homes for orphans and lending money to the house in Madrid where a group of Spaniards ran a kind of . . . Never mind. It was all very hush-hush. Except for the information that went out on the sly, to other countries on the continent. Many rich customers. Some pretty high-born, titles and all."

"And your Lady Athlone was mixed up in that?"

"I guess it's because she couldn't have children and it seemed appalling to her that these children might not even be born because others didn't know how to find them. Anyway, for my own sake, I'm damned glad Lady A and the others saved me from – but enough of that. They say it was a very nice place. Secretive, specially from the Spanish Government, as you can imagine. Well, the Civil War put an end to that."

"And all for rich women who had betrayed their husbands?"

"Not necessarily. Wives who felt no more children were needed. That kind of thing."

That's what I am, Julie reminded herself. Not needed. By someone. Funny, she hadn't thought too much about the unwanted part lately. Long ago she had buried that part of it.

"What are you thinking about?" he asked suddenly.

"I'm thinking about my nightmare, when I was very little."

He leaned forward, looking into he eyes. "Maybe I can exorcize your nightmare."

She was not used to the concern in his eyes and his voice which was suddenly hoarse with emotion. It seemed the most natural thing in the world to describe that unforgotten nightmare.

"It's just pieces of the dream. It's night and I'm in a shed where animals used to be kept. There are little creatures around me in the straw, all tightly wrapped against the cold. Some of them are crying. I've been

274

told to stay with them until the lady comes back. She is a nun, I think."

"Are these lambs? Puppies?"

"Children. Infants."

"God." He wiped his hand over his face. "Go on."

"I think they've taken as many as they could and will come back for us. Only, they don't come. I don't remember parts of it. I must have slept. I wake up when the lights explode over the shed. And there is horrible noise, like thunder. I lean over the babies. There are four, I think. One wears something on her little wrist that shines when the light explodes over our heads. Something throws me back. A terrible wind, like a cyclone. It throws me off the babies. I knock my head against something and then I go to sleep."

"Bombardment?"

"I don't know. When I wake up nothing is moving except me. The babies, they are all – all – very – still."

She swallowed hard and found his hand gently caressing her hair. She gave him a tremulous smile. "Well, the nightmare goes away."

"You don't remember reaching England?"

"No. Only being with other girls my age and older. They all speak different kinds of English. Busy ladies in nurses' uniforms bustle around. This part is no dream. It's my real life. I was in some kind of children's asylum, I think. It's my first real memory." She blinked the tears off her eyelashes and added brightly, "It hasn't been bad at all, since. I'm no Oliver Twist, you know."

"I know."

Then she remembered his own childhood. On a note of incredulity, she asked, "Were you really unwanted too?"

He laughed. "Impossible as it seems, I must have been."

"Did it bother you?"

"Lord, no! There was Lady A, you see."

"How nice! She took a fancy to you."

He said nothing for a minute or two while the music wavered sadly in the night, but he kept looking at her in a way that made her nervous.

"I hope you are not pitying me. I don't know anyone who needs it less."

"I wouldn't dare pity you," he admitted in his joking way.

She did not find this amusing and was glad when the gypsy took his balalaika to another table.

Their order was set down before them, redolent of delicious flavours and spices. Brett reminded her, "You see? You've heard that music all this time and it never bothered you. You've been running away, instead of facing it. That's all." Then, abruptly, "How's the *gulyas*?"

"Wonderful. I love it." She skipped his other remark.

True to his prediction, the dessert was a wonderfully rich pastry, and he teased her, "Are you going to take this home wrapped in a tabloid?"

"I'm going to eat every bite."

She did so under his watchful eyes and his complaint that she was far too thin anyway.

By the time they left the restaurant they were in excellent spirits with each other and when they were driving back across town she allowed him to joke about how fat he was going to make her. He stopped all this light-hearted talk only to point out a heavy stone building four storeys high and formerly a hotel used by

276

the local Nazis and a meeting place of the SS during the late war.

"Not a pretty place," Brett agreed when Julie turned from it in disgust. "Seems quite suitable for its present use. Headquarters of Vukhasin's 'Democratic People's Party'."

Julie looked back over her shoulder. "Speaking of parties, seems like they're having a party tonight."

"Oh, the big light in the foyer. Yes. Rumour says they're celebrating some kind of comradeship – if you will excuse the expression – between the People's Party and the Kuragin Supporters."

So Brett knew about that, did he? And poor Prince Max was sitting home in the Chalet, imagining his supporters were out to swallow Vukhasin's Communists.

She was suddenly agitated by another thought: suppose Prince Max had gone to that ugly grey building anyway. His reputation would be ruined forever. All decent Lichtenbourgers and the Western World would despise him.

They had already passed the grey building with its unsavoury reputation and still Julie worried. Brett glanced over at her. "Does it matter terribly? A traitor is a traitor, even if he is a prince. He's betraying the legal elected chancellor, the ruler of his country. Not a very savoury business."

All perfectly true. Prince Maximilian was betraying her hero, Prince Stefan, but if her suspicions of Brett's father were correct, the Athlones were also meddling in the political affairs of Lichtenbourg. She wanted to say so but decided it would be wiser to let Stefan deal with the Athlones. That problem was not as clear as this one, which involved the naïve ignorance of a sick man who might be dying.

She reminded Brett, "It isn't as if Prince Max had actually gone to that building. He is like a child, playing a game he doesn't understand. All to impress his wife."

Brett shrugged. "True. I hope to God he minds his own business and stays at the Chalet."

The white car climbed the Chalet hill and pulled in around the semi-circular drive to the front steps. Brett pulled up and greeted the sentries on duty. Two of the four inspected his passport, saluted him and one of them smiled at Julie as Brett gallantly helped her out of the car.

She felt very much the Lady of the Chalet when Brett walked into the reception hall with her. She was surprised to see the interior of the Chalet so dark and silent but it was late and doubtless, most of the staff had gone to bed.

Brett stopped her as she offered her hand to say good-night. He asked her whimsically, "Don't I deserve something more, love? All that balalaika music and the *gulyas* and the pastry?"

"Not to mention the *Tokay*." She was smiling and he took that for assent, framing her cheeks with the palms of his hands and holding her still. Looking into her eyes he explained, "This is to prevent you from biting me."

He almost caught her laughing but this time he closed her mouth with his kiss. She found her body trembling with excitement and put all that feeling into returning his kiss. She wanted only to draw his lips hard over hers so that he would control her body as he controlled her senses.

When she could no longer breathe, he guessed her

problem and drew his lips away. He looked into her eager eyes again. She was delighted to see that he too was out of breath.

"All right, love. I'll let you go. See you tomorrow?"

She wanted to, desperately but she had to remind him, "If I can. It depends on whether I'm needed."

"Fair enough. I'll arrange something." He pinched her nose, then touched it with his lips and started towards the front doors. She was just going up the service stairs when she heard his voice, calm now, but slightly puzzled. "Julie?" He stooped and picked up something near the staircase, a wadded-up piece of paper.

She joined him, wondering why a little wad of paper could be important. When he spread it out, she understood. It was a quarter page of a scandal tabloid. She could see part of some worldly figures there before her.

"Seems to be grease-stained," he said, turning it over. He looked at Julie. "You wrapped that custard pastry in one of these on our first date; didn't you?"

"Of course. Later, I tore up the paper, wadded up the pieces, and threw them into my waste-paper basket to be destroyed."

He moved closer to the lights that illuminated the steps outside and examined the torn paper he had smoothed out. He showed her the wrinkled paper.

"Either it's the tabloid we found, or someone has gone to the trouble of making it look that way. There is a bit of tape on the back, as if the tabloid you tore up has been mended with tape."

She stared at him with gradually mounting terror. "Someone wants to get me in trouble. But why? What do they have against me?"

"No one went to this trouble just to incriminate you, love." He looked around and then up the white and gold main staircase towards Prince Max's suite. "It's my suspicion this is much worse. The destruction of Max Kuragin, at which time, if I don't miss my guess, his Kuragin support will be pushed to join Vukhasin."

She caught her breath. "It can't be. They would bring down the present government."

He nodded. "Pro-Western democracy here. None of this phoney People's Government. Then it would be straight from the Kremlin." He took her hand. "I'll need you to get to Old Max. He probably wouldn't open up to me. If he is still here."

"Don't say that. Hurry."

He was already on his way. She ran up the stairs after him, reaching him as he stopped before the prince's door.

He whispered, "Call him in the normal way. Ask if you may speak to him."

Her hand shook a little but she raised it and knocked. Then she called out in a tone more plaintive than customary, "Your Highness, it's Fräulein Jones. May I speak to you?"

There was no answer. She tried again, louder. Nothing.

Brett tried the door latch gently. It yielded under his hand. He pushed the door wider, stepped in and glanced around. He looked over his shoulder at her.

"He's gone. And I'm afraid he has seen that filthy rag."

Julie stared at the floor as he crossed the room which was littered with torn and crumpled pieces of the foreign tabloid.

CHAPTER TWENTY-TWO

Brett began to pick up pieces of various pages. He was too busy to put them together until he reached the chaise longue where the trail appeared to have begun. The chaise had been pulled out from its place with the white wicker table on one side and a long bookcase of leather-bound yearly journals on the other side.

The books were all topsy-turvy, some lying open to one of the gilt-edged pages, others lying closed on the floor and a few on some shelves still untouched. Julie noted that the books remaining neatly on the shelves covered the first years of Max's reign, from 1918 to 1932 as well as many after the war, from 1946 through last year, 1955.

Having gathered every torn piece of printed paper he could find, Brett was arranging them on the wicker table. Julie glanced at the pieces he put together. Then she rummaged through the yearly Maximilian II journals that had been most carefully examined. She had known the minute she saw the journals just what the prince had been doing.

"He was matching the dates on the tabloid pictures with the things he wrote in the journals. Here's one about how he misses his beloved Garnett but that she is doing this for him: acting as his unofficial ambassadress with the Royal Family in Italy, and here in Spain, six – no, seven months later, she is bringing his hopes for a peaceful relationship between Lichtenbourg and the new Republican government in Madrid. It's an awful thing for the poor man to find out after all this time. He thought she was helping him."

Brett muttered, "My God! What a thing like this for an adoring husband to see! He was always a fool over her, from the beginning. I suppose it's—" He looked at Julie and to her astonishment he added, "possible for some women to inspire belief in their lies." He smiled faintly. "But not you, love. You're much too transparent, that's one of your charms."

She wondered if that was a compliment of sorts. Considering the moment, she would have thought it in very bad taste, but she was grateful for it, all the same.

She studied the torn scraps which Brett had put together: one of them, a photo taken on a beach somewhere, obviously one that permitted nude bathing. Garnett looked gorgeous between two very young males. They were in jockstraps with towels slung over their shoulders. One of the muscular beachboys had his arm hanging down at full length which prevented most of Garnett's pubic area from being seen, and his arm shadowed a part of her well-developed left breast. Otherwise, she was happily nude and laughing.

"Are the men important?" Julie asked, trying not to be embarrassed. "Imagine! A woman that age!"

Brett laughed shortly. "My love, you are as naïve as her poor husband. The woman was probably in her early thirties at the time."

Julie was offended at this picture and the others,

including Garnett on a dance floor in a lamé evening gown somehow cut on the bias and revealing every gorgeous line of her body. This time her partner was definitely a gigolo type, all sleek and dark in immaculate formal attire. Whether deliberately or accidentally, the camera avoided the gigolo's face.

There were other photos on the torn pages, some of the Duke of Windsor, when he was Edward VIII, in swimming trunks, beside Mrs Wallis Warfield Simpson on a yacht in Greek waters. But it was later than the other pictures of Garnett and clearly had no interest for Prince Max, since the pieces of these pages were tossed away uncreased by any angry hand.

"What do the books have to do with it?" Brett asked, beginning to riffle through one.

"But don't you see, the dates he has opened them to were around the months when these photos were taken. Look at the dates and the sly, dirty remarks under the pictures: 'Fun in the sun for enchanting Princess Garnett at a very close friend's private beach off Cap Ferrat'."

Brett looked at the date on one of the journal entries and compared it with the photo of Garnett and her beach boys. "Pretty disgusting. All the snide innuendoes. Individually, they could mean nothing. It's the amount. Three, four? And this is only one of the rags. All the time she was gadding about with these swines, poor old Max was fussing around here trying to keep Hitler off his tail."

He raised his head and threw aside a handful of the torn photos he had carefully put together. The room around them looked as if a cyclone had torn through it.

"Where the hell is Max right now?"

She reminded him, "We must call the New Palace

first." She added with a shudder, "No wonder everything was so quiet here. Where has everyone gone? And why didn't the sentries see him leave, if he did?"

"You're right. I'll call the palace."

He reached for Max's private phone. After a long minute or two he turned from the receiver frowning. "The whole exchange is busy. The call should be taken by a second or third number. Damn it! Something has happened."

Surrounded by the evidence of Prince Max's belated tragedy, Julie could only feel pity for him. Brett, however, was concerned with the political significance of what had happened. He probably thought Max was stupid for having ignored all the hints and sly innuendoes that must have been exchanged behind his back.

She started to say, "I hope this doesn't cause an attack. I could almost bet it was some agent of that Russian – "

"This is it. The palace, is on the line."

She listened, growing more nervous every second. Besides her pity for Prince Max, her own position was appalling. Would they believe she had given him the tabloid?

Brett gave his name and the Consulate number for verification, then explained that he had called to see Prince Maximilian and found no one at the Chalet except the sentries in the front of the building. Before he finished speaking Fräulein Steib cut in and he repeated her explanation to Julie. Even before he spoke, Julie guessed from his expression that the news was as bad as possible.

"Where did he die? The Marktstrasse Hospital." He turned to Julie, covering the mouthpiece of the phone.

"The prince called his valet, Biddicombe, and insisted he wanted to make a secret visit to some building on the Bahnhofstrasse Nord . . . You know the one. They went down through the woods path, eluded the sentries, and took Biddicombe's car. In the car Prince Max had an attack and was suffering so much Biddicombe took him direct to the hospital."

Sickened by the prince's desperation, Julie whispered, "No, no. Tell her the valet misunderstood about the house on the Bahnhofstrasse."

Brett nodded his agreement. "Fräulein Steib, Biddicombe misunderstood. Earlier this evening His Highness mentioned to a stenographer, Fräulein Jones, that he might have a checkup himself at the Marktstrasse. He felt – better. Said he wanted to prove it by making the trip himself."

Julie cut in, "Has anyone else heard Mr Biddicombe's story?"

Brett repeated the question to Fräulein Steib and went on, "Then His Serene Highness and the two princesses were present when he died. I see. Prince Max was too ill to recognize his wife. That is obviously the explanation for his behaviour. After all, the man was in his death throes. I'm glad Prince Stefan understood that it was just a mistake on Biddicombe's part. We'll leave at once to – er – testify to Their Highnesses. At the New Palace. Thank you."

He set the phone back. "Well. That's that, I guess. Poor devil. He wouldn't speak to Garnett when they were attending him. Just avoided her and closed his eyes."

She closed her eyes. "Oh, God! If she ever loved him that must have hurt worse than his death."

Brett was touched by her concern for the feelings of Garnett Kuragin, of all people. He put his arm around her and drew her close. "Love, these are the problems of princes and other fine-feathered birds. I'm happy to say they aren't mine. And I don't think they will be yours, in spite of the trouble caused by that dying old woman in London."

"Who?" She felt the beginnings of a chill.

"Never mind. Don't think about it."

In her whole life she had been alone in her fight for survival. How comfortable it was to have Brett on her side and fighting her battles!

She turned her head. Her lips touched the knuckles of his hand. "Thank you." She gazed up at him mischievously. "If you keep on like this, I could learn to love you. Be careful."

All he could think of to say was: "Well, I certainly hope you are working towards that idea. It's been in my mind for some time now."

Prince Stefan asked Julie in a gentle voice, "Has Mr Athlone explained His Serene Highness's decision to visit the hospital? I think that seems agreed upon."

"Yes, sir." But Julie wondered what they did to people in Lichtenbourg who committed perjury. She had carefully avoided Brett Athlone's eyes, though he sat beside her with an arm casually draped over the back of her chair.

Little Mr Biddicombe stammered, "I was g-grossly m-mistaken. I know that now, Your Highness. I owe everything to Prince Maximilian. I couldn't do less."

Princess Alexia, in a neat black suit with a white

blouse, sat besides her husband; yet she appeared to be completely alienated from him.

She said, "I am willing to accept the word of these witnesses. My father believed his health was improving. His last heart seizure was brought about as an indirect result of his first blow, the loss of his country. In short, political dealings."

There was an uneasy silence before Prince Stefan began to close a plain scratch pad on which he had made notes with one of the modern Biro pens. He impressed Julie as always by his quiet authority. Also, he hadn't tried to browbeat her. He looked around at the others in what seemed to Julie, a forbidding room whose walls suffocated her with their layers of books in foreign languages, on most of the walls and only one window to see the blue July sky beyond.

Every member of Prince Max's household had been questioned, including the sentries who would be reprimanded for failing to note Max's secret departure.

When the last of them had left the room, and Brett Athlone had spoken for Julie and himself, Prince Stefan said, "Thank you, Mr Athlone, and Miss Jones. I realize how much the family and ultimately, the nation, owes you. Now, if you will excuse me, there is a Council waiting to hear the conclusion we have reached and the Royal funeral in the Cathedral to arrange."

Before anyone could move, Princess Alexia stood up, looked around with painful sadness at her husband and walked out of the room. Even her husband had been caught by surprise and she opened the door before he could reach it.

He let her go without speaking, came back and held out his hand to Julie who took it while rising from a trembling curtsy. Then he offered his hand to Brett and the little valet. Biddicombe seemed overwhelmed by the honour and hurried out.

Before Brett and Julie could leave the prince repeated his thanks. "We know Vukhasin must have been in this somehow, but he hasn't been near the Chalet and we still don't know who his spy may be. Anyway, many, many thanks. At least, Max's reputation is secure now. And if it is any satisfaction for you to know, my mother-in-law seems to be genuinely overwhelmed by all this. She won't even talk to my wife. She keeps complaining amid floods of tears that it is all her fault. 'If only she had known . . .' et cetera."

"I'm afraid I am inclined to agree with her, sir. I'm sorry." At Stefan's understanding nod, Brett added, "Everyone in the Chalet seems to have a clean slate. Julie tells me His Highness didn't see any strangers while she was there."

The prince smiled at Julie. "Our little agent in the Chalet was certainly faithful to me about matters that counted, although I am happy to say, they amounted to nothing, in the end. You might tell General Athlone that, my boy." Brett's eyes opened wider but Stefan went on. "If only we knew the person who brought Max that infernal rag. But I suppose we will never know after all this."

Something in his words brought back an odd little memory to Julie. "Wait!"

The men stared at her.

"We do know, I think. It may be a silly notion."

Brett's laugh had the new tenderness she was beginning to find in him but Prince Stefan did not laugh. "Yes. I believe you."

"No one counts her. People don't even know she is there. She hasn't even got a name."

"Go on," Stefan urged her.

"I think of her as the kitchen slave. She follows the housekeeper around and does the menial work. She cleans the rooms on the upper floor under the eaves. She could have found the tabloid I tore up and threw in my waste-paper basket."

Stefan nodded and she went on. "Twice I heard voices in His Highness's rooms. Each time he snapped on the radio when I came in. I passed the girl going out at that minute. And when His Highness was dictating and I made some little remark about his trusting Colonel – " She broke off, then went on. "He said he knew what he was doing. He had a spy in the enemy camp."

Brett and Prince Stefan glanced at each other. Stefan said, "Obviously, it was the other way around. I think you've hit on it, Just Julie."

As they were leaving, Stefan remarked, "I only wish you could be as persuasive with my wife."

Brett said, "Excuse me, sir, but Tige Royle has always been sensible. Couldn't he get her to understand?"

Stefan shook his head. "Tige has gone to Madrid on some expedition of his own. If he had been here my wife and her mother might have been more understanding." He added after a moment, "Thank you both once more for handling poor Max's troubles so well. You may have saved his name from disgrace. Unfortunately, the investigation that looms up ahead of us won't be very pleasant."

CHAPTER TWENTY-THREE

The last day of official mourning for the late Prince Royal of Lichtenbourg saw practically everyone in the tiny country present in or around the centuries' old cathedral. The fact that they were there for the most part to gape at official representatives from both Western Europe and the Communist Bloc had something to do with the crowd which made a monumental traffic jam in Kuragin Square.

Julie could see some of the procession's activities when she stood on the commode seat in her bathroom at the New Palace.

"House arrest, I think that's what they call it," she told the stout chambermaid who was straightening her rooms. No use in hiding the fact. Everyone in the palace knew why she was here and under what might be interpreted as "house arrest".

"*Ja*, Fräulein Jones."

The maid was obviously dying of curiosity but managed to tuck in the bed sheets and settle the bolster just right while she remarked, "But to keep you locked into these rooms like a prisoner, it is strange; not so?"

Days ago Julie would have bristled at this talk of "prisoners" but days ago she had still been free. Now, she felt considerably older and wiser. She adopted a

mood that lifted her spirits, whether it would help her
cause, she had no way of knowing.

She laughed. "Oh, no. It's unpleasant to be singled
out as special, but I was told I am what you might call
the "Star Witness". The Royal Council has to hear my
story before final judgment is made."

"About what, Fräulein Jones?"

"About what caused His Highness's heart seizure and
killed him. That's all."

The maid shook her head, picking up the linen that
had been discarded. "I do not think I like this "Star
Witness" if I am called. *Nein.* I climb from the window
– maybe not on this third floor but I think of excuse and
get out another way. Then I run to the railway station. It
is too quick from this "house arrest" you call it, to the old
prison back of the Chancellery. Rats, and bugs, all things
like that in the old cells. *Guten morgen*, Fräulein."

And a *guten morgen* to you with your bugs and rats,
Julie thought as she began to watch the excitement
down the busy old boulevard at Kuragin Square around
the cathedral. But she couldn't help thinking of what
lay behind the ugly old chancellery on the south side
of the square. Would it really come to that? "Julie
Nobody" finds her true level at last: the Lichtenbourg
old Prison!

Brett Athlone had come to see her every day, often
several times in the day and always in the evening. It
seemed now, as she looked back, that in spite of her
house arrest, she had never really known what it was to
be entirely alive. Until she came to Lichtenbourg she had
made do with what life gave her, her own self-reliance, a
generally cheerful disposition, cynicism, and her dreams
of what she called "getting somewhere".

Alone.

How curious that she had never felt the deep loneliness of a person attached to no one in the world! Then, along came the thrilling and kind-hearted Prince Stefan to show her that some of her dreams could come true. Somehow, she had never really expected to marry that great prince. She was no Sleeping Beauty, but he had put her on the way to meeting a fellow orphan who had just as many romantic qualities as any prince. No one could have demonstrated more than Brett, the romance, companionship and comradeship, of a true lover.

She was used to his caresses and lovemaking now. He was grooming her to be what he thought of as a whole woman. The fact that he restrained himself from taking her sexually had made her all the more hungry for his love.

Meanwhile, he blamed himself and his father and of course, Princess Garnett, for Julie's present predicament. It didn't matter that Prince Stefan either came himself every day or sent a kind and caring message to her, reasuring in its very presence. Brett had come this very morning before she was out of her bath, to tell her he couldn't see her at the usual time because General Athlone worried over the reflection on the honour of Great Britain if his son did not show up at the cathedral to pay his last respects to the late prince. Instead, Brett promised her, he would come to her immediately after the service "and to hell with the honour of Great Britain".

That had made her laugh and she reminded him, "I am a citizen too, I think. At least, the passport Mrs Tenby got for me says so."

He had kissed and held and cuddled her, making her

feel that only good would come of this Star Witness business. He acted more worried over her than she was.

Darling Brett! How awful her life would be if she had never gotten over her first dislike of him.

Waiting for him now, and wondering what was going on down there in that crowded old cathedral, Julie was able to pass the time by thinking how good life would be after the Council's investigation of Prince Maximilian's household staff.

The minutes passed. Doubts began to creep in. Suppose Brett couldn't do any more to help her. Suppose his adoptive father not wanting another orphan in the family, had managed to persuade Brett that it would be better to drop his impossible relationship with a young woman of no past and an even more dubious future.

Shortly after one o'clock, before the crowds were herded aside in the Square for the dignitaries to leave the cathedral, one car swung out between rows of spectators and headed up towards the New Palace at the east end of the Boulevard. It was a white Porsche.

Bless Brett. He hadn't let her down. Surely, everything would go well now. She got down from the commode and stood briefly in front of the heavy, oak dressing table with its three mirrors, smoothing her hair, pinching imaginary threads and hairs off her skirt, then surveying the lineaments of her face.

She no longer seemed to have the independence of her youth: but that didn't matter so much. What mattered was that her eyes looked larger and more uneasy than they had been a week ago. She had always been proud that she could stand up to anything except the nightmares of her babyhood. Now, she looked frightened all the time. Julie, who had twenty years of an occasionally hectic life, should not let these silly foreigners in a microscopic country scare her like this. She had a quick mental flash of medieval dungeons, unnamed horrors from old movies suddenly come to life.

Thank God for pride.

"I'll show them," she told herself when the polite guard in the hall knocked and then opened the door to let Brett in.

"What's this, love? Aren't you glad to see me?" Brett wanted to know, lifting her off the floor to kiss her on an even keel.

She explained when she had hugged him and returned his kiss. "Talking to myself. His Highness told me yesterday morning that the slave-girl from the Chalet kitchens sneaked off to East Germany. Thanks to Colonel Vukhasin, I expect."

Brett frowned. "That's a big help. But it doesn't change your testimony. You heard Max say he wanted to visit the hospital for a quick onceover, because he felt perfectly well. I'll be there to volunteer the same information. I hope Tige Royle gets back from Spain in time. He and Vukhasin were old friends some years ago, during the late fracas with Hitler. It might help."

"I don't see how. Tige Royle never liked me. He thinks I'm conniving. As you did, for some reason."

He laughed and then apologized. "It had to do with our both being born in Spain. Now, don't argue. When we get to the root of it, you're going to be glad to have it out in the open. That's what Tige is doing in Spain. Remember your pal the Reverend Tenby and a dying ex-midwife in London a month or so ago. The dying woman used to contact my mother, Lady Athlone, when there were infants in the hospice in Spain. When she heard your vicar mention his home in Miravel, the old woman mumbled some odd things. They had to do with Spain and, the nurses thought she said 'Miravel'."

"How silly! Mr Nick Chance questioned me. He was quite insistent that it had nothing to do with me."

"Don't shiver so, love. Come and sit down here on this nice sofa and forget about midwives and Spain and all that . . . Good God! This couch is hard as nails. Are you all right?"

"Don't worry about me, I'll be fine. But I am so scared! Being mostly innocent doesn't seem to help me a bit. Anyway, we can talk about it tomorrow. I don't want to think of prisons and chancelleries and inquisitions right now." She looked soulfully into his eyes. "They won't put me in a dungeon with rats and spiders and things?"

He kissed her and promised, "No dungeons or rats or even things that go bump in the night, if Stefan or I have anything to say about it. But sweetheart, I'm afraid we've run out of time. Unfortunately, Colonel Vukhasin and one or two of the Council are trying to get the Communist oar in as soon as possible. All they need is the truth about Max being on his way to the Vukhasin party headquarters to celebrate a union with his party. If they get that, we're all done for."

"You mean the Hearing is today?"

"As soon as Vukhasin, Stefan and the others in the Council get back from the cathedral."

She sat still, thinking this over. In some ways, she would be happy to see the end of this business, one way or the other. But she was in a situation that few except Vukhasin's gang knew anything about. They couldn't betray their part in it without antagonizing the country and making the Communists themselves sound like a party to Maximilian's death. They would much prefer an admission that Max had instigated the union.

Julie said slowly, "Princess Alexia and her mother would never forgive me if I told about Prince Max's letters to Colonel Vukhasin. They'd think he started the talks. As for Princess Alexia and her mother, they would blame her husband if he defended me. It would be dreadful, maybe ruin him politically."

"After all," he reminded her reasonably, "Vukhasin would have to admit he had a spy in the household, which wouldn't go down very well with the rest of the country. Then, too, Stefan's party is the majority party in Lichtenbourg by a considerable margin. Anyway, we can only hope. Between us, and Tige, if he gets back in time, we may be able to get you out of this without a scratch. Stefan won't let you dangle." He saw her face and added with a contrite smile, "I didn't mean that the way it sounded. We will get you out of this mess if we have to blow up the Chancellery. It used to be the German Consulate under Hitler. The country would be well rid of it."

She shook her head at him. "I don't know which is worse, your joking about it or your serious notions."

They both started as a heavy hand knocked on the door.

Julie got up. She didn't need Brett to tell her this must be her summons. She tried to laugh. "I feel like Marie Antoinette on her way to the guillotine."

He laughed too, but he took both her hands in his. "I swear to you, love, we are going to get you out of this."

"But you don't know how."

296

"Not yet. But I will."

She tried to be content with that.

Alexia had not been in the Council Chamber of the old Chancellery Building since her father's illness and she dreaded entering the big chamber now, with its banks of seats all crowded together and the eyes of the public turned to watch the widowed princess make her entrance.

As Alexia had feared, Garnett made the most of her moment in the sun, mostly from habit. Widow's weeds required great dignity but her position permitted her to drip pearls if not flashy diamonds. Pearl drops glowed in her shapely ears. They matched the flawless ropes of pearls which gave life to her black silk suit. Her gloves, unfortunately, precluded calling attention to her famous engagement ring with the celebrated "Lotus" diamond.

All this glamour was for nothing. Alexia wondered if her mother realized how much she had aged in the last few days. Even her smile was old and her lips pursed. The tiny wrinkles around her mouth and eyes couldn't be disguised. These details seemed to Alexia more proof than all her mother's words, of how deep was her sense of loss.

After the first three days of desperate sobbing and self-blame, she had pulled herself together and set out for vengeance. During the rest of the week she had talked of nothing but "avenging my Max".

"They wanted to be rid of him. Don't you see, dear? It's so plain. Somehow, they persuaded Max to make that trip to the hospital when he should have been safely in bed at the Chalet. Someone made him go," Garnett had stated.

"Mother, for heaven's sake!"

"And your beloved Stefan had Max's suite cleaned and swept so quickly one would think he couldn't wait to get rid of every sign of the man whose throne he usurped."

Alexia did not know why Stefan had been in such a hurry to have Max's suite "cleaned", or why he asked the ambitious little Miravel girl, Julie Jones, to do the job. But perhaps there was a reason. Just as there must be a reason beyond fear of some personal revelation that made Stefan say to her before the funeral, "I hope to God there won't be questions about the contents of the letters Max dictated."

"Will you be hurt politically?" she had asked, trying not to sound suspicious.

And then, there was Stefan's quiet answer, "No, Max."

Whatever that meant.

Still, there was no question that Stefan knew more than he had told her about the death of her unfortunate father. Something to do with Max's little valet, and in odd circumstances, that girl Julie again.

The crowd in the Assembly Hall stirred when Garnett and Alexia entered. There was a loud scraping of feet on the aged wooden floor. Everyone arose as Garnett came down the narrow aisle to the row of cushioned chairs reserved at one side of the rostrum for the Royal Family to witness sessions of the State Council.

Automatically, Garnett took the first of those chairs without noticing that the Council usher had been about to seat her in the second chair. Alexia took this chair and glanced over at the eight council members. They had risen from their chairs at the long table facing the ranks of assembled Lichtenbourg citizens.

Stefan, in the centre, caught her eye and smiled a greeting. It was a warm smile and there was understanding in it, because he knew that the funeral service had been very painful for her. Almost in spite of herself Alexia returned Stefan's smile. She had never loved him more, but so much lay between them. Her father's cruel death wasn't the worst. The physical change in her mother was more shocking.

Everyone settled down again and only a low buzz of gossip, obviously about the two princesses, remained. Looking across the rostrum Alexia noticed Biddicombe, her father's valet, tiny, gaunt and frightened, standing at one side of the rostrum where he had retreated at the entrance of Alexia and her mother.

Colonel Vukhasin was seated at Stefan's left, having said, for publication, "It would not suit my constituents if I were now to favour the Right elements." He had a heavy jaw and thick lips which he somehow used to his advantage, playing the sly humourist and the bombastic – not to say frightening – Inquisitor when he chose. He was personally very popular. More so than Stefan, Alexia suspected. But luckily, his personality did not control the ballot boxes.

Vukhasin leaned forward now, both his elbows on the wide table. "We are to understand that His Serene Highness – " He glanced at Stefan and apologized elaborately, "Did I say that? A slip of the tongue." As he had anticipated, this was greeted by a titter from the crowd. "I mean to say, of course, His Royal Highness, since his worthy son succeeded him as in all ancient dynasties."

Stefan corrected him, likewise smiling. "*Son-in-law*. We do everything strictly by the law in Lichtenbourg."

A nice little laugh from the crowd met this remark. Alexia was pleased for her husband. Beside her, however, her mother was growing more and more white with some deep, poorly-controlled fury. Alexia could feel her mother's tension and her quick breathing.

Vukhasin noticed the public enthusiasm. "His Serene Highness has so many devoted fans. Like a master of the soccer. But no matter. We must get beyond theatrical entertainments and return to the tragic death of our worthy chancellor's predecessor. Biddicome you say you drove to the Marktstrasse on the wrong street by the order of His Highness?"

"*Nein*, Herr Vukhasin. By my mistake. I misunderstood His Royal Highness."

"Ah, yes. My hearing. Deplorable." The colonel shook his head. "You keep to this story?"

"*Ja*, Herr Vukhasin."

Alexia, who didn't know what they were getting at, was still glad the valet stuck by his story, whatever the reason. It hadn't pleased Grigori Vukhasin.

The colonel looked along the row of councillors and asked indifferently, "Does anyone else wish to question the witness?"

"I think not," Stefan said. "Biddicombe has always been a trustworthy friend and companion of His Royal Highness. Who is our next witness?" he asked the council clerk who sat at the end of the table, paying more attention to his shorthand than to what went on around him, once the witness was excused.

The clerk glanced through his notes. "Bergin the housekeeper, the chef, the cook, the footmen, the sentries on duty, and the maids. One more. The stenographer on loan from the Foreign Secretariat at the New Palace."

Stefan looked at the young man in the front row of spectators. Alexia wondered who it was, and saw that the man was the British Consul's son, Brett Athlone. Athlone sat forward, obviously interested.

The narrow door at the left end of the rostrum was opened by a young page in Lichtenbourg livery rather than that of the new royal house. He did it neatly, not turning around but reaching behind him and opening the door. The girl who entered looked to be in her late teens. Her boyish honey-coloured hair and her thin figure in a neat but obviously inexpensive green suit aroused interest but Alexia could understand the admiring comments a few made considering Julie Jones' noticeably fine big eyes.

Young Julie had captured the sympathy of the fickle crowd, for the moment. She managed her curtsy, first to Prince Stefan and then to the two princesses, with a kind of coltish grace.

No wonder Stefan had taken a fancy to her, Alexia thought.

In answer to the first calm, easy questions by Stefan the girl gave her name, and the address of the Royal Chalet, her occupation as stenographic help to the late Prince Maximilian II. She had been well rehearsed like most witnesses, and made a good impression. When she described the remark of His Late Highness that he would take a trip to the Marktstrasse Hospital himself soon, to prove how healthy he was, everyone believed her.

Alexia looked around and discovered an odd circumstance. Colonel Vukhasin had a curious little smile, what she thought of as a 'smirk' when Julie Jones testified.

301

Julie stated further that she had not dared to reprimand His Highness and only hoped he was joking.

"It is quite clear, *liebe* Fräulein, that he was not joking," Vukhasin put in, then, as the girl started, obviously afraid of him, he apologized pleasantly. "But I interrupted, please continue, Fräulein Jones."

"That is all, sir. When we returned that night we discovered that Prince Maximilian had actually gone to the hospital with Herr Biddicombe."

"Are you satisfied, Colonel?" Stefan asked coolly.

"It is always good to be precise, if His Serene Highness will forgive my pointing out the obvious. For example, the girl returned alone. Interesting."

"Very interesting to me, Your Excellency," Brett called out from the front row of spectators.

"Oh?" Vukhasin pursed his heavy lips. "And how is this matter of Prince Maximilian's tragic end of interest to a member of Her Britannic Majesty's Government?"

There were gasps in the audience and a catching of breath. Was the death of Lichtenbourg's late ruler somehow connected with Great Britain? Was the late prince murdered, in fact?

Alexia stared at Vukhasin, hating him, but fearing him too. For some reason Stefan wasn't upset. He leaned forward. "Herr Athlone, would you care to explain the interest of Her Britannic Majesty's Government in Fräulein Jones?"

To almost everyone's surprise, Brett Athlone chuckled. "With great pleasure, Your Highness. I had just asked Miss Jones to marry me. My happiest day waits only for Miss Jones to be done with this red tape."

Two of the council members, one of them stately old Count Thallin, muttered at this dismissal of an important investigation. Colonel Vukhasin leaped onto Brett's remark. "We understand the ardent desires of a lover, even a staid British lover – if the young man will forgive me – after all, one remembers the recent antics of King Edward VIII. Pardon, the Duke of Windsor." There were titters in the audience. He pretended to ignore them. "But I have one more witness to call." Julie Jones, obviously relieved, curtsied again and turned to leave. She was stopped by Vukhasin's syrupy command. "But what's the hurry, Fräulein Jones? One more minute, if you can spare it . . . will the usher call Willy Krantz?"

Alexia looked quickly at Stefan. She wondered if he recalled the name of the boy he had set to work cleaning the pavements one night a few weeks ago. She thought Stefan looked puzzled for a minute. Then he understood. He was on his guard.

The lanky, trembling boy shuffled in, holding his cap between his fingers. He kept staring at the floor. Vukhasin asked him in his friendliest voice, "You remember seeing Fräulein Jones deliver envelopes to a certain building on the Bahnhofstrasse Nord?"

"*Ja*, mein Herr."

"Is she present in this hall?"

The boy nodded. Still with his attention on the floor, he indicated an astonished Julie Jones with a tilt of his head. "Her."

The tension in the Assembly Hall suddenly increased. The crowd stared at Julie. Watching her, Alexia could not believe the boy's testimony. The girl looked so indignant there seemed to be no room in her slender body for fear or guilt.

"What a liar he is!" Julie cried furiously.

Brett Athlone caused another furore by leaping forward

303

and grabbing the boy's shoulders. "You contemptible little bastard! How much did the Old Bear pay you for this lie?"

Everyone was shaken back into silence by the hammering of Stefan's fist on the table. "Silence, if you please. Has anyone coached you in your testimony, Willy?"

"N-no, Your Highness." The boy wouldn't look at him.

Stefan pointed a long finger at the boy. "You are under age; aren't you? You have a guardian? Who is he?"

For the first time Willy looked up and around, as if for help. "Y-yes, Your Highness. My f-father."

Colonel Vukhasin, suspecting which way the wind would blow, cut in to protest mildly, "How can this concern the doings of the young woman, Your Serene Highness?"

Stefan ignored him. "Willy, if you have lied, it is your father who must pay for your crime. I will ask the usher to have the gentleman in question summoned."

As the boy had done that night Alexia remembered so well, he broke down again. "No, Your Highness. Please. My father had nothing – He is not a friend to – to the Communists. He would never – I lied." He reached out across the table to Stefan, pleading. "He told me my father need not be called."

"In short," Stefan said amiably, "your testimony is a lie, and someone coached you, perhaps threatened you. Is that true?"

The boy avoided Colonel Vukhasin with great care. "It was like that. Someone – I don't know who. It was dark. I could never say who, because I didn't see her. Not once."

"Shall we pursue this, Colonel?" Stefan asked politely.

Vukhasin examined his nails with great care. He shrugged his heavy shoulders and answered in his most bland way, "We seem to have wasted our time. Children this age are notoriously unreliable, as you will be the first to admit, I am sure, Your Highness."

"Excellent. Then, if there are no more witnesses, I think we may dismiss these proceedings."

In the midst of the sounds along the rostrum, feet shuffling, chairs being scraped back over the floor, a buzz of low voices, and the beginnings of a movement among the assembled audience to get out, Princess Garnett arose.

What was she up to? Alexia reached out instinctively to stop her. She knew her mother was not satisfied with the way the investigation had gone, but she also sensed that there was something about her father which Stefan had spared her.

"Mother," she whispered. "Be quiet."

But Garnett's clear, imperious voice rang through the chamber. "Don't let her go. She knows something. She is hiding it." Her finger, with the glove removed by her nervousness, seemed to light up the room with the flash of its great Lotus Diamond. "Let them proceed."

"Mother!" Alexia tugged at her sleeve. "Sit down!"

Stefan had looked over at them and saw Alexia's gesture. Alexia shook her head at him, shrugging in her despair. He was about to ignore the woman and dismiss the council when Garnett burst out again.

"I demand justice for my poor dead husband!"

A shiver seemed to go over the crowd. People began to sit down again. Suddenly, to everyone's stupefaction, and none more than Colonel Grigori Vukhasin who had been trying to suppress a grin, the door at the top of the rows of seats opened quietly, and a man came down the aisle. He was a big man, and his shock of white hair told Alexia, even from the front of the hall, that this was her great-grandfather.

Garnett had not seen him yet. She was pointing to Stefan. "Why do you close this meeting without the whole truth?"

Another voice, quiet, but powerful as it had ever been, cut into her tirade. Alexia wondered if she heard him right. He called out, "Merribelle?"

Garnett's frame stiffened. She looked as if she had been turned to stone. Alexia got up, ready to hurry to her. Stefan reached her first. Garnett pushed him away but the entire assembly could see that she was hardly aware of anything around her.

Someone murmured, "She's going to faint."

Garnett circled around, saw her grandfather, and raised her shaking hands to him. "Tige, I didn't mean it, I swear."

He had reached her by this time and Stefan stepped back to join Alexia. "Did Tige say 'Miravel'?"

Alexia shook her head. She, as much as Garnett, welcomed the warm arm around her. Garnett looked up into Tige's face. "I've got to get away. Tell them I didn't mean it. I don't know anything about the girl, or Max's death. Nothing!"

Tige glanced around over his shoulder. He spoke to the genuinely astonished Colonel Vukhasin. "I think, Colonel, you also have had enough of this political rubbish. Prince Maximilian died from over-exertion. Don't you agree?"

"I, my dear old friend? Absolutely." The crowded assembly hall began to empty, though the whispers and exchanges of conversation were loudly divergent. Vukhasin added in a lower voice, for Tige's benefit. "There are other times, other places. Eh, old friend?" He indicated to Stefan, "Cut the business off now. It has become a circus of small yapping dogs." He added after a moment, "I would give a million rubles to know why Princess Garnett acted so oddly at the mere mention of Merribelle."

"Miravel," Stefan corrected him, signalling an "OK" to Brett Athlone who was trying to calm the badly shaken Julie.

But Colonel Vukhasin contradicted him, "I have excellent hearing, Your Highness."

Alexia was revolted by his smile.

CHAPTER TWENTY-FOUR

"I'm all right. Never been better," Julie said crossly. "If I can face that lying Mr Vukhasin, I can certainly handle Mr Royle and your father."

Brett did not make the mistake of soothing her prickly temper. "Certainly, you can."

He kissed her faintly perspiring forehead. They started down the corridor of the New Palace towards the ground floor and Prince Stefan's study behind the public rooms.

As they approached the room where she had gone through Stefan's gentle interrogation the day after Prince Max's death, she hesitated, and almost stopped. "It's not that I'm scared, but I don't know what they want me to say."

"Just the truth," Brett said with a belated addition, "within reason."

Her cynical education in life made her ask, "You mean, sometimes lies are necessary?"

"Precisely. Ah. Here we are."

An usher pushed the study door open and Julie was surprised to see only Prince Stefan, Tige Royle and a greying stranger with dark eyes that seemed to have a poignant interest in her.

The meeting was a far cry from her entrance into the Assembly Hall. These men stood up to greet her, even

Tige. Maybe Brett Athlone, with his arm protectively around her shoulder, had something to do with their treating her like a lady. Prince Stefan came over to her, shook Brett's hand, and led her to an arm chair next to his own.

She felt herself surrounded, but pleasantly so. She smiled at Brett. "I told you there wasn't anything to be afraid of."

He looked somewhat taken aback at her denial of her earlier terror but found a seat beyond the kind, sad-eyed foreigner. Julie's gaze followed Stefan to the stranger who was still standing.

"This is Dr Francisco Ventura, Julie. He was with Generalissimo Franco's armies. The nurses and the midwife at the hospital in San Juan de la Cruz made their way through the lines and asked asylum for the infants. Several infants were removed and three remained with you to be taken out next. You were nearly as small as they were, Julie. Am I right, Doctor?"

"Quite right, Your Highness." The stranger came to stand before Julie. She drew back, more in fear than revulsion, but Dr Ventura did not take offense. He reached for her hand and she let it lie in his like dead flesh.

"This brave child remained with those last infants until their refuge was struck by mortar fire and she seemed to have been knocked out. The infants were dead when we reached them half an hour later. Our Julie was taken to England by friends. That is all."

"Not quite, doctor," Tige Royle said. "According to Young Athlone, who heard what the girl Julie called 'her nightmare', there was something bright, maybe a bracelet that flashed on an infant's tiny wrist. Isn't that true, Julie?"

She glanced over at Brett. She felt betrayed by all this, but his anxious expression made her admit after a minute, "I think so. The nightmare was with me so many years. Maybe it will go away now."

"I pray that it will," Dr Ventura said. He leaned over to kiss her hand. Then he moved back to the chair beside Brett and added, "The bracelet was found by one of our troops. The English midwife, Mother Beechum, recognized it among the ruins but we could not be sure the infant had died. You know this for a certainty, Senorita?"

Julie nodded and started to explain hoarsely. "She was dead. I knew. I saw the – " She covered her mouth. "The arm."

Brett pushed his chair back and reached her before Stefan could do so. "You've done wonderfully, love. Don't think about it any more." With Julie close against his body he turned to the others. "She's had enough. No more of this. The Reverend Tenby simply misunderstood that dying woman. Even the nuns in the London hospital a month or so ago thought Beechum might have said 'At Miravel. A great lady's orphan'. Or as they first thought, 'Merribelle.' Obviously, this seems to have been the case."

Tige Royle got up and walked to the window, looked out over the palace gardens and came back. "It seems to have been 'Merribelle.' That is the name on the bracelet Dr Ventura brought with him. It is now in the hands of my granddaughter, Princess Garnett." He passed his hand over his eyes. "But the name Merribelle wasn't good enough for George Athlone or me. No! We had to conjure up a wild theory that young Brett here might be the child, which would have meant that the blood of the Royles would have been perpetuated in the male line."

Brett shook his head. "The general put two-and-two together. My mother, that is, Lady Athlone, persuaded the general to adopt me by hinting that I was the child of a noble house. When the nuns told the general of the dying woman's words, he leapt to conclusions, as Mr Royle says."

Dr Ventura put in, "The name 'Merribelle' was engraved on the little bracelet at Princess – that is, the mother's request. I believe she hoped to adopt the child some day. Unfortunately, we had to inform her of the infant's death."

Tige asked, "Did Garnett suffer much at the news?"

Dr Ventura hesitated. "She was most anxious that His Highness, her husband, not discover it."

"I'll bet!" Tige said bitterly. "Who was the father, by the way?"

"A man of no importance, Señor. An accident, the lady said. It was long ago."

There was a small silence. The men looked everywhere but at Tige Royle.

At last, Tige uttered everyone's thoughts. "I've no doubt it was my granddaughter's fear of discovery and not the unfortunate child she was concerned about."

"Let us be charitable, Señores," murmured the Spaniard.

"Well, there you have it," Tige said, ignoring the charitable view. "For a little while during the past weeks, I thought the child might have been Max's. Garnett never wanted more children, even his. They aged her, I reckon. She had less motherly instinct than an alley cat. And she was over-sexed." He bit his lip. "Sorry. That slipped out. It's just that if the child had

311

been Max's and a boy, he would be the next Prince Kuragin."

"And I definitely would not be the reigning prince of Lichtenbourg." Stefan smiled without humour. "I knew you and George Athlone were up to something . . . Well, I devoutly hope the poor little cause of all this has gone to a better world."

Julie stared at Tige Royle. Apparently, a possible male descendent with his blood had meant something to this tough old patriarch. When his great-granddaughter, Alexia, died, there would be no more 'Royles' to move the world.

The terrible day was nearly over. There had been a visit to Julie's room by General Athlone, jovial as ever, trying hard to assure her that he welcomed her into the family. He kissed her wetly on the cheek, chuckled at Brett's frown, and managed to change the frown to a grin when he added, "How proud Lady Athlone would have been, dear boy. Here you are, planning to marry one of my wife's little foundlings and provide the name Athlone with a long and happy line."

"It takes one to know one, General," Brett reminded him. "I'm a foundling too, you know."

The general laughed but stopped in the doorway of Julie's little suite to add thoughtfully, "I wonder what other royal ladies left their infants in San Juan de la Cruz at the time you were born, Brett."

Julie did not laugh until Brett had closed the door noisily on his adoptive father. She was laughing at Brett's revolted expression.

Stefan and Alexia met the two lovers as Julie's luggage

312

was being removed to Brett's car, parked, with Brett's usual self-confidence, inside the royal gates.

Stefan, after asking Brett's permission, kissed Julie goodbye on the cheek and wished her every happiness.

Julie thought Princess Alexia looked pretty happy herself as she shook Julie's hand, murmuring, "After all the pain my mother and the rest of us have given you, Just Julie, I do apologize most humbly. I will not return with my mother to Miravel. I find I am far more needed by my husband."

When they had gone Brett asked Julie, "Is it really over?"

She watched Prince Stefan and his wife as they disappeared down the great stairs. There would never be anyone as wonderful and superior to other men as the prince. But he was much too unreal for Just Julie. She would settle for the very real and passionate Just Brett.

"We orphans stick together," she told him and hugged him to clinch the discussion.

Brett was helping her into the sleek white car minutes later when they both heard a woman's high heels clicking down the palace steps to a black limousine. Julie murmured. "It's Princess Garnett. Shall I curtsy?"

"Not on your life." Brett took his hand off the car door and kissed Julie's lips in the most public way he could think of, just as the limousine roared past them.

Julie whispered, "She saw us. She looked awfully sad."

"I must contradict you, sweetheart. She looked bloody awful. Arrogant and cold. Funny, I always wondered what all the dashing hangers-on at court saw in her."

"But she is beautiful."

He looked skyward in feigned astonishment, boosted

her into his car, and went around to his own side. When he got behind the wheel he put his arm around her and she rested her head against his shoulder.

Then he said, "Goodbye, Lichtenbourg." He ran his thumb along the sleeve of her dress. "Would you mind too much if I put in for another post in the Service, somewhere without any Kuragins, Elsbachs, Royles and even Athlones?"

She shifted her head and looked into his eyes. "You read my mind, love."

In the distance down the boulevard the palace limousine pulled up before the cathedral and both Garnett's maid and the chauffeur assisted her to the great doors. She looked small and frail to those citizens who bowed to her as she passed.

Brett and Julie drove out between the main gates of the New Palace down the Boulevard Kuragin, past the cathedral and on towards Britain and home, wherever that might be.